Beau

Remington Ranch Book Four
Beau and Corinne

SJ McCoy

A Sweet n Steamy Romance

Published by Xenion, Inc

Published by Xenion, Inc.
First paperback edition 2016
www.sjmccoy.com

Cover Design by Dana Lamothe of Designs by Dana
Editor: Mitzi Pummer Carroll
Proofreaders: Aileen Blomberg and Kristi Cramer

ISBN 978-1-946220-02-8

Dedication

This one is for my 'lil sis' in Australia.
You've been with me since the beginning of this journey
Caryn, and we've still got a looong way to go.
I know someday you and Ruby will find your cowboy. In the
meantime, Beau is all yours.
Love ya, lil sis.
OXOXO

Chapter One

Beau shut down his computer and cleared off his desk. Just as he was locking the desk drawer, Wanda stuck her head around the door to his office. She laughed when she saw what he was doing. "You know, they say it's only untrustworthy people who don't trust anyone, right?"

Beau rolled his eyes and tried not to smile. "Are you saying I'm not trustworthy, Wanda?"

She shrugged. "I'm saying nothing of the kind. I just find it amusing that in a town where no one locks their front door and most people leave their car running when they stop at the store, I work for the only guy who locks his desk drawer every night. It tickles me, that's all."

"Well, good. I'm glad I can give you a laugh. I'm going to head on home."

Wanda nodded. "Do you want me to forward any messages, or leave 'em till Monday?"

"Why don't you let the machine handle them? I'm sure you wouldn't mind getting out early either?"

Wanda's eyes widened in surprise. "You're saying I can clock out and go home?"

"Yeah, why not?"

"Why not? Because I work for a slave driver who'd give Ebenezer Scrooge a run for his money, that's why not." She narrowed her eyes and gave him a suspicious look. "Are you going to dock me the hour and a half, if I go now?"

Beau laughed and shook his head. "Well, if that's how you're going to thank me, forget it. You can stay till six."

She held up both hands. "Oh, no! You offered. I'm accepting. Consider me gone. My ample ass is waddling its way out of here as we speak."

Beau laughed again as he watched her retreat. She couldn't have described it more aptly. "Quick," he called after her, "if you're not out the door before me, I'll lock you in and you'll be here till Monday."

Wanda grabbed her purse from the reception desk and grinned up at him. He knew what she was smiling about. Her desk, unlike his own, was littered with piles of documents, post-it notes and various and sundry office supplies, coffee cups and snack packs. It drove Beau to distraction, but despite the apparent chaos, Wanda was the most efficient assistant he'd ever worked with—and he'd worked with a lot. Most of them found him too demanding, or abrasive, and quit on him. Wanda had been with him for two years. She drove him nuts, but she'd become his right hand. He couldn't imagine having to work without her now. And she didn't have a problem with his so-called abrupt manner. She didn't have a problem with him at all. She gave as good as she got, and somehow she had him smiling and laughing more than he ever had in his professional life. More than he had in his whole life, if he cared to admit it. He held the front door open and stood aside as she barreled toward it, making him think of her as a one-woman stampede.

She stopped to wait on the sidewalk while he locked up. Once he was done, she linked her arm through his as they walked around to the little parking lot at the side of the building.

"Seriously, Beau. Are you sick or something? It's not like you to leave early."

Beau shrugged. "We've been working hard lately…"

Wanda laughed. "When don't we?"

"Okay. Even harder than usual lately. It's Friday. I just figured we could both start the weekend early. I feel like vegging out with a movie and a good bottle of wine. I'm sure you have things you'd like to do." He made a face at her. "Whatever those things might be."

She squeezed his arm and smiled up at him. "You have no idea what those things might be, do you? I don't exist for you once we leave the office."

He let go of her arm and gave her a quick hug. "No. Your boss is a heartless bastard. I don't know how you put up with him. Say hi to Terry for me. I hope his foot's doing better now he's got the cast off. And don't you go chasing little Nolan around all weekend. Make his momma do some of the work for once."

Wanda shook her head with a rueful smile. "Will do, you heartless bastard."

Beau had to laugh as she turned and opened her car door.

"One day, Beau Remington, you're going to have to drop the front. You've got a big soft heart lurking behind the tough shell exterior. I don't know why you're so scared to let people see it."

He shrugged. "You see it. That's all that matters."

Wanda shook her head. "I don't matter one bit; I just worry that when you finally do meet someone who matters, you'll scare her away. I don't want that big soft heart to wither and die from never being allowed out to see the light of day."

He raised a hand and turned to open his own car door. "Yeah. You were doing well there for a minute, Wanda, but you lost me. You're boring me now. I'm going home. Don't be late on Monday."

Wanda laughed. "Coward," she called after him.

"What was that?"

"Nothing, boss. Just calling you a heartless bastard. See you Monday."

Beau grinned and slammed the car door shut. Wanda made him smile. When she'd first come to work for him, he'd thought she wouldn't last long. She'd appeared to be disorganized and didn't know much about real estate at all. But she was the only applicant, she was a fast learner, and best of all she was thick-skinned. She didn't take any of his crap, was what it came down to. And more than that—better than that, if he was honest—she called him out on it. She saw through the façade, in a way most people didn't, not even his brothers. Well, Carter saw through it, but he was too nice a guy to call him on it most of the time.

He waved as Wanda pulled out and, on a whim, blew her a kiss as she drove away.

Once she'd gone, he sat there for a few minutes longer, letting the engine idle. Why had he wanted to finish early? It wasn't as though he had any pressing plans. Or any plans at all, for that matter. He had a couple of movies he'd been meaning to get around to, and a decent bottle of wine sounded like a good idea, but that was all. Maybe he was just tired. Things had been really busy for a while now. The market was picking up. He'd sold quite a few houses that had been on the books for months. All his rental properties were full for the summer. He smiled. Except the one out on Mill Lane. That one was due to close in a couple of weeks. It had sold—to Carter and his new fiancée, the country singer, Summer Breese.

He shook his head to clear it. There was no point finishing work early if he was just going to sit outside in his car grinning to himself like an idiot. He should get going. He could hit Deb's wine store on the way home, treat himself to a bottle of something good.

~ ~ ~

Corinne looked around the cabin and wondered for the umpteenth time what on earth she was doing here. This was going to be home? This two bedroom log cabin, on a ranch, in the middle of nowhere, Montana? This was where she was going to live, work, and raise her daughter? What in hell's name had she been thinking to accept this job?

She sighed, as she sorted through the last of her clothes and put them away in the dresser. That desperate times called for desperate measures! That's what she'd been thinking. Since the Williamsons had sold the hotel, life had been tough. She'd worked for them since college, starting out with summer internships and working her way up till she was hotel manager. She'd been devastated when the buyers had turned out to be a big chain. They brought in their own people and systems. During the handoff she'd met the guy who was to be the new manager. He'd encouraged her to apply—for the job of his assistant. She hadn't though. She was used to running the place, not pandering to a guy who had made it abundantly clear that he liked the idea of having her under him!

At first she'd thought it would be easy to find another job in Napa Valley. She had a good reputation, so did the hotel. It hadn't worked out that way though. It seemed everyone was adjusting in the new economy. There were many older, more experienced managers looking for work, and they were snapped up when positions became available. Corinne was a little way down the list. She'd thought it would just take time, but after a year of working three jobs, she'd had to face reality.

Her sister, Carly, had come up to Montana on vacation with her husband. They'd brought Ruby with them, just to give Corinne a break. She'd thought it was a joke at first when Carly had called her to say there was the possibility of a job managing the lodge at a guest ranch. It wasn't a joke though. And now she was here, moving into this cabin, getting ready to start work, and start her and Ruby's life—in Montana of all places! No joke. No joke at all!

She started at the sound of a knock on the cabin door. She hurried to open it. "Oh, hi, Shane. Is everything okay?" Her new boss was one hell of a hunk of cowboy. All six and a half feet of him. It was a good thing he wasn't her type. He wasn't! And besides, he was engaged and she didn't need a man in her life. She had Ruby to think of. And as Corinne knew from bitter experience, single moms with small kids were better off staying away from the dating scene.

"Everything's fine. I just wanted to make sure you're settling okay. See if you need anything?"

"Mommy?"

Damn. Ruby was up from her nap. "We're fine, thanks."

Shane gave her a puzzled look. "Do you have any groceries or anything yet? We only stocked you up with bare essentials and you haven't left the ranch once since you arrived."

She smiled. Hoping to fob him off, though he did have a point. "We've been busy getting settled. I'll drive to town tomorrow."

Shane cocked his head to one side. "Are you okay to drive by yourself?"

She nodded. "Of course!"

"Mommy?" Ruby wasn't going to wait much longer before she started to yell.

"Are you sure?"

"Absolutely. Thank you. Now if you don't mind?"

He looked a little taken aback, but covered it quickly with a smile. "Okay. I'll get going, but if you need anything at all, you just holler."

"Thank you." She closed the door behind him and turned back to go see Ruby. How could she admit to her new boss that, yes, she was a little worried about driving around out here? That she was worried about taking Ruby on the half hour drive up to town and the grocery store, while she herself was still unsure of the roads? She felt stupid, but she was used to knowing her environment, knowing what challenges might put themselves in her way and how she would handle them and the headstrong Ruby at the same time!

She opened the door to Ruby's room and smiled when she saw her daughter sitting there cuddling her favorite bear. "Are you all right?"

Ruby nodded and held her arms up. She was always snuggly when she first woke up, it didn't last long though.

Corinne sat down on the bed and wrapped her in a hug. "I love you, Ruby."

"I love you, too."

Corinne smiled and rested her chin on top of Ruby's head. No matter what else might be changing in her world, this was the one constant. Her daughter, and the love they shared. Ruby was a handful, there was no denying it. But she was Corinne's handful. Her reason to keep going, to keep trying. Her reason to build a great life, and be a great example. She sighed. How she hoped she could do that, that coming here hadn't been a mistake.

"Are you okay, Mommy?"

"I'm great, sweetie. Just a little tired from getting us moved and settled in."

"You should have taken a nap, too."

She smiled. "You're right. I should have. But it's too late now. I need to start thinking about dinner."

Ruby's eyes lit up. "Can I have chicken fingers?"

Corinne sighed. They were Ruby's favorite. Her comfort food, and, of course, she didn't have any. She didn't have much of anything yet. Shane had been right. She really did need to get to the grocery store. "We can have them tomorrow."

"Oh, but please!"

Ruby had been very good so far with the move and all the upheaval, but Corinne knew that edge to her voice.

"Tomorrow, sweetie. We've got a lot left to do for today and it's a long way to go to the store."

There was another knock on the cabin door. Corinne sighed. And she'd been worried about never having anyone around! Ruby climbed down from the bed and followed her to the front door.

"Cassidy!" she squealed when she saw the woman standing there. "Is Summer Breese with you?"

Cassidy smiled at Corinne. "Hi. Shane said you were busy, I won't keep you." She looked down at Ruby. "Summer isn't here, no. It's just me."

"That's okay," said Ruby. "I like you."

Cassidy laughed. "Well, I'm honored. Thank you."

Corinne gave her an apologetic smile. "Sorry. Ruby is the biggest little fan girl when it comes to Summer."

"Don't worry. I know how she feels. Summer's awesome. You're going to have to come out for lunch with us both as soon as you're settled."

"Yes!" cried Ruby.

Cassidy laughed. "You get to go out with everyone all the time. I was thinking it would be nice for your mom."

"Oh, she can come, too." Ruby turned around. "I'm going to find a dress to wear."

"I don't mean right now," said Cassidy.

"I know." Ruby smiled back over her shoulder. "I just need to have one picked out."

Corinne laughed once she'd gone back into her new bedroom. "Sorry. She likes to be included, and to take charge!"

"I noticed. I don't know how you do it. I mean, she's awesome, but wow. She must be a handful."

"She can be."

"How do you even get anything done? You're like wonder woman, getting moved in and settled and keeping up with her the whole time."

"Don't you believe it. We're nowhere near settled in and I haven't even made it to the grocery store yet."

Cassidy nodded. "That's what Shane was worried about. Do you want me to run up and get you some stuff? You can do me a list, I don't mind."

Corinne considered it for a moment. It would make life easier—especially if she were to put chicken fingers on the list! But no. She couldn't bring herself to ask for help like that. Shane and Cassidy had been so kind already, and he was her boss after all. She needed to appear capable and confident, and she was—even if she didn't feel it right now. "No, it's kind of you to offer, but I'm fine, thank you. After Shane stopped by I realized he was right. We're about to drive up to town. I need to get familiar with where everything is."

Cassidy looked doubtful. "Are you sure? I really don't mind."

"I'm sure. Thank you."

"Okay. Well, I guess I'll leave you to it so you can get going. You'd better go soon so you can get back before dusk."

Corinne wanted to laugh. "Should I be worried? Do the vampires come out at dusk or something?"

Cassidy laughed. "No. You're safe from them. It's the suicidal deer that like to throw themselves in front of your vehicle. They do it all the time, but it gets worse at dusk and daybreak."

"Oh. Great. Thanks."

Cassidy shrugged. "At least they're not vampires."

Corinne liked her. She hoped they might become friends. "That's true. I should be grateful for small mercies, I suppose."

"Yep. Have you got your cell phone handy? I'll give you my number in case you ever need it for anything. You've got Shane's, right?"

Corinne nodded. She was relieved to think that if a deer did throw itself under the car, or if she were to break down, she'd at least have someone to call.

Once Cassidy had gone, Corinne found Ruby in her room, with all of her dresses laid out on the bed. She sighed. All of the dresses she'd unpacked and hung in the wardrobe this morning.

"Do you think I should wear the purple one when we have lunch with Summer?"

Corinne smiled. "Yes. It's lovely. But for now, we need to get going."

"Going where?"

"To the store to get your chicken fingers."

"Yay! Thank you." Ruby came and flung her arms around Corinne's legs. "You're the best mommy in all the world."

Corinne smiled. Moments like this made it all worthwhile.

Chapter Two

Beau opened and closed the fridge door for the third time. There was nothing in there he wanted to eat. He knew that from the first two times he'd looked. He checked the wine rack. Nothing he wanted to drink either. He picked up his car keys off the counter. He should have stopped at Deb's on the way home. He'd go get a bottle of something decent and see what she had on offer in the deli. He didn't feel like cooking.

He locked the front door on his way out, and smiled. Wanda was right. No one locked their doors around here. But he did. Every time. Why was that, he wondered. He had a nice house, full of nice belongings, but Jesus, he lived in Livingston. It wasn't exactly a hotbed of crime. He knew it had more to do with his desire for privacy than a fear of thieves. He kept his house locked, his car locked, his desk drawer locked, and he kept his true thoughts and feelings locked up, too. Why? Because he didn't trust anyone.

He had to wonder as he backed out of the driveway just what it was that he didn't trust. That people would hurt him? Dislike him? He just didn't know. He shrugged as he pulled out onto Main Street. What did it matter anyway? It was just a part of who he was. He didn't need to be getting into self-analysis mode. What he needed to be doing was setting himself up for a nice relaxing evening. As he pulled into the parking lot by the old railroad depot, he spotted someone waving at him. Ugh. He shuddered. Angie! He lifted a hand to wave back and drove straight through the parking lot and out the other end. He'd rather make a loop through town and come back when she'd gone than have to get stuck talking to her.

He'd taken her out a couple of times. The dating pool was pretty small in this town—and it could use a good shot of chlorine. Angie was a good-looking woman. But she wasn't a nice person. He'd tried to kid himself that she was all right really. He'd given up the pretense after what she'd done to Carter and Summer. He'd taken her along as his date to a dinner at Cassidy's place and she'd taken photos of Summer and Carter and gone to the local paper with some bullshit story about them. Beau had felt guilty as hell. The story had caused all kinds of problems for Carter and Summer. Carter had gone AWOL for a while, then Summer had left the valley and gone back to Nashville. All because he, Beau Remington, would rather show up with a stupid date than no date at all. What was his problem? He didn't need a woman in his life. So why didn't he like to be seen out without one? He drove back down Main and looped his way back. He checked the parking lot, but there was no sign of Angie anymore. Good. He didn't need to hear her apologies, yet again, or to tell her, yet again, that he wasn't interested.

He checked the coast was clear before he got out of the car and locked it before hurrying into Deb's wine store. He loved this place. Deb knew her wines, and her cheese for that matter. He could spend hours in here browsing and talking wine with her. She wasn't around today though. Lisa looked up from her perch behind the counter when he walked in. She was a nice enough girl and quite knowledgeable, but Beau wouldn't be stopping to chat with her.

"Hi, Mr. Remington."

He nodded. "Lisa." He walked past her and on down to the Cabernet Sauvignon section. Tonight he wanted something big and bold. He browsed the shelves; there were some familiar favorites that might do the trick, and a couple of non-starters. Deb worked with a couple of importers, a couple of distributors, and even directly with a couple of California wine makers. Beau was always impressed by the selection she stocked. As he ran his gaze over the upper shelves, he stopped and grinned. There were two bottles of a California Cab he absolutely loved. Deb couldn't always get it and, at over two hundred dollars a bottle, that was maybe a good thing. When she did have any he had to buy it. He reached up and grabbed both bottles, then made his way to the little deli counter at the back of the store. He'd want some good cheese to go with this.

While Alice, who ran the deli counter, was cutting his cheese, the doorbell rang as someone came in. He could hear a woman's voice talking to Lisa. It was such a sexy sounding voice, he had to turn to see its owner. He couldn't though. A wave of goose bumps ran down his spine as he continued to listen. He couldn't make out the actual words she spoke, just the soft gentle tones. He smiled. Getting shot of Angie had been a good thing, but that had been a while ago now. He hadn't thought he missed a woman's company, but from the way his body was reacting to just the sound of that sweet voice, it seemed he did miss something. He rubbed his hands together, surprised at how sweaty his palms were. His heart was beating fast and loud. So strange. He really needed to catch a glimpse of the owner of that voice. He had to bite back a chuckle, she was probably hideous. One look at her would no doubt bring him right back down to earth.

Alice placed the cheese on top of the counter. "Anything else?"

He shook his head. "That's it, thanks."

"Okay. You give my best to your momma for me when you see her next."

"Will do. Have a good weekend, Alice."

"And you, Beau."

He tucked the two bottles under one arm and picked up the cheese then started making his way up to the counter at the front—toward that voice that seemed to be drawing him in like a siren. He deliberately walked along the second aisle, so he wouldn't be able to see her until he got to the counter. He wanted to live with his beautiful fantasy as long as he could before reality shattered the illusion.

When he was halfway down the aisle, she appeared at the end of it. The fantasy fell short of the reality! He sucked in a deep breath and hugged the bottles tight to his chest. She might be the most beautiful woman he'd ever seen, but that was still no reason to drop four hundred dollars' worth of wine on the floor. Once he had them secured, all he could do was stare. She was gorgeous! She looked like her voice sounded. Beautiful. Brown hair fell around her shoulders. She had the perfect hourglass figure. Her V-neck sweater showcased full breasts above a narrow waist, and her jeans flattered rounded hips. Hips that he wanted to take hold of and…

She met his gaze. Her eyes were wide, he could see a little pulse fluttering in her neck. Could it be that he was having the same effect on her as she was on him? God, he hoped so. He smiled. She smiled back, her full lips turned up and a dimple appeared in her cheek.

"Did you find it?" Lisa's voice cut through the magic of the moment like a knife.

"What? Err, no…"

Beau cocked his head to one side. "What are you looking for? Can I help you find it?"

She stared at him. "I don't know."

Lisa appeared behind her, apparently coming to help her find whatever it was she was looking for. She grinned when she saw Beau. "Oh, see. You did find it. It's right here." She pointed at him.

Beau was confused as hell. He wondered if he'd somehow slipped into a parallel universe. He'd just asked this woman if he could help her find what she was looking for, and Lisa had told her that he was what she was looking for. What the fuck?

Lisa laughed. "Sorry. I mean the wine."

Beau looked down at the two bottles he was grasping tight to his chest. "You mean these?"

Lisa and Beautiful Woman nodded at him. She wanted his wine? He clutched them tighter. "They're just a little farther down," he said.

"They're the last two we have," replied Lisa.

Shit! Shit, shit, shit, shit, shit! But they were his! He'd found them first!

Big green eyes looked up at him. Oh, for fuck's sake. She could have them. She could have anything she wanted.

He walked toward the counter. Lisa followed him. Beautiful Woman just stood and stared. Lisa rung him up and gave him a sour look. What? Did she think he should just hand over one of the bottles and let Beautiful buy it instead of him? Hell no!

Once he'd swiped his card and tapped in the number, Lisa put everything in a paper bag and handed it over.

"Enjoy," she said, with a look that said, I hope you choke on it.

Beau shook his head. He really was misunderstood. "Thanks, Lisa. Can you spare me another bag?"

She huffed as though he was adding insult to injury, but handed one over.

"Thanks." He took one of the bottles and slid it into the second bag.

Lisa watched openmouthed as he approached Beautiful Woman. His heart raced as he held out the bag toward her. She looked down at it and then up at him. Then she shook her head. "Oh, no. I couldn't."

"Please? I'd like you to have it."

She shook her head again. "I couldn't." Her cheeks were flushed, that little pulse was fluttering on her neck. Damn she was as attracted to him as he was to her. He knew it! He needed to get a grip. He must seem like a crazy person. He smiled and took a gamble. "You're new in town." He hoped to hell she was, she had to be, he'd have found her before now if she wasn't. "Consider this a housewarming gift." He thrust it toward her, making her grab it instinctively.

He grinned when she had hold of it. "I'll see you around," he said, and practically ran before she could argue. He heard his name being called as he sprinted across the parking lot. He wasn't about to stop and see who it was though. It sounded like that little kid who had been here with Carly and James. He didn't need to deal with that right now! He unlocked the car and pulled away as fast as he could. In the rearview mirror he saw Beautiful Woman emerge from the store and look around. He'd find her. She was new in town. She hadn't denied it. He grinned. It looked like he was a bit rusty on how to impress a woman, but he was about to brush up his skills in a hurry.

Corinne stood outside the store and looked around. There was a silver Mercedes pulling out onto the road. Was that him? Had he just disappeared into thin air? Had she just imagined the tall, dark, gorgeous stranger who had given her a two hundred dollar bottle of a wine, at the same time he'd stolen her breath and her senses?

She came back to her senses in a hurry. Ruby was in the car. She'd only intended to leave her for a minute and had thought she'd be able to keep an eye on her through the store window. She hadn't planned on getting distracted by a gorgeous looking guy and his ridiculous gift! She opened the car door, feeling immensely guilty for having left Ruby in there. Ruby wasn't in the least concerned.

She smiled. "I saw Beau!"

"Bow?" Corinne wondered what she meant.

"Yes, Beau! I like Beau. Beau's handsome."

Corinne looked around wondering what kind of bow she was talking about. There was an oversized bottle in the display window of the wine store, tied with a gold ribbon bow. She must mean that. "Oh, I see. That is nice."

Ruby's eyebrows knit together as she looked up at her. "You don't know Beau."

Corinne sighed and put her seat belt on. She really didn't know what Ruby meant, but she didn't want to get into an argument with her now. She needed to get them home before it got dark. They'd braved the grocery store and now it was time to get back to the cabin, get Ruby her chicken fingers, and...she looked down at the bottle of wine. She couldn't drink that. Or maybe she should. She'd been about to buy a bottle for herself, it was her very favorite, and though it was a crazy splurge, she'd planned to settle down with a glass after Ruby was in bed. She was celebrating the beginning of her new life, after all.

"Thank you for my chicken fingers, Mommy," Ruby said once she'd cleared her plate.

Corinne smiled. Serving chicken fingers was the only time Ruby was guaranteed to finish her food. "You're welcome. Now are you going to come and help me with the dishes?"

Ruby grinned and climbed down from her seat at the table. She loved to help in the kitchen. Although the cabin did have a dishwasher, they'd started what Corinne hoped would be a new tradition of bringing Ruby a chair to stand on so that she could wash the dishes in the sink and Corinne dried them.

"Are you going to work tomorrow?" Ruby asked as she sloshed water all over the draining board.

"Just for an hour. I'm going to meet with Shane."

"While Mr. Mason teaches me to ride?"

Corinne nodded. She had another week before she was supposed to start her job, but she'd set up a meeting with Shane so she could learn how he liked the place to run. She wanted to get a feel for what he expected. His brother, Mason, had offered to let Ruby ride one of the ponies and Corinne had seen that as her chance to get an hour with Shane. Ruby was going to start Pre-K when she started work, but until then, she'd have to take any opportunity she got to take care of other things.

"I like Mr. Mason. He's handsome."

Corinne smiled. He was, too! All the Remington men were very handsome indeed. Shane was flirty and outgoing, Mason was broody and commanding, Carter was the strong silent type. There was one brother she hadn't met yet. She almost dropped the plate she was drying. It couldn't be! She looked at Ruby. "Who did you see when you were waiting in the car today?"

"Beau."

"Who's Beau?"

"Summer Breese's friend."

"Is he Carter's friend, too?"

"Of course he is, silly. He's his brother."

Corinne's heart started to pound in her chest. So the tall, dark, expensive wine drinking stranger, was the fourth Remington brother? She didn't know whether to laugh or cry. She was bound to see him again then, but he was totally and utterly off limits. She blew out a big sigh. Who was she kidding? All men were off limits to a woman in her situation.

Beau put his feet up on the coffee table and took a sip of his wine. Damn, that was good. He shook his head with a rueful smile. And now he only had one bottle of it to enjoy. What the hell had he been thinking? Two hundred bucks! And he'd just thrust the bottle at that woman. That breathtaking woman with the voice like warm honey. The one he would no doubt never see again. What an idiot! He picked up a piece of cheese and a cracker. Ah well. Maybe it'd do him good to make a fool of himself now and then. He hadn't done anything so stupid in a long time, if ever. Normally he liked to make sure every move was well thought out, every word was carefully chosen. He smiled. Wouldn't it give Wanda a laugh to know what he'd done? She'd probably demand a raise, if he could give two hundred dollars' worth of wine to a complete stranger, he could damned well give her a couple more bucks an hour! He could hear her.

He picked up the remote and turned on the TV. Time to get the movie going and get his mind off Beautiful Woman. She'd been the highlight of his Friday night, and that was a good thing. But wasn't it really a bad thing? That he had so little going on in his life that a chance encounter with an attractive stranger was the best thing that had happened to him in a long time.

He stared at the TV for a few moments. He didn't really have a life outside of work, so when was anything good supposed to happen? These last few months he'd been getting together with his brothers and their girls for dinner once a week. He enjoyed that. But that was the sum total of his social life. He sighed. He didn't normally care. Hell, it suited him, it was his choice. He couldn't let bumping into Beautiful Woman change the way he felt about himself and his world. Maybe he just needed more going on. He stared at the TV while he wondered about it. The commercials came on and he watched a wild black stallion gallop across the screen. That was it. There was one thing he enjoyed doing and hadn't done in way too long. Tomorrow he'd go down to the ranch and take his horse Troy out. He rarely made time to ride any more, but he always felt happier when he did.

He smiled and lifted his glass up in a toast to thin air. "Thanks, Beautiful." He'd never see her again, but the green-eyed beauty at Deb's had still managed to give him something to smile about.

Chapter Three

The next morning Beau took his time showering. He decided not to shave. It wasn't like him, but he didn't want to feel like him today. At least not the him he'd become. He wanted to go back to being the old Beau. The one who would tumble out of bed at the ranch with his brothers early on a Saturday morning so that they could all ride out checking fences. That Beau would never have even stopped to think about whether or not he should shave.

He toweled himself down and walked into his closet. Riding jeans, where were they? He had to go all the way to the back and dig to the bottom of his jeans shelf. Wow. It really had been too long. He found his favorite shirt back there too, the red one. Why hadn't he worn it in so long that it was folded up all the way back here? He shook his head. It'd get worn again today.

When he was ready he locked the house up and ran down the front steps. He drove the truck whenever he went down to the ranch, but he had to stop and check the Merc was locked on his way out. Of course it was. He climbed in the truck and started it up. Today was a good day. The sun was shining, he was going to take Troy out. He'd go say hi to his folks. He hadn't stopped in on them for a while, though he did call every other evening to make sure they were okay. He had a big surprise he wanted to spring on them soon, too. Not today though, that could wait a while yet.

When he got to the ranch he spotted Mason out in the arena. He had a kid on one of the ponies. Beau smiled. It seemed he wasn't the only one wanting to go back to an earlier version of himself. Mason hadn't given kids riding lessons in years. He focused on the stud these days, and training the horses himself. He only gave occasional clinics, and they weren't for kids.

Beau parked by the barn and wandered down to lean on the fence and watch. His smile faded a little when he recognized the blonde curls. Ruby! He almost turned around and walked away before she spotted him. He'd named her the two-foot tyrant when she was here visiting with her aunt and uncle. Now she was back. To live apparently. Beau didn't even want to imagine what the mother must be like. What kind of woman could have spawned that little monster?

"Beau!" Mason called to him before he could make his escape. He led the pony and its rider over to the fence. "Good to see you. What are you doing out here?"

He shrugged. "I thought I'd take Troy out."

Mason grinned.

"Who's Troy?" asked Ruby. "Can I come?"

Beau shook his head rapidly and looked to Mason for help.

Mason gave Ruby a stern look. "Do we talk when we're having a riding lesson?"

Ruby hung her head. "Only when you ask a question."

Mason grinned at Beau again. Apparently he had somehow managed to tame the mini demon. For his part, Beau would rather just avoid her.

"He's out behind the barn," said Mason. "I was thinking I might take him out myself, since you can't get out here that often."

Beau nodded. It wasn't a criticism, he knew that. Mason just liked to look out for the horses, make sure they weren't left out to graze without proper exercise for too long. It sure felt like criticism though.

Mason pushed his shoulder. "Don't look like that. I'm glad you're here to take him. He rides better for you than anyone else. You're his very own human."

Beau's smile returned at that. Mason sure knew how to handle him. He usually managed to push all the right buttons to keep him smiling.

"Can I come?" Ruby asked again.

Mason gave her the same stern look.

"But I want to go with Beau!" This time she didn't back down.

Mason shook his head. "How about you wait here with Beau a minute while I just run inside?" He looked at Beau. "I'll be right back."

Beau could hardly refuse, much as he'd like to. He climbed over the fence and took hold of the lead rein.

"This is Gypsy," said Ruby.

Beau nodded. He'd rather not engage in conversation if he could avoid it. He started walking, leading Gypsy and her mini rider around the arena. It beat standing around and hopefully would keep Ruby quiet.

"My mommy…"

Beau turned to look at her with what he hoped was the same stern look Mason had used. "Do we talk while we're having a riding lesson?"

Ruby's eyebrows knit together and her bottom lip started to slide out. Oh, shit! All the warning signs of a storm about to hit.

"That's right. We don't. Good girl." He turned back and urged Gypsy into a trot, hoping that would avert disaster. It did.

Mason came back out from the barn and smiled as he let himself into the arena. "Good job, Ruby. You're doing great!"

That brought a smile back to her face. Beau led her back to Mason and handed over the lead rein. "There. I'm out of here."

Mason laughed. "Coward."

Beau tipped his hat with a grin. "That'd be me! See ya!"

He let himself out of the arena and started walking back to the barn. Then he stopped in his tracks. Could it be? There was a woman walking down the path from the lodge toward him. A very beautiful woman. Either his eyes were playing tricks on him or it really was Beautiful Woman.

He held his breath as he watched her approach. Her stride faltered as she recognized him, too. Then she continued toward him, her beautiful smile causing that dimple to deepen. Man! She was gorgeous.

"Hello again," she said when she reached him, her voice slid over him, wrapped him in its warmth and, if he wasn't mistaken, slipped its fingers inside his pants for a moment.

"Hello." That was all he had? Hello? He really had to up his game here.

"Thank you for the wine. You really shouldn't have, though."

He shrugged.

"Look at meeee!" For God's sake. All he needed was Ruby ruining this for him. He was making enough of a mess of it by himself. Then a thought struck him. He didn't want Beautiful Woman thinking that the kid was his! He didn't want her to think he was an asshole either. He turned to look. "Good job, Ruby. You're doing great." So what if he had to borrow Mason's words? The only ones he could come up with himself weren't the kind he could say out loud to a five year old!

He turned back to Beautiful Woman, she was smiling. Apparently impressed by his ability to appease the monster. He smiled back. "She's not mine."

He couldn't figure out the look on Beautiful's face, she was still smiling, but there was something strange in her eyes. "No?"

He shook his head. "Hell, no. I don't have kids."

"You don't like kids?"

Oh, shit. Was he walking himself into an ambush here? He shrugged. "I don't really know many." Hopefully that was an acceptable out.

"Except Ruby?"

He nodded. "Yeah, and she's a monster. She gives kids a bad name."

"I see."

The look on that beautiful face said he had well and truly blown it. That was hardly fair though, was it? They'd known each other for a grand total of five minutes. Surely she couldn't be judging him on his parental potential already? Time to change the subject. He held his hand out. "I guess we've made it to the stage where we should introduce ourselves. I'm Beau."

She nodded and shook his hand briefly. Her smile was still there, but it was merely polite now. "It's nice to meet you, Beau. I'm Corinne." She raised an eyebrow, apparently waiting for some reaction. Should he know her name for some reason?

She sighed. "Ruby's mom."

He could feel the blood drain from his face. He didn't know which was worse: the fact that he'd just told this beautiful woman that her daughter gave kids a bad name, or the fact that she was the two-foot tyrant's mother. He nodded. He didn't have any words.

She pursed her lips and nodded back at him. She wasn't happy. Not happy at all.

"Well, it was nice meeting you." He tipped his hat at her and beat a hasty retreat to the barn. Wonderful! Just wonderful. Wasn't that just his luck? He took his hat off and ran his hand through his hair.

The most beautiful woman he'd ever met and she had to be the mother of the brat! He blew out a big sigh. "Fuck it!" He muttered under his breath.

"Are you okay?" Summer popped her head out from one of the stalls.

What the hell? Was everyone out here today?

He nodded. "I'll survive."

She came out and closed the door behind her. "Are you sure? You sounded pretty upset. What is it?"

Beau shrugged. He wasn't into talking about his problems, or his personal life, with anyone. If he was he might start with Summer. She was good people. She had a kind heart. She seemed like she cared about everyone, even him. He smiled. "It's nothing. Really. I just messed up. I made a fool of myself."

She gave him an inquiring look.

He shook his head. "Explaining it would be reliving it, and I'm still cringing from the first time."

She laughed. "I know how that goes."

Beau couldn't believe that, but it was sweet of her to say it. "Anyway. It's good to see you. I'm just on my way out to get to Troy."

"Okay. Have fun."

"Thanks." He made his way down the aisle of stalls, headed for the back door. He'd almost reached it when Summer called after him.

"Oh, and Beau. Dinner's at our place this week. Wednesday. Can you make it?"

"I'll be there. Thanks, Summer." He went out through the door with a smile on his face. At least that was something to look forward. He enjoyed the family dinners they'd been taking turns to host. He was feeling closer to his brothers than he had in years.

He'd even hosted himself one week. Of course all the girls had helped. It had been fun.

He spotted Troy grazing down by the creek. He whistled and smiled as Troy's head came up and he looked around. When he saw Beau he gave a loud neigh and came cantering over. That made Beau smile. Troy hadn't forgotten him, though he had every right to. He came and butted his shoulder, then snuffled around his pocket. Beau hadn't forgotten either. He pulled out one of Troy's favorite mints. "There you go, old fella."

Troy crunched the mint then lifted his head and peeled his lips back looking for all the world as if he was laughing. Beau laughed with him. He had to laugh. What else could he do? He'd just blown his chances with Beautiful, from now on to be known as Corinne, mother of the monster. He may as well laugh, saddle up his old buddy and get out into the back country for a few hours.

Corinne walked down to the arena with a heavy lump of disappointment lodged in her stomach. What could she expect? Her tall, dark stranger was heavy on the good-looking. And good-looking guys never seemed to like kids. Why would they? They could have their pick of all the young, pretty girls who came with no strings and no complications. She shook her head. It wasn't even that. Yes, she found him attractive, but he was a no-go anyway. It was his obvious dislike for Ruby that hurt her. Ruby was a good kid. Okay, so she was strong-willed. That was a good thing. Beau had said she gave kids a bad name! That was a horrible thing to say about any child. She reached the fence and sighed.

"Look at meeee, Mommy!" Ruby called again as Mason led her around the far side of the arena at a trot.

Corinne smiled. Ruby looked so happy. Screw Beau Remington! The guy must have a heart of stone not to find her adorable.

Mason smiled and led the pony over to where Corinne was standing. They stopped when they reached her.

"I'm a natural," said Ruby with a big grin. "Mr. Mason said so."

Corinne grinned back.

"What's a natural?"

Mason laughed. "It means you ride like someone who was born to ride."

Ruby nodded solemnly. "I was born to ride. I love Gypsy. I love riding. Riding is my new favorite thing in the whole world. I'm going to ride every day now."

Corinne exchanged a look with Mason. That wasn't going to be possible. Corinne wasn't going to have either the time or the money to make it happen.

Mason smiled. "Not every day, Ruby, no. But sometimes, if your mom tells me you've been a really good girl, then you can have a lesson."

"I'm always good."

Mason gave her a stern look.

"Sometimes. I'll be good all the time if you let me ride Gypsy."

Mason caught Corinne's eye and she gave him a grateful smile. It seemed he'd already figured out how to handle her daughter and get the best out of her. It was a pity his brother…No. She had to stop that line of thought before she got started with it.

"Well, I'll be checking in with your mom. So you'd better be good, okay?"

"I will."

"Okay. Do you remember how to dismount?"

Ruby nodded and put both reins in one hand before sliding her feet out of the stirrups. She swung one leg over behind the saddle and slid down to the ground. Corinne had to smile, she really did look like a natural.

"Good job!" said Mason.

Ruby grinned at him before turning to Corinne. "Some people leave one foot in the stirrup to help them climb down. Around here we don't do that, just in case the pony moves away. We don't want to fall and get dragged along by our foot."

Corinne wanted to laugh. It was obvious she was reciting word for word what Mason had told her.

Mason grinned. "I couldn't have put it better myself. Now, if you'll excuse me, I'm going to take Gypsy in and get back to work."

"Thank you so much," said Corinne. "What do I owe you?"

Mason shook his head firmly. "Not a thing. If Ruby's going to live here, she needs to know how to ride. He tipped his head back and looked out at her from under the brim of his hat. "You should, too."

That took her by surprise. "Oh. I…"

He smiled. "You can join Ruby's lessons if you want to."

"I don't know if I'll get time. I need to see how the job is going to work out. But, thank you."

Mason nodded. "We'll work something out."

"Thanks again. Come on, Ruby. We need to go, and Mr. Mason needs to get back to work."

Mason started to walk away, but Ruby tugged on his sleeve. He looked down at her with a smile.

"Thank you, Mr. Mason. I had fun."

Corinne was relieved that she hadn't forgotten her manners.

"You're welcome, I had fun too."

The smile on Ruby's face melted Corinne's heart. She didn't think she'd ever seen her daughter look so happy. As she smiled up at Mason she crooked her finger and beckoned him to come down to her level. Corinne thought her heart might overflow when Mason bent down to her and she planted a kiss on his cheek. He straightened up with a big grin on his face. Apparently even broody and commanding could be melted by her daughter. Even if tall, dark, and handsome couldn't. Oh, well. At least Ruby was winning over one Remington brother. One of the two most important ones, since Mason and Shane were the ones she'd be around the most.

Ruby took hold of her hand as they walked back up the path. "I saw Beau."

"So did I." Corinne didn't like the idea of Ruby being so enamored with a guy who didn't like her. "And you had a good time riding with Mason?"

Ruby nodded. "Yes. I like Mr. Mason."

"I do too."

"I like Beau more though."

Corinne sighed.

"You don't like him? Do you like Mr. Mason better?"

"I don't really know him. I like Mr. Mason because he's been kind to you. And to me."

"Beau's kind, too."

"He is?"

Ruby nodded sagely. "He's a good guy. He's just got his head up his ass."

"Ruby!" Corinne was caught between the urge to laugh and shock at hearing her daughter say such a thing.

Ruby shrugged. "That's what Cassidy said."

Corinne bit back a smile. She could just imagine that. Cassidy wouldn't be one to bite her lip, and she didn't come across as someone who was used to being around little kids—or watching what she said when she was. "Maybe so, but you know you shouldn't repeat what you hear people say."

Ruby simply shrugged again. They carried on walking in silence for a few minutes and were almost back to the cabin before she looked up and asked. "What does it mean?"

"What does what mean?"

"That he's got his head up his ass?"

Corinne wanted to laugh again. "Well, first of all that's a word you shouldn't be using."

"Ass?"

"Yes, that one."

"But what does it mean?"

"An ass is like a donkey."

"Oh! I thought it meant his butt! But how could he get his head up there?"

Corinne did let out a little chuckle at that, she couldn't help it. There was no pulling the wool over Ruby's eyes.

Those eyes widened as Ruby pondered. "So he's got his head up his donkey's butt?"

"No! It's just a saying. It's not real."

"But what does it mean?"

"It means that…" Corinne had to think what it really did mean. "It means he's not always aware of the people around him. Or of how he affects them with the things he does."

"Does that mean he's mean?"

"No. I don't think so. Just that he might seem mean even when he's not trying to be." Corinne considered her own words along with Ruby. It was insight into Beau's character that she wouldn't have had. So maybe he wasn't trying to be mean about Ruby before he knew he was talking to her mother. She sighed. What did it matter anyway? And besides, apparently he had his head up his ass. Just one more reason that she should steer well clear of him—in case the fact that he didn't like her daughter wasn't enough!

Chapter Four

Beau jumped down from Troy and patted his neck. They'd been out for a couple of hours and it had done them both good. He took the saddle off and carried it into the tack room. Troy followed and waited at the door for him. He came back and slid the bridle off, too. He'd never liked to tie Troy up. He wasn't going to wander off; he always waited patiently and followed Beau around like a dog. Troy was the one person he did trust, even if he was a horse.

Beau came back and gave him a mint before he started to brush him down. Troy turned to watch and tried to nibble his butt, making him laugh. "Would you quit that, buddy?" He straightened up and came back to rub his nose.

"He's telling you he missed you."

Beau hadn't spotted Mason standing in the shadows. He smiled. "I've missed him, too. I just didn't realize how much till I got out here."

"You should get out here more. It'd do you good."

He nodded. "You're right."

"Wow. No arguments? No telling me that you don't like to be around here?"

That took Beau by surprise. He was normally the one to go there while Mason tried to steer clear of the touchy subjects.

"Not today, Mase, no. Today's a good day. I don't want to argue. I want to enjoy being here. And besides he's not even around. Maybe that's why I feel more comfortable." That last part wasn't true at all. He hadn't even given Chance a thought until now. He couldn't resist making the dig though.

Mason shook his head. "Why can't you just let it go? He's never done a damned thing to you."

Beau clenched his jaw. His fist curled into a ball at his side. Then he deliberately relaxed. "I'm trying. I know you're right. But it's hard."

"Why? What's so hard about it? I don't get it. I never have."

Beau shrugged. He wasn't sure he got it either. Why did he resent Chance so much? Their dad had brought Chance to the ranch when Beau was still a teenager. Chance had done a stint in prison. He had some murky, tragic past and their dad had wanted to give him a second chance. He was a great guy like that. Beau loved that about him. He liked to help people improve their lives, improve themselves. He was ashamed to admit it, but he'd been jealous of Chance. He worshipped his dad and had spent his childhood doing whatever he could to try to impress him. To win his love, his approval, his affection. It just didn't seem fair to him that he'd worked so hard to earn all of that from his own father, while Chance had screwed up his own life and still benefitted from Dave Remington's love and generosity.

"Sorry," said Mason. "I don't want to push it. Not when you're out here to enjoy yourself for once. I guess I'm just getting antsy about the whole deal with the wedding coming up. I know you don't like the idea of me and Gina taking over the big house. To be honest, it weirds me out. It belongs to all of us."

Beau shook his head. "No, it's right. With Mom and Dad going down to Arizona for the winter, it'd be weird for the place to stand empty. I don't really have a problem with you guys moving in there at all." He hesitated, wondering whether he should let Mason in on his plans. What the hell, Mase was trying to open things up between them, to talk honestly about the changes they both knew were coming. Their dad was going to divide the ranch between them all. The four brothers and Chance. Beau's problem with Chance getting an equal share didn't have anything to do with the cottage though. He smiled. "I'm going to tell you something if you can keep it under your hat till I'm ready to tell the folks."

Mason raised an eyebrow. "You're pregnant?"

Beau had to laugh. "Nope. I'm relieved to say I'm not. Though sorry to say that it'd have to be an immaculate conception if I was."

Mason patted his shoulder. "Poor Beau. You just need to get laid, that'd help you chill a bit I'm sure."

"Yeah. Whatever. Do you want to know what I'm up to or not?"

"Course I do."

"Okay. Well, since you and Gina are going to be moving out of the cottage, I'm going to give it to Mom and Dad."

"Wow! Give it to them?"

Beau nodded. "What do you think?"

Mason nodded slowly. Then looked up at Beau with a grin. "I think it's awesome. I mean it's one thing me and G living in the big house while the folks are down in Arizona for the winter. But I have been wondering what we're going to do when they come back in the spring."

"Exactly. I don't see the four of you sharing the place. It's big enough, but that's hardly the point."

"I know. Dad was talking about maybe buying a little house up in town, but I can't see either of them being happy there."

"I can't imagine them not being on the ranch. I figure this is the best of all worlds. You're going to be running the place, you should be here. But the cottage is right there." He turned and pointed past the barn to where the roof of the cottage was just visible. They'll still be on the ranch, still be around everyone, but not responsible for everything."

Mason grasped his shoulder. "It's a great idea, Beau. And I know they both love the place. Every time they come over Mom goes on about how sweet it is."

Beau nodded. He should be happy at that news, but part of him couldn't help thinking that they never came over to his place in town. That was dumb though. They went to the cottage because it was right there on their doorstep. "Well. Don't say anything to anyone yet. I'm going to tell them in the next couple of days. I'm just waiting for the right time."

"Of course not." Mason turned at the sound of neighing inside the barn. He smiled. "That's little Gypsy by the sounds of it. I'd better go turn her out." He gave Beau a look he didn't quite understand. "She's got as much to say for herself as her little rider does."

Beau made a face. "She's not that bad."

Mason laughed. "Neither's Ruby really. She gave me a kiss after her lesson today."

Beau shuddered at the thought, making Mason laugh again.

"I saw you chatting with her mom."

Hmm. What was he supposed to say about that, he wondered. He didn't know, so he just nodded.

"She's a good-looking woman," said Mason.

"She is."

Mason raised an eyebrow. "Not your type?"

It was Beau's turn to laugh. "Physically, she's my type, but she's the mother of the monster."

"So?"

"So how in the hell could a guy take her out on a date?"

"Quite simple. You ask. You go out."

"Yeah, right. And then you see each other a couple of times, and you want to do something fun on the weekend. What do you do? You have to take the monster with you anywhere you go."

"And?"

"And where's the fun in that? She's a two-foot tyrant! A menace to society. You can't have any fun with her around. She has to be the center of everything."

"She's five years old. That's what they do."

"Exactly!"

Mason chuckled. "So you're not interested then?"

Beau shook his head rapidly. "No. I find Corinne attractive." Talk about an understatement! "But not attractive enough to have to get involved with Ruby as well."

Mason rubbed his chin looking thoughtful.

"Why?" asked Beau. "What does it matter to you?"

"Nothing. Doesn't matter to me at all. I just wondered. Seems like most of the guys find her as attractive as you do. I don't think they mind Ruby though." He shrugged. "I guess I'm just curious to see what'll happen. There aren't too many young, attractive single women around here are there?"

"No." Beau sighed. And it was just his luck that the one who had shown up had decided he was an asshole. And why wouldn't she? He'd told her that her daughter was a monster who gave kids a bad name!

"I'd better get moving," said Mason. "It's good to see you."

"You too." Beau watched him walk back into the barn before turning back to Troy who had waited patiently while they talked. "Come on then, buddy. Let's get you back out."

Troy snorted and nodded his head as if in agreement, making Beau laugh.

After he'd turned Troy out, he made his way up to the big house and let himself into the kitchen. He was surprised to find Carter and Summer in there.

"Hey," said Carter. "I hear you took Troy out."

"Yup. We had a good time of it too."

"Good for you. It does you good. At least I know it does me good. I've been riding a lot more since Summer's been learning, and I'm loving getting to spend time with Jake again."

Beau smiled. He was happy for Carter. "Yeah. I might not have as good a reason as you have for riding again, but it did do me good."

"I can see it, darling," said his mom who had appeared in the hallway. "You look more relaxed than I've seen you in a long time. You work too hard, you should play more."

He nodded. "I'm trying. I took off work early yesterday and I came out to ride today."

Summer smiled at him. "And you're coming out to dinner on Wednesday."

He nodded.

"Oh good." His mom had an odd gleam in her eye.

"We've all been having dinner once a week for a while now, Mom. You know that."

"Yes, but this week the numbers will be even for the first time."

He cocked his head to one side, not understanding.

Carter grinned at him. "Shane's new manager is going to join us. Corinne. She doesn't know anyone yet, so the girls wanted to invite her."

Beau didn't know how to react. His heart was racing and his palms were sweaty. Just like the first time he'd heard her voice. But that had been because he found that voice, and then her appearance, very attractive. Now he wasn't so sure how he felt. He'd made a fool of himself this afternoon talking about Ruby. And he'd no doubt pissed Corinne off in the process. Spending an evening in her company wasn't going to be too comfortable after that. And it wouldn't be comfortable at all if she was going to bring Ruby! How could that work? Their family dinners were a time to catch up and laugh—and talk freely, not mind their language and explain things to a five year old.

"Do you mind?" Summer was giving him a puzzled look.

He shook his head. "Of course not. It just hit me that I might not be able to make it on Wednesday. I have to go over to Billings and I'm not sure what time I'll be back."

That was bullshit and the looks on the faces staring back at him told him that they knew it. Well? What was he supposed to do?

"Anyway. I was just stopping in to say hi, before I left. I need to get going." He went to his mom and gave her a hug.

"Your dad should be back any minute. Don't you want to wait so you can see him?"

"I'll catch him next time. See ya." He turned around and let himself back out, then he ran back to his truck and started it up. He drove the length of the driveway and out onto East River Road before he let his breath out. What the hell was that all about? So he was disappointed that Ruby was going to spoil his night with his brothers. That was no reason to turn tail and leave, was it? He thought about it while he drove back up the valley toward town. No, it really wasn't. But the thought of being around Ruby for the evening wasn't really what had unsettled him. It was the thought of being around Corinne that had done that. He knew damned well that his brothers would immediately spot what was going on—how attracted he was to her. He didn't need that!

Corinne had just got Ruby down for a nap when she heard a tap on the front door. She wasn't sure she liked this. She hadn't even been here a week, yet there was always someone stopping by. She wasn't used to it. She had to smile when she opened the front door and saw Summer standing there. Summer was a sweet, kind person, but it was weird to be hanging out with someone she'd only previously known as a voice singing on the radio.

"Hi. I hope I'm not disturbing you?"

"It's okay. I'll step outside. I just got Ruby to sleep." She pulled the front door to behind her.

"I'm sorry," said Summer.

"It's not a problem. It's as much for your sake as mine. If she wakes up and sees you, she'll want to keep you."

Summer smiled. "She's a little sweetheart."

Corinne liked to think so. But what Beau had said this afternoon had upset her. And it did have her wondering. She knew Ruby was strong-willed. She encouraged her to speak her mind, but she tried to teach her to do so respectfully, and to understand that adults were the ones in charge. She was a character, but she wasn't rude or naughty. At least that's what Corinne had thought. Beau seemed to think otherwise. "Do you really think so?"

"Of course I do, why?"

Corinne sighed. "Sorry. It's just someone said something today that made me wonder."

"Oh no. Who? Said what?"

"That doesn't matter. I just wanted a reality check. He had me wondering if I'm blinded by my love for her and if she really is a little monster like he thinks."

"Beau!" Summer shook her head.

"How did you know that?"

Summer gave her an apologetic smile. "Ruby took quite a liking to him when she first met him. He didn't know how to handle that. Or to handle her. It's not that he doesn't like her or anything. He's just not used to kids. None of the Remington brothers are."

"Well, the others seem to do just fine with her. Mason had her eating out of his hand. He didn't think she was a monster!"

Summer touched her arm. "I don't think Beau does either. He just doesn't know how to deal with her. He's a good guy really."

"Yeah. He's just got his head up his ass!"

Summer laughed. "Oh, so you have had a chance to get to know him then?"

Corinne smiled. "Sorry. I shouldn't have said that. But it's what Ruby came out with. Apparently she overheard Cassidy."

"I'm sorry. Cassidy's another one who doesn't know how to behave around children. I'll tell her to watch her language."

"No. You can't do that. We can't just come in here and make everyone change their ways. I do understand that."

"It's not exactly a big deal. It's what you do, when you're used to kids. It's just that these guys aren't. They'll get used to it, just give them a chance."

"I suppose. You sound as though you're used to kids."

Summer nodded. "I have a lot of cousins who are much younger. I haven't spent much time with them in the last few years, but in our family there were always little ones around. And, believe me, compared to most of them, Ruby is an absolute angel!"

"She is a little strong-willed."

Summer smiled. "And that's a good thing. She knows her own mind and she's not afraid to speak it."

"That's true. I should forget it. Forget Beau."

Summer raised an eyebrow.

Oh, no. Corinne had to hope that Summer didn't realize that it was more than his opinion of Ruby that had gotten to her. "He's just a guy who doesn't like kids. It's not as though we're going to run into him that often."

"He's a good-looking guy," said Summer.

Corinne nodded. There was no point denying it. All the Remington men were.

"And you'll probably run into him on Wednesday evening."

Corinne's heart leaped, and then sank. "We don't have to come."

"Yes, you do! We invited you. We want you there."

"But I don't want to spoil things. You're used to having a grown-ups night. I'm sure Beau won't want Ruby spoiling it for him."

"She won't spoil it for him. Or anyone. He might not even make it. He says he's got some meeting to go to and might not be back in time. I just wanted to warn you." Summer smiled. "And to see what your reaction might be. You like him, don't you?"

Corinne met her gaze. She didn't know what to say. She couldn't deny it, but she didn't want to admit it. She shrugged. "He's a good-looking guy. That's all I know about him. That and the fact that he doesn't like my daughter. How could I like him when he thinks Ruby's a monster?"

Summer gave her a knowing look. "He doesn't. Anyway. I just came over to give you my number before we go home. I realized you didn't have it. If ever you want me to keep an eye on Ruby for you, you just give me a call, okay?"

"Thank you!" It was so strange to think that she was living out here in the middle of nowhere and now if she needed someone to watch Ruby, she could call the country superstar, Summer Breese! Once she saved the number in her phone, she looked up at Summer. "Do you mind if I ask you something?

"Ask away."

"How's your voice doing? You sound perfectly fine most of the time."

Summer smiled. "I am. It's doing great. It gets a little bit scratchy if I talk too much for too long, as you'll probably notice on Wednesday, but it's so much better than it was. It seems it was stress that made it worse, and I was stressed about a lot of things. Now I'm not. I'm happy." She certainly looked happy. Who wouldn't be if they were engaged to Carter? He was gorgeous and he obviously adored her. They made such a cute couple.

"And that's all down to you coming here, and to Carter?"

Summer nodded. "It is. When I came here I thought all I was looking for was some peace and quiet and a rest. I had no idea I'd find everything I didn't know I was looking for. Everything I need to be happy."

"I'm glad it worked out that way for you."

"You never know, it might work out that way for you."

Corinne shook her head. "I came here for a job, and hopefully to build a good life for Ruby."

"And who knows what else you might find."

They both looked up at the sound of a truck approaching. Summer smiled. "I told him I'd walk back up."

Corinne smiled at the sight of Carter leaning out of his truck window. She would have waved, but he only had eyes for Summer. That was a man in love if ever she'd seen one.

"I'd better go."

"Okay, see you. And thanks for your number, and the offer."

"It'll be my pleasure. I do love Ruby, don't you go thinking anything else okay?"

"Thanks."

Chapter Five

"What in hell's name is wrong with you today?" asked Wanda.

Beau turned to scowl at her. "Is that any way to talk to your boss?"

She laughed. "It is when he's behaving like a butt hurt five year old. What's your problem?"

"I don't have a problem. Unless you count having an assistant who can't keep her nose out of my personal business as a problem. Then I'd say you're my problem."

Wanda shook her head. "Okay, so it's your personal business that's got you in a tizzy, is it? As long as you're not losing money, or about to go bankrupt. I need this job. I didn't know you had a personal life. I thought you just locked yourself inside your fancy house at the end of the day and ceased to exist until business needed you again in the morning. So come on, tell your Auntie Wanda. What's upsetting my Beau-Beau?"

Beau pushed his chair away from his desk and leaned his head back against the wall. He looked up at the ceiling and let out a reluctant laugh. "You know I should fire your ass?"

Wanda smiled. "Apart from two small details. For one, you wouldn't know what to do without me anymore, and for two, no one else in this town would work for you. You're screwed, you're stuck with me. So why don't you tell me why you've been stomping around all day like a toddler in a tantrum?"

"A toddler in a tantrum?"

Wanda folded her arms across her ample bosom and leaned in the doorway to his office. She nodded her head firmly.

"That's harsh."

"It's true is what it is."

Beau sighed. "If you really want to know, I'm supposed to go to dinner at Carter and Summer's place tonight." He stopped. He wasn't really going to explain to Wanda what had him on edge, was he?

"And?" She raised an eyebrow. "I thought dinner with your brothers was one of the few things in life you actually enjoy?"

"It is. Usually."

"So what's different about this time? What's got your panties in a wad?"

He had to laugh. "Okay. If you really want to know…" He stopped again, not quite believing he was going to admit it.

"I do. So spill. Tell your Auntie Wanda all about it."

He shook his head at her. "I can't believe I'm going to tell you. We both know you're only going to give me shit."

She nodded eagerly. "Just tell me already."

He blew out a sigh. "Okay. Well, you know Shane brought in a new manager for the lodge at the ranch?"

Wanda nodded. "She's the one who came from California. Carly's sister? Corinne, is that her name?"

Of course Wanda had dealt with Corinne's sister Carly when she was here looking at property. "Yeah. That's her. Well, she's invited to dinner, too." The glint in Wanda's eye made him nervous.

"And this is a problem because…?"

Beau scooted his chair back up to his desk, folded his arms on it and leaned forward. "Because she is the mother of the two-foot tyrant. You remember that little kid that was running around with Carly and James?"

"Ruby? She's a little sweetheart."

Beau snorted. "She's a little demon."

"And she's going to dinner too? You're going to let a five year old scare you away?"

"I don't even know if she's going to be there."

Wanda came into the office and pulled up a chair. She was trying to conceal a grin, but she wasn't succeeding. "Okay, so let me get this straight. You're not happy that Corinne is going to be at the dinner. The only thing you have against her is that she's Ruby's mom, but you don't know if Ruby is even going to be there. So..." She folded her own arms on the desk and leaned toward him. "Why would it be a problem that she's Ruby's mom?"

He shrugged.

"Come on now, tell me. You like her, don't you?"

He shrugged again.

A victorious smile spread across Wanda's face. "I knew it. You've been weird all week."

"No, I haven't!"

"Yes, you have! And now I know why. This Corinne's caught your eye, and you're pissed that you finally met an attractive woman, but she has a five year old kid in tow. Am I right or am I right?"

"You're right." There was no point denying it. "But I don't know what you're looking so pleased about. It sucks."

She patted his hand. "Aww, poor Beau."

He shook his head at her. "It's not funny, Wanda. I managed to thoroughly piss her off."

"Uh-oh. What did you do?"

"Well, I didn't know Ruby was hers."

Wanda raised her eyebrows and waited.

"I may have mentioned that Ruby was a monster and that she gives kids a bad name."

"Why the hell would you say something like that?"

"Because it's true!"

Wanda shook her head. "So you haven't exactly endeared yourself to her then."

"That's an understatement if ever I heard one. I think she hates me. So even if Ruby doesn't go tonight, it's not exactly going to be comfortable to be around Corinne. And if Ruby does go…"

Wanda laughed. "If I were you, I'd be hoping Ruby does go."

Beau looked at her as though she'd lost it.

"That way you could start to show her momma how good you can be with her."

Beau shuddered. "No way. I'd rather not go. In fact, I'm thinking I won't."

"And that's what got you all pissy. You want to go."

"Yeah, but either way it's not worth it."

Wanda gave him a stern look. "Just like I said. A toddler in a tantrum."

"Yeah. Thanks for the understanding. Glad I opened up to you. This little chat is over."

Wanda laughed. "No, it isn't. I'll tell you when it's over. You're so closed up you never let anyone in. I've barged my ample ass through the walls you keep up, and I ain't leaving till I've said my piece."

Beau wanted to laugh. She was right. He didn't let anyone in, didn't confide in anyone. This was weird, opening up to Wanda of all people, but he kind of liked it.

"You listen to me, Beau Remington. You're a good man. You're smart, and you're used to making things happen. You're not used to things getting out of your control and because you're not used to it, you don't know how to deal with it. Right now you're stropping around like a little kid who can't have things his own way. And I'm only telling you that so that you'll see the truth of it and quit it. When you do admit it, then you can man up and deal with it. Either you'll decide that this Corinne is worth you getting used to Ruby for, or you'll accept—graciously—that you can't have what you want this time and move on."

When she'd finished Beau stared at her for a long moment.

Eventually she cocked her head to one side. "So say something already. Even if it's just that you're firing my ass!"

He laughed. "Sorry. It's hard."

"What is?"

He gave her a rueful smile. "I might choke on the thing I have to say."

"Which is what?"

He nodded. "Thank you."

She grinned at him "You are more than welcome. I really thought I'd blown it for a minute there. No one talks to you like that, do they?"

"No and it's not easy to hear. But that doesn't make it any less true."

She nodded.

Beau smiled at her. He didn't have the words to tell her how grateful he was for the verbal ass-kicking. And he wouldn't have spoken them if he did. No one did speak to him like that, ever. Maybe his family used to, but these days they tended to just avoid the subjects that set him off. That wasn't good. Why had it taken Wanda to make him see it? He looked up and met her gaze. "Why do you care so much?"

She looked flustered for a moment and then grinned at him. "Care? All I care about is my job. I need the pittance you pay me, so while I have to be around you every day I'll take any chance I get to make you into an almost-decent human being."

That made him laugh. What else could he do? If she hadn't walked down the path to her banter, he might have had trouble swallowing the lump in his throat.

"Of course. I'm just a paycheck to you. I knew that. So, if you want your day to be bearable tomorrow, what do you think I should do?"

She smiled. "Go to dinner. Don't make excuses, go. If Ruby's there, be nice to her. That kid loves you."

"Jesus! What would she be like if she hated me?"

Wanda laughed. "You're just not used to little kids. They're just little people, like you and me only with less filters."

"Is that why you relate to them so well?"

"I'm trying to help you here. If Ruby's there, make an effort with her, play with her. And if she's not, well, you don't need me telling you how to make an effort with her mother, I hope?"

He shook his head. Women liked him. Well, they usually did. Corinne had, until he'd goofed up about her daughter. He sighed. "What's the point though?"

"What do you mean?"

"Yeah, I like her, but what's the point? Why make an effort with Corinne?"

"Because you'd like to go out with her?"

"Exactly, but what would that look like? We'd get maybe one or two dates before Ruby was tagging along too."

"That's how it goes when you date a single mom."

Beau glared. "That's why I don't date single moms. And this one especially. The thought of having a kid tagging along is bad enough, the thought of that kid being Ruby is a deal-breaker."

Wanda sighed. "Then I guess all you can do is accept that things didn't work out for you this time. And if you could work on the gracious part, I'd appreciate it."

He stared at her. The humor was gone from her face and her voice. He nodded. He didn't know what to say. He felt like he'd disappointed her—and it wasn't a feeling he liked, but what choice did he have?

Wanda stood and made her way to the door. She paused and looked back when she reached it. "I hope you'll still go to dinner though. You shouldn't let the things you can't have screw up the things you do have."

"Wow, that's deep." He wanted to make her smile again. It didn't work.

She shrugged and made her way back out to the reception desk. She'd left him with a lot to think about.

Corinne checked the mirror. She looked good. She just hoped it was right. She had no clue what people wore to dinner around here. In fact, she hadn't seen anyone wear anything but jeans to do anything at all. However, did that mean that they all dressed up to the nines whenever they got an excuse to? She hoped not. She could have asked, she could have called Summer or Cassidy, she supposed. She hadn't wanted to though. She needed to appear capable and confident as she moved into her new role managing the lodge. She sighed. She'd erred on the side of caution and chosen her nicest jeans and paired them with a green top. If she had it all wrong, she shouldn't be too far underdressed or overdressed—she hoped.

She turned at the sound of a knock on the door. It seemed that door might wear through with all the callers she'd had since she'd moved in. At least this wasn't a surprise.

"Hi, Susie," she greeted the woman standing there with a smile. "Come on in."

Ruby came flying out of her room with a big smile on her face. She wrapped her arms around Susie's legs and smiled up at her. "Can we do letters?"

Susie smiled back. "Maybe in a little while. I need to talk to your momma first."

Ruby looked at Corinne. "You look pretty."

"Thank you." Corinne hadn't been sure about this arrangement at first. Susie worked at the lodge and Shane had suggested that Corinne talk to her about watching Ruby when she needed help. That had turned into what sounded like an ideal arrangement for both of them. Susie worked from eight to two everyday so she could get her grandkids to school and pick them up. Now she was going to take Ruby, too. And she was happy to watch her whenever Corinne needed. Her first meeting with Ruby had been a great success and Corinne was hopeful that this would all work. She wasn't holding her breath on it, though. She looked at Susie. "I shouldn't be too late back."

Susie gave her a reassuring smile. "You just go and have yourself a good time. That's what we'll be doing."

"Yes," said Ruby. "We're going to do letters."

Ruby had spent a couple of hours at Susie's yesterday afternoon. Apparently she'd had a grand time, made fast friends with the grandchildren and was now eager to get started at Pre-K with them.

"You'll do as Miss Susie tells you, okay?"

Ruby nodded.

"Honestly, you don't need to worry about a thing. I've had lots of practice at this and I have your number in case we need anything."

"Okay. Thank you." Corinne was nervous, but it wasn't only about leaving Ruby. She was confident in Susie and her ability to handle anything that came up. If she was honest, she was more nervous about the evening ahead. She shouldn't be. Summer and Cassidy were great. Shane may be her new boss, but he was a great guy. Carter was an absolute sweetheart, even if he didn't say much. Mason had been so kind to her and to Ruby, and his fiancée, Gina, had been pleasant on the few brief occasions they'd met. No she wasn't nervous about any of them, or about spending an evening with them. It was Beau.

"Are you okay?" asked Susie, making her realize that she'd been standing there staring while she thought about it.

"Yes. Sorry. I'll just get my purse and be on my way." She stopped at the front door and hugged Ruby to her. So what if Beau thought she was a monster? What did he know? "You be a good girl."

"I will. You have a nice time."

Corinne kissed her cheek. "Thank you, sweetie."

Susie held the door open for her.

"Call me for any reason, okay?"

Susie smiled. "Stop worrying. But yes, I promise I'll call you if we need you."

"Thanks." As the door closed behind her, Corinne wanted to run back inside. She felt as though she was being pushed out into her new world, her new life, and she wasn't ready for it yet. She took a deep breath and made herself get a grip. That was ridiculous. Of course she was ready. She was going to get this new life off to a great start. Screw Beau Remington! She chuckled as she walked down the path to her car. No! That was one thing she was not going to do.

It was just a short drive up East River Road from the ranch to Summer and Carter's place. Mason and Gina had offered to pick her up on their way there, but she'd declined. She didn't want to seem rude or standoffish, but she did want to be able to make her escape whenever she was ready. She needn't have worried. Gina had given her an understanding smile and had stopped Mason from trying to insist. Corinne had a feeling that she and Gina might become friends given the chance.

She didn't have any problems finding the place. She'd driven by yesterday just to make sure she knew where she was going. She turned in and drove down the long driveway. Once she'd pulled up in front of the house she took a good look around. It was a beautiful place. A gorgeous log built home that was far too grand to be called a cabin. It sat on the bank of the river and there were beautiful views of the mountains in every direction. She started to regret her decision to wear jeans. Maybe she should have dressed up more. She turned to look as a truck pulled up beside her.

Gina grinned at her through the window. Corinne was relieved to see that she was wearing a nice, but not dressy, top.

"I told you, you should have let us give you a ride," said Mason as he got out of the truck and came around. He too was wearing jeans, and a shirt she'd seen him wear at the ranch.

Gina smiled at Corinne. She really had understood. "I know I'd have driven myself if I were you. There's nothing like being able to make a quick exit when you want one."

Corinne smiled back. "It's only because of Ruby though. I'd hate to have to cut your evening short if Susie calls."

"We could have taken you home and then come back," said Mason.

Gina patted his arm. "We all know you can take of us, Mase. We get it. But I think Corinne is used to taking care of herself." She linked her arm through Corinne's and started up the steps to the front door.

"I do appreciate the offer." Corinne smiled at him. He seemed like he was used to taking charge and taking care of people. Even though she didn't want or need his help this evening, she didn't want to offend him.

He grinned. "That's okay. I'm learning. Gina here says I can be a bit domineering, but I'm only trying to help. Apparently you ladies like to be a bit more independent than I give you credit for."

Gina linked her free arm through his and smiled up at him. "You really are learning. And I do love you for trying."

The two of them were obviously very much in love. It made Corinne smile to see the way they looked at each other. She'd never had a love like that; she'd doubted that it even existed, but Gina and Mason were living proof that it did.

As they reached the top of the steps the front door flew open and Shane appeared. "You made it!"

Mason laughed. "Of course we did. We're not even late."

Shane rolled his eyes. "I didn't mean you, asshole. I mean my new best friend, Corinne." He took hold of her arm and led her inside.

"Hey everybody, Corinne's here!" he called as he led her into the kitchen.

She already knew Shane well enough to know that this was just his way. He was full of life, and energy—and loud!

Cassidy caught her eye and laughed. "I'm sorry. You'll have to excuse the asshole I call my fiancé."

Shane grinned. "Ignore her. She's mean to me. Mean I tell you."

Summer laughed. "Don't buy it for a minute, Corinne. No one is ever mean to Shane. He just likes to go for the sympathy vote every chance he gets."

Carter gave her a shy smile, and nodded. "It's true. Can I get you a drink?"

She nodded. Wondering what might be on offer.

"I already poured you one."

Beau! He'd made it then. Part of her had been hoping he wouldn't, but she couldn't deny that part of her had been hoping he would.

Chapter Six

Corinne had to catch her breath at the sight of him standing there. Wow! She'd seen him in a suit in the wine store, in riding gear—complete with cowboy hat—at the ranch on the weekend, and now here he was rocking the casual GQ look. He was gorgeous! She tried to recover her composure when she realized that everyone was watching.

Beau came toward her with two glasses of red wine. He held one out to her. She looked down at it then up into deep brown eyes. She ran her tongue over her lips, not sure she'd be able to speak, her mouth had gone so dry. She didn't miss the way his pupils dilated before he smiled.

"It's good stuff. I know you like it."

She looked down at the glass again. More of the expensive Cab?

He nodded, seeming to have heard the question she hadn't asked as she took it from him.

"Thank you."

"Can I take it you two have met before?" asked Shane.

Corinne wasn't sure she liked the mischievous gleam in his eye. She simply nodded, unsure how best to answer.

Beau surprised the hell out of her when he came to stand beside her. "We have."

Her traitorous body was loving the closeness of him. Waves of goose bumps chased each other down her spine as he rested his hand on the counter behind her. Why could her brain not take charge and remind her racing heart and butterfly-filled stomach that this man thought Ruby was a monster?

"Hey, Corinne," called Cassidy. "You need to come out on the deck and see the view from here."

She knew Cassidy was trying to rescue her—from the brother that she thought had his head up his ass! Part of her wanted to stay by his side, but that was crazy! Cassidy was offering her weak-willed self a lifeline, and she needed to grab onto it while she could.

"If you'll excuse me?" She didn't dare look into his eyes; she just hurried over to where Cassidy was waiting by the doors that led out onto the deck. She could feel him watching her with every step she took.

Once they were out on the deck, Cassidy closed the door behind them and held up her glass in a toast. "You can thank me anytime, though now would be good."

Corinne laughed and chinked her glass against Cassidy's. "Thank you."

Cassidy raised an eyebrow. "So how do you know Beau?"

"I don't know him. We just ran into each other a couple of times already."

"Oh, shit! You don't like him, do you? I didn't screw up, did I?"

"No! I appreciate you springing me from what could have been an awkward moment."

"Why awkward? And why didn't you say no?"

"No to what?"

"To the question of whether you like him."

Corinne blew out a sigh. "Okay. I can answer both questions in one go." Why not? She may as well admit what was going on.

Cassidy was going to be a part of her life, she hoped they would become friends, and friends shared confidences. "Awkward because, yes, I do find him attractive."

Cassidy shrugged. "I can see that. He is a good-looking guy."

"However, he can't stand Ruby and," she had to smile, "I have it on good authority that he has his head up his ass!"

Cassidy chuckled. "Umm. I'm guessing I may have screwed up and said that when Ruby was around?"

Corinne nodded. "Just a heads-up, if you don't want something repeated, make sure she's not within earshot when you say it."

"And try to make sure I don't use any bad words, right? I'm sorry."

Corinne held up a hand. "No, I wasn't…"

"It's okay. You're too nice to say it, but I should know better. Anyway, where does all that leave you with Beau? Torn, I guess?"

Corinne shook her head. "No. It has to be cut and dried. How could I like a guy who thinks my daughter is a monster?"

Cassidy pursed her lips. "I'm sure Beau thinks all kids are monsters. It's nothing personal."

"It is to me!"

"I know, but…Damn, I can't believe I'm going to stick up for him, but I guess he and I are the same in this. He's not used to kids. He doesn't know how to treat them, and well, more than that even, Beau's not used to anyone telling him what's what. From what I've seen, Ruby speaks her mind." She smiled. "You know, I just realized that maybe I've struggled with Ruby because she and I are pretty much alike. Strong, smart and not afraid to speak our minds." She nodded. "She's a good kid!"

Corinne had to smile, thankful that Cassidy's breakthrough regarding Ruby had come so easily. If only the same thing could happen for Beau! "Okay, so you figured out what your problem with her has been." She noticed that Cassidy made no attempt to politely deny that she'd had a problem. "What do you think Beau's problem is?"

"Like I said. She speaks her mind. She tells it like it is." She thought about it for a few moments. "I guess they're too much alike as well. He's used to getting his own way. And he's used to being in charge, in control."

Corinne nodded. That certainly described Ruby even though she didn't like to admit it. "But they're traits that are acceptable in a little girl, even if not desirable. But she's just exploring her world and finding her place in it. Describing a full-grown man in the same way doesn't make him sound very appealing."

Cassidy shrugged. "Maybe I'm being too harsh."

"But you don't like him?"

"It's not that. It's just. I don't know. He's not as open as the others, I don't know him as well, but I think that's because he's not easy to get to know."

"Hey, ladies," Summer stuck her head out the door. "The coast's clear in the kitchen now if you want to come back in?"

"Thanks." Corinne followed Cassidy back inside

"Where've they gone?" asked Cassidy.

Summer smiled. "Carter decided he wanted to show them his new greenhouse he's working on. Though I think it was really just an excuse to get all the guys out of the way so us girls could talk."

Gina smiled. "He's such a sweetheart. He makes out he's so clueless, but he keeps an eye on everything, doesn't he?"

Summer's eyes shone and she nodded her agreement. "He's the most amazing guy ever."

Corinne smiled at the way Cassidy rolled her eyes. "Forgive our little love-struck missy here."

"Nothing to forgive," said Corinne. "I think it's awesome."

"Thank you," said Summer.

"Looks like someone else is love-struck from what I could tell, too," said Gina. She raised an eyebrow at Corinne. "What's the story with you and Beau?"

She sighed. "There isn't one. I mean, he's an attractive guy. I know none of you will argue with that, he's a Remington after all, but that's all there is to it."

"You don't like him?"

"Whether I like him or not is irrelevant."

"But why?"

"Because he doesn't like Ruby!"

"Oh." Gina's face fell. Corinne had to notice that she didn't have any arguments to offer. She shrugged. "It's okay. I'm used to it. Being a single mom and dating don't exactly go well together. If I'm going to take a risk on a guy I need to have a pretty strong inkling that he's worth it. From what I've seen," she looked around at the others, "and heard, Beau doesn't exactly inspire the right feeling."

"Aww," Summer looked upset. "I wish you'd give him a chance. He means well."

"If it was just about me, I probably would. But I have Ruby to consider. It's hard knowing that she thinks the world of him, when he can't stand her."

"I think it's more like he's scared of her," said Gina.

"Whatever it is, I don't want to take the risk of her getting hurt. It's just not worth it." She turned at the sound of guys coming back in. "I'm glad I got to talk to you all about it, but I'd rather we just dropped it?"

The others nodded their agreement.

"What's going on in here?" asked Shane as he came and wrapped an arm around Cassidy's shoulders. "What kind of trouble are you ladies brewing?"

Cassidy turned to look up at him with big wide innocent eyes. "Nothing. What makes you ask?"

"Now I'm worried," said Shane with a laugh. "I didn't think you were up to anything till you gave me the Little Miss Innocent look. Now I'm pretty damned sure you are."

Cassidy laughed and pushed him off her. "What are you saying?"

Shane shrugged. "That you, my love, can be accused of many things, but being innocent isn't one of them."

Cassidy huffed as she pushed him again. Corinne loved the banter and the sparring those two had going most of the time. She turned away and found Beau watching her. A jolt of electricity shot through her veins, making her scalp tingle—and other places too.

He raised his glass to her and came toward her. He really was a good-looking guy.

"Listen, I wanted to apologize for what I said about Ruby."

She nodded. She didn't know what to say, she hadn't thought he'd address it directly.

He leaned his head down and looked into her eyes, making her heart flutter, just the way he had when she'd first laid eyes on him. "I mean it. I'm sorry."

For a moment she stared back into those big brown eyes. It'd be so easy to get lost in them and to believe that he meant it. Like she'd just told the girls, if it were only about her, she'd take the risk and see where it went. But it wasn't just about her. It was about Ruby too. "Thank you."

He held her gaze for a moment longer and then gave a brief nod.

Beau turned away. What was he supposed to do? He couldn't lie and say that he thought Ruby was great really. He didn't! He did want to get to know Corinne, but he wasn't sure that Ruby was an obstacle he wanted to overcome in order to do so.

He was relieved when Summer called them all to sit down. Though when he made his way to the table he found himself seated beside Corinne. He gave her a rueful smile as he sat down.

"Do you think you can stand it?"

"Stand what?"

"Having to sit next to me."

Her smile took his breath away. She was so goddamned beautiful! "Of course I can. And since Ruby's not here, I'm guessing you can stand to sit by me as well."

He nodded. "I didn't mean to offend you."

"I know." She shrugged. "It's hard not to be defensive about her though. I'm all she's got. She's all I've got."

Beau thought about that. The perspective of a parent wasn't one he'd considered before. He nodded. "I'm sorry."

She gave a little laugh. "You don't need to keep saying it. How about we move on from there?"

"Gladly." He looked up to see the others watching them. He caught Mason's eye and lifted a shoulder.

He was pleased that Shane seemed to be in great form tonight. He kept everyone entertained with tales about the guest ranch. Occasionally Beau stole a glance at Corinne. She was enjoying herself, laughing with the others, not afraid to throw in a comment here and there. On more than one occasion their eyes met as he caught her looking at him. Why, oh why did she have to be Ruby's mom? It'd be a no-brainer if she wasn't. He was pretty sure that she felt the same way, but she did have a kid to consider. No matter what he thought of the kid, he did respect that. He thought again about what she'd said earlier. She was all Ruby had, Ruby was all she had. What must it be like to be wholly responsible for someone else's life? He shuddered at the thought. He'd never really given much thought to the matter of parenthood. Yeah, he'd assumed he'd be a dad someday. But someday was a long way away.

When they'd finished eating, the conversation turned to Corinne. Beau sat up a little straighter, eager to get to know more about her.

"Yeah," she was answering Mason. I did love Napa, I would have stayed there if I could."

"Just as long as you don't plan on hightailing it back there the first chance you get!" interjected Shane. "I need you."

Cassidy pushed at him. "Then start behaving like a grown-up or poor Corinne will want to get out of here as fast as she can."

Corinne laughed. "No, I like it here." She grinned at Shane. "Even though I'm not sure about my new boss yet."

"You should have a probationary period," said Cassidy. "Only the opposite of the usual. He needs to be on his best behavior if you're going to stay."

Corinne nodded. "That could work."

"And how about Ruby?" Beau couldn't figure out the look Summer shot him as she asked the question. "How's she settling in?"

Corinne nodded. "So far, so good. She's looking forward to starting Pre-K. And Susie's going to be picking her up and dropping her off."

"I'm glad that worked out," said Shane.

"Me too. Thanks so much for suggesting it."

"Sure thing. I knew she was looking after her grandkids, and I figured it might help you both out. Plus it gives Ruby some built-in friends before she starts school."

"Is she with Susie tonight?" asked Beau. He'd wondered where she was, but hadn't liked to ask.

"She is." Corinne checked her watch. "And I should probably get going. I don't want to leave them too long on their first night together.

Damn! Beau hadn't intended to scare her off.

"Don't go yet!" said Shane. "It's early! Susie will think you don't trust her if you go back now!"

Corinne shook her head. "I'm sure she'll understand a nervous momma."

Summer nodded. "You go if you want to. There'll be plenty of other times you can come for the whole evening."

Corinne gave her a grateful smile. Beau had to wonder how it must feel to be her. He had no clue.

He went with the others as they all gathered in the hallway to say good-bye to her. He hung back as hugs and kisses were exchanged. He came to his senses when he watched her hug Carter. No way was he about to miss out on that. He stepped forward and held his arms open to her. "It was good to see you again."

She froze as she stared up into his eyes. She looked like a rabbit caught in the headlights. He wasn't going to let her escape though. He stepped forward. He felt a tremor run through her as she leaned in to hug him. It passed through her and made him shiver too. Whatever this current was that was running between them, it had him letting her go far more quickly than he'd planned—but only so that he didn't make a fool of himself by giving in to the desire to kiss her—right there in front of everyone and to hell with it!

She looked stunned as she stepped back awkwardly. She backed into Mason and dropped her purse, sending its contents spilling all over the floor. She managed to push everything back inside, well, almost everything, Beau saw something she'd missed. She gave them all an embarrassed smile. "Well, now I really am going. Thanks for tonight this was great guys."

As he watched the girls walk her down the steps and to her car, he wondered if he should go after her. He shook his head. He knew he should, but he'd wait a little while first. As the guys made their way back to the living room, he bent down and picked up her cell phone from where it had slid under the bench in the hallway. He wouldn't leave it too long, he needed to follow her with it. He hated the thought of her driving alone with no phone if she needed it. He waited until she'd pulled away and the girls were making their way back up the steps.

He went out onto the front deck and held up the phone. "Look what she lost when she dropped her purse!"

"Oh, no!" Summer turned around to check but Corinne had already disappeared down the long driveway.

"We can drop it off to her on our way home," said Gina.

Beau shook his head. "What if she has a problem on the way home? I'll go take it to her."

"Thanks, Beau!" Summer looked genuinely relieved.

"Are you coming back?" Cassidy looked skeptical.

He shook his head. "I was about ready to head home anyway."

"Yeah, right!" Cassidy laughed. "Good luck. And you know, I've been with you on the whole Ruby thing, but if you think about her being just like you, only smaller. It gives you a whole different perspective."

Beau stared at her. He didn't know what to say. How did Cassidy even know that Ruby was a problem for him? Had Corinne told her? And if so, why?

She grinned at him. "Go give it a shot cowboy, we're not stupid. We can see what's going on, just think on before you screw either of them over, okay?"

He nodded. He didn't know what else to say.

Summer gave him an encouraging smile and Gina patted his arm as he walked past them and down the steps to his truck. As he climbed in, the thought struck him that he never bothered to lock it out here. He shook his head and started it up. That was hardly a detail he needed to be focusing on at the moment. What he needed to do was figure out what he was going to say to Corinne when he got to the cabin. What he probably should be figuring out was why the hell he hadn't told her about her phone before she left.

Chapter Seven

Corinne smiled to herself as she drove home. It had been a good evening. She'd enjoyed the company. When Carly had first told her about a possible job here in Montana she'd wondered what kind of people she might meet, whether she'd be able to make any friends in the back end of nowhere. Now she felt as though she couldn't ask for a nicer group of people anywhere.

Even Beau.

Watching him laugh with his brothers, chat with the girls, he did seem like a nice guy. There was no denying the effect he had on her. All he'd needed to do was put his hand on the counter behind her when he'd given her that glass of wine, and she'd gone all swoony! Then when he'd moved in for a hug before she left! Wow! If she didn't have Ruby to think about she would have been dragging him home with her! She chuckled at the thought. She wouldn't, that had never been her style, but it had been a long time since she'd had sex. And Beau seemed to have awakened her desire.

He'd even apologized for what he'd said about Ruby. He hadn't said he didn't mean it, or that it wasn't true, but he had at least apologized for saying it. She sighed. But what did it matter? Even if he was willing to give it a go, she couldn't. She couldn't do that to Ruby, couldn't expose her to a guy she already liked, knowing that he didn't like her. It wouldn't be fair to her. She got attached to people.

As she drove back down East River Road she realized she was lost in her thoughts and missing the opportunity to just take in the beauty of the place. The sun was setting, touching the mountains with gold and the sky with crimson. It was absolutely beautiful. She decided to stop in the pull out by the river. She was going home very early and she deserved to take just five minutes to take this all in. She cut the engine and sat to watch the sky change color with a big smile on her face. This was the first time since they'd arrived that she'd taken a minute to just sit and be and appreciate where she was. This felt like a sign, an omen that she was in the right place and good things were to come. She rolled down the window to let in the cool air and breathe it all in.

A few moments later she looked up at the sound of a vehicle approaching. It was a big, dark blue pickup truck. It didn't look like anything local though, it wasn't old and dust covered, but new and still shiny. A momentary panic swept through her—and she was sitting out here in the middle of nowhere, all alone. What was she thinking?

She watched as it pulled in behind her. She was torn, part of her wanted to follow her instincts and flee. Another part of her thought she was being silly. She was in Montana, bad things didn't happen here, people were friendly, they looked out for each other. It was probably someone stopping to see if she was okay. Not someone coming to murder her—she hoped. She put her hand on the key ready to start the car up and drive away in a hurry if she had to.

Her heart beat faster as she watched in the rearview mirror. The driver's door of the truck opened and a man climbed out. A tall, dark, very good-looking man. Beau! She let out a slightly hysterical laugh. Thank goodness it was him. But what on earth was he doing here?

Her heart was still racing, though it wasn't with fear anymore. She opened the door and got out as he approached.

"Are you all right?" he asked. His eyes were full of concern.

She nodded. "I am now I know it's you. You had me scared silly for a moment there."

"Did your car break down?"

"No. I'd just stopped to watch the sun go down."

"I see. Well, I'm sorry I scared you, but you scared me, seeing your car sitting there like that. I wondered what had happened."

She smiled. He really did seem relieved that she was okay. "I'm fine, like I said, I just stopped to take it all in for a few minutes. What are you doing out here anyway? I thought you lived up in town."

"I do." He looked shifty. "I came after you."

"Oh." She didn't know what else to say to that. "Why?"

He dug in his pocket and held out her cell phone. "You missed this when your things fell out of your purse."

"Oh, wow! Thank you! I didn't even know I didn't have it."

"I'm glad. When I saw your car parked there, I was worried that you'd broken down. I was just praying that you were still in the car and hadn't wandered off to find help since you didn't have your phone."

Corinne shuddered at the thought. It wasn't too far back to the cabin, but it wasn't a walk she liked the idea of taking at this time of night by herself.

He held out the phone and she took it from him. She looked up in surprise as their hands touched. She felt the same rush of heat, the same fluttering of her insides as she had every time he came close, but the touch of his hand intensified everything a hundred fold. Oh, he could be dangerous! Especially to a sex-starved woman living alone in the middle of nowhere!

From the look on his face he felt it, too. He smiled down at her. "I'm sorry we got off on the wrong foot."

She nodded. So was she. Looking up into his big brown eyes, she wished he was the kind of guy who loved kids and would enjoy hanging out with Ruby.

"Maybe we could try again? Start over?"

She sucked in a deep breath as he stepped closer. What exactly did he have in mind? He put his hands on her shoulders and looked down into her eyes, leaving her incapable of words, incapable of doing anything other than lifting her lips to meet his. It was the briefest kiss, a mere touching of lips before he lifted his head, but it left her senseless. His closeness eclipsed common sense, any sense at all. She stood there, looking up into his eyes, wishing he'd do it again.

One corner of his mouth lifted in the hint of a smile. "So what do you say?"

"To what?" She couldn't even remember what the question had been.

"To us starting afresh. To you forgetting what I said about Ruby."

Oh, damn! If only he hadn't mentioned Ruby! That had gone and broken the spell. She shook her head slowly.

"No?"

"There's no point, Beau. I like you, you like me. That's all well and good. However, I love Ruby and you can't stand her. That's not a recipe for anything good to happen, is it?"

"I'm not asking you to let me into your lives and become a permanent fixture or anything. I just thought we could see each other sometimes. Just you and me."

She raised an eyebrow at him. Was he suggesting what she thought he was? And was her heart beating so fast because she hoped he was? "What are you saying?"

He shrugged. "That maybe you'd like a grown-up night now and again."

She still wasn't sure that he meant what she thought he did. There was only one way to find out. "Are you suggesting we just…"

He held a hand up before she could finish. "Stop." His tone was so commanding that she did.

He stepped toward her and the look on his face made her take a step back. Now she was trapped between him and the car. He closed his arms around her and held her close to his chest. She wanted to moan and melt in his arms, his presence surrounded her, engulfed her. His lips came down on hers. There was nothing brief about this kiss, it was deep, and long and thorough as he tasted her and explored her. He pressed her back against the car and thrust his hips against hers. She did moan at the feel of his hard-on pushing between her legs. She couldn't help it, she rubbed herself against him, wanting more. So, of course, he lifted his head and smirked at her.

"So now, before you ask if I'm possibly suggesting what you think I am, answer me this."

"What?" she breathed.

"Can you honestly tell me you don't want to?"

She stared at him. How could she deny it? How could she admit it?

He brought his hands up to cup her face and smiled. "Just think about it, beautiful." He covered her mouth with his own and she clutched his shoulders, kissing him back hungrily, knowing it made her answer plain as day.

Then he stepped back. "I'll be waiting." He turned around and walked back to his truck. He didn't pull away though. He waited while she got into her car and started it up.

She kept an eye on him in the mirror as she drove the last few miles home and he followed. Who the hell did he think he was? Who did he think she was? It seemed he had a pretty good idea who she was, actually. A sex-hungry woman in the middle of nowhere who didn't have many options. She shook her head. That wasn't fair. It was him. He made her feel that way. She hadn't had sex in way too long, but it hadn't bothered her until she met Beau! And it wasn't that she wanted sex all of a sudden, it was that she wanted him!

Beau pulled over as she turned into the driveway at the ranch. She was home safe. It was crazy that he'd followed her the last couple of miles back here, but for some reason he'd had to. When he'd seen her car pulled over at the side of the road like that, all kinds of horrible scenarios had run through his head. He'd been worried sick until he'd seen her step out of the car. He wasn't the kind of guy who went around worrying about people. Like Wanda said, they ceased to exist for him when he wasn't around them. It wasn't that he was cold or heartless, at least he didn't think so, it was just that he was pretty much self-contained. People came into his world for a few minutes, or hours, then they were gone again, until the next time. Usually. Corinne was proving to be the exception. He hadn't managed to get her out of his head since he'd first heard her in the wine store. And when he'd watched her drive away after he'd kissed her, he couldn't stand the thought of not knowing that she'd made it home okay.

He turned the truck around. So, yeah. Now he knew she'd made it home. Home to Ruby! Life could be a bitch when it wanted to. Why couldn't he just meet a gorgeous woman who didn't have a kid? Or even one who had a sweet kid? He sighed as he headed back up to town. He had to wonder what she'd made of his offer, and whether she'd allow herself to take him up on it. He wasn't stupid, he'd known his fair share of women. More than his share if he was honest. He knew when a woman was attracted to him. There was no doubt in the world that Corinne was. He knew from the way she'd kissed him back that at least some part of her would love to have a grown-up night with him now and then. He shifted in his seat as one part of him grew bigger and harder at the thought of such a night.

The idea had come to him while he was driving after her to give her phone back. He'd been trying to figure out what the hell he was playing at. Why hadn't he given her the phone before she left? Because he'd wanted to go after her, to see her away from the others. He was attracted to her, but didn't want to get involved with her—because he didn't want to get involved with a kid. So he'd decided he may as well go after what he did want and lay it out for her. He'd love to spend time with her, and he'd love to get to know her better—in every sense. He could only be honest about it, and if she was in, great. If not, tough luck.

It was dark by the time he arrived home. He unlocked the front door and went through to the kitchen to pour himself a glass of wine. He'd been back to Deb's and bought another four bottles of the Cab. He needed to finish the one that was open.

His cell phone rang in his pocket and he pulled it out. Shane.

"What's up?"

"Just making sure there's nothing up with you."

"What might possibly be up with me, oh littlest of the brothers?"

Shane laughed. "Umm, my new manager maybe? It was hard to miss the fireworks flying between the two of you. Then you shot out of Carter's place to chase after her. Want to tell me what's going down?"

"Nothing."

Shane waited.

"Yet."

"Yeah, that's more like it. But how's it going to work?"

Beau thought about it. He didn't really want to tell Shane that he'd just made his newest employee an indecent proposal. He wasn't sure what Shane would make of it. He wasn't sure what he made of it himself really. "I don't know yet. It might not even work at all, but there's a spark there."

"Jesus, Beau. That's no spark, that's a big-ass flame waiting to ignite a wildfire."

Beau laughed.

"Seriously, bro. You're getting into something big there."

"You sound concerned." Beau might have expected that from Carter, but not Shane. It seemed his littlest brother really was growing up. Or maybe it was just the love of a good woman that helped him see farther than jokes and sex.

"I am. I don't see you taking on Ruby. And I don't see Corinne being interested in a guy who doesn't like her kid. I don't want to see you screw yourself over."

"And you don't want to lose your new lodge manager?"

Shane laughed. "No, I don't. Though I wouldn't mind seeing her turn into my next sister-in-law. I mean, then we'd have a full set."

Beau stared at the phone for a moment. "What the fuck, Shane? Have you lost it? This is me you're talking to, remember? Even if I was looking to settle down, it sure as hell wouldn't be with Ruby."

"Yeah. I know. Just pulling your leg." He didn't sound as though he was.

"Okay, well is that all you wanted to know?"

"I guess. Will you be out to the ranch this weekend?"

"Yeah. I want to ride Troy again, and I need to see the oldies."

"Uh-oh. Are you still on the warpath about the ranch?"

He sighed. "No. As a matter of fact, I want to do something nice for them. Not that you'll believe that of me. See ya."

He hung up, pissed that everyone got so antsy about his opinion on the division of the ranch, or more specifically on Chance getting a share. He stared out the window. Why shouldn't they get that way, though? He never missed an opportunity to make his opinion known. He felt bad. Shane had only been trying to talk honestly with him, and he'd shut him down. He needed to stop doing that. Wanda's words about him putting up walls and keeping people out echoed in his head. He picked his phone up and called Shane back.

"Hello?"

"It's me, asshole."

"I know."

"I'm sorry."

"Can you just wait while I find a way to record this conversation and then repeat that?"

He had to laugh.

"I'm sorry, too, Beau. I didn't mean to piss you off. I guess we've just gotten so much more relaxed with each other lately. I felt comfortable enough to say it before I remembered I shouldn't go there."

"Damn."

"What?"

"Am I that bad?"

"You haven't been lately, no."

"Well, I guess that's something, at least."

"It is. Anyway, we don't need to be on the phone for hours doing kissy, kissy make up stuff. I'm sorry, and I'm thrilled that you called me back."

"I'm sorry, too. I think I'm getting a bit better. And I'm glad I called you back, too."

"Great. Then everything's just peachy again. Kissy, kissy, smoochy, smoochy, love you big bruv. Talk to you soon."

Beau laughed. "Yeah, right. See you soon, Shane."

Beau hung up smiling to himself. Not so long ago it would never have occurred to him to call Shane back. Nor would he have given the conversation another thought. It seemed he was changing. Was it just because Wanda had pointed out his shortcomings? He didn't think so.

Chapter Eight

Corinne woke early the next morning and lay staring at the ceiling, running over her encounter with Beau. At dinner at Summer's house, she'd seen a guy she liked, in personality as well as looks. Well, apart from that one minor detail about Ruby! He was someone she could be friends with. Then when he'd come after her on the way home she'd seen a guy she liked even more, and someone she'd like to be more than friends with. Was that true though? What he was offering was sex. That wasn't more than friends. It was different from friends, wasn't it? She sighed. And was it something she was interested in? A wave of heat washed through her. Hell, yes! Her body, at least, was more than interested. The question should be whether or not it was a wise move. It'd be the odd night here and there. He was her new boss's brother. He was an integral part of the social life she was going to have here. How would it be when they were out with everyone else as they no doubt would be? Would they just screw each other on the quiet and then be civil acquaintances when anyone else was looking? She wasn't sure how she felt about that. And the most important question was, what about Ruby?

"Mommy? Are you awake?" As if on cue, Ruby came into the bedroom clutching her favorite bear.

Corinne sat up. "Yes, I'm awake, sweetie. I'm just getting up."

Ruby climbed onto the bed and sat beside her. "How many days until I start school?"

"Four more."

Ruby smiled. "That's not many."

"Are you excited to go?"

"Yes, I get to play with Tara and Josie, and I get to go to Miss Susie's with them after school too."

Corinne nodded. Ruby was an outgoing little person. She was glad she didn't have to worry about her being shy or nervous. "Did you have fun with Miss Susie last night?"

Ruby nodded enthusiastically. "Yes. We did letters and we went for a walk and she told me all the horses' names. When can I ride Gypsy again?"

"I don't know, sweetie. We'll have to ask Mason."

"Tell him I've been good, won't you?"

Corinne smiled. "I will, because you have. You've been very good. Now, do you want to come and help me make us some breakfast?"

"Yes! Can I squish the oranges?"

Corinne laughed. "You can help."

Once they'd had their breakfast and were dressed and ready for the day, Ruby wanted to take Corinne for a walk to show her where she'd been with Susie last night. Although she still had a lot to do before she started work on Monday, she agreed, knowing that once she did start work there wouldn't be many opportunities like this to just enjoy time together.

As they walked down the path from the cabin toward the barn, Ruby chattered about the horses she'd seen last night.

"Do you want to know who's my favorite?" she asked.

"I bet I can guess."

"Go on then."

"Gypsy?"

"Nope."

"Oh, I don't know then."

"Him!" Ruby pointed to a tall dark horse grazing by himself.

"And what's his name?"

"Troy! Isn't he handsome?"

"Yes, he is." He really was a beautiful horse.

"He belongs to Beau."

"Oh." Just the mention of his name sent shivers racing through her as she remembered the feel of his lips on hers. Thinking about the way he'd felt as he held her to him, she wondered if there was any way she could turn down his offer.

"Are you okay, Mommy?"

"I'm fine, sweetie." There was her reminder why she should turn him down. She'd have to keep secret from Ruby where she was going, and that just wasn't right.

They'd reached the fence and Ruby called to Troy. He lifted his head and looked in their direction, but didn't come over.

"I don't think he likes me." She looked so disappointed.

"I'm sure he does."

Ruby shook her head forlornly. "He wouldn't come last night either. All the others do."

"Maybe he just likes to be by himself more than the others do."

Ruby shrugged. "Gypsy!" The pony lifted her head and neighed loudly when she saw them. She came cantering over and stopped at the fence, poking her head between the rails to nose at Ruby.

Ruby giggled. "See, I know Gypsy likes me."

Corinne nodded. It certainly seemed that way.

"Hi, ladies." Shane came out of the barn and striding toward them. "I wondered what was up with Gypsy, now I know she's just excited to see her friend."

Ruby grinned up at him. "She is my friend. I'm excited to see her, too. Can I ride her?"

"Ruby!" Corinne didn't want her pestering for rides every time she saw Shane. That would get old very fast.

Shane smiled. "Not right now, I'm afraid. Maybe this weekend."

"Thank you!" Corinne was relieved that she was appeased with that, and that she remembered her manners. It was important to her that Ruby should be polite to her new boss and not get too familiar with him. Shane was easy to be around, but he was still her boss.

He smiled at her. "So, you got home okay last night?"

She nodded, willing herself not to look embarrassed. He couldn't know what had happened between her and Beau on her way home, could he? She forced herself to smile and to speak. "Yes, thanks. It was a lovely evening."

"It was. You'd better get used to it, we do that once a week at someone or other's house."

"I did enjoy it, but don't feel you have to invite me all the time. You gave me a job, you don't need to provide a social life too."

Shane grinned. "Sorry, too late. You're stuck with us. Can you imagine the…" he hesitated and looked at Ruby, "...the grief Cassidy would give me if you weren't there? You're one of the girls now. You'd better get used to it."

She nodded. "I do enjoy their company."

"And I hope you enjoy the brothers' company, too. We're not so bad when you get used to us. And I know one brother in particular is more than happy to have you even up the numbers."

She willed her cheeks not to flush. "I enjoy everyone's company," was the best neutral response she could come up with.

Shane raised an eyebrow. "You do?"

Oh, no. Was he reading more into her reply than she'd intended?

She nodded, deciding that least said, soonest mended was a good one to try for.

Shane winked. "Good to know."

She smiled. Hoping that was the end of the awkwardness.

"How would you feel about joining us on Saturday evening? We're having a cookout for all the guests. They'll have checked in Saturday afternoon, so they'll be your first guests when you start Monday. I thought it might be nice for you to meet them before you're in your official role."

"That'd be great," she smiled, relieved to move the conversation back to work matters.

"Great. I need to get going for now, but I'll see you around."

"Okay, boss."

Shane laughed. "I have a feeling when you get started I'm going to be the one calling you boss."

"Probably. I won't deny I like to take charge once I find my feet."

"Good; that's what I need you for." He looked down at Ruby. "What are you two doing today?"

"I wanted to go for a ride." Ruby's bottom lip was starting to slide out.

"But since we can't ride every day, we're going to go up to town and do some shopping," said Corinne.

Ruby's smile reappeared. "We are?"

"Yes, we are. After you finish telling me all the horses' names."

Shane lifted a hand. "I guess I'll catch you later, then."

"Bye, Shane," called Ruby as he walked away. He turned back and gave her a wave. "I like Shane," she said when he'd gone.

"I like him too. And it's a good job, since he's going to be my boss."

Ruby nodded. "He won't be a mean boss."

"You don't think so?"

"No. I can tell."

Corinne smiled. Her daughter did tend to be a good judge of character. She had good instincts about people. So what did that say about Beau? She still claimed he was her favorite.

~ ~ ~

It was twelve-thirty by the time Beau got to the office. Wanda peered at him over the reception desk and gave him a questioning look. "I hope you've had a busy morning?" she asked.

He laughed. "I thought I was supposed to be the slave driver around here?"

"Well, it's almost lunch time and I haven't heard a peep out of you yet today. I figure there are two possibilities. Either you've been a busy little Beau, making pots of money so you can give me a raise. Or, you're avoiding me because you don't want to tell me how last night went."

Beau came in and closed the door behind him. "I've had a very busy morning, if you must know."

"And you don't want to talk about last night?"

He laughed. "Why wouldn't I?"

"Because you know I'm going to interrogate you about Corinne and Ruby!"

He shrugged. "Ruby wasn't there. It was a nice evening."

Wanda gave him a stern look. "And?"

"And what?"

"What happened between you and Corinne?"

"Nothing."

"Don't lie to me, Beau Remington. I can tell by the gleam in your eye that something happened."

He shrugged. "It wouldn't be very gentlemanly of me to go talking about it though, would it? I need to protect the lady's reputation."

Wanda's hand flew up to cover her mouth. "Now you really have to tell me! What happened?"

He laughed. "Nothing!"

"Something! Or you wouldn't have said that."

"I just said it to get you going. You're too easy to wind up."

"I'm not buying it, Beau. Something happened."

"Okay." Beau couldn't believe it, but he was about to tell her what he'd done. Part of him wanted to know what her reaction would be. He'd been rationalizing his offer to Corinne as a practical solution for two people who were attracted to each other, but who didn't want to get involved in each other's lives. A little voice in the back of his head kept telling him it was wrong though. He knew Wanda's reaction would give him a good read on that. "I made her an indecent proposal."

Wanda laughed. "And what exactly does that mean?"

"I suggested that since we're obviously physically attracted to each other, but we both know I wouldn't be any good with her daughter…" he hesitated. Here it came. "…we should just get together to have sex sometimes."

Wanda's eyes widened and she stared at him, seemingly speechless. That didn't last long. She laughed loudly. "You son of a gun, Beau! You take the biscuit. What did she say?"

"I didn't give her chance to answer. I left her to think about it." He smiled, remembering the way she'd felt, rubbing herself against him, kissing him back so hungrily. "I think she's giving it some serious consideration though."

Wanda grinned. "Well, good for her!"

"Really? You don't think I'm an asshole for even suggesting it?"

"I don't. I think you may live to regret it, but it's probably just what a girl like her needs."

That took Beau by surprise. It was pretty much the opposite of what he might have expected—Corinne might live to regret it, but it was just what he needed! "Why would I be the one to regret it?"

Wanda grinned. "Oh, I dunno. I just have a feeling that you like her a lot more than you realize. And by the time you do realize, she'll just see you as bonking material, not boyfriend material!"

He laughed. "Bonking material?"

Wanda laughed with him. "Or whatever you call it these days. Someone to screw around with, but not someone to settle down with."

"That's fine by me. That's exactly why I suggested it. I'm not looking to settle down and most definitely not into a life that includes Ruby."

Wanda nodded sagely. "Only time will tell."

Beau nodded. She had him wondering now. "I guess it will. In the meantime, how are the docs coming for Hickory Lane?"

She tapped the top file on the pile beside her. "All done and ready to roll."

"Thanks, Wanda. You're the best."

"And don't you forget it!"

"No worries there, how could I forget when you remind me every day?"

"I just need to make sure you appreciate what you've got."

"I do, and to prove it, how about I go pick us up some lunch from the coffee shop?"

"That'd be great! Thank you."

"The usual?"

"Yeah, and don't forget my cookie!"

He laughed. "I won't. See you in a few."

He let himself back out and walked the few blocks to the coffee shop. He was making his way to the counter when he stopped in his tracks. Ruby was sitting at one of the tables by the window. Corinne had her back to him, but Ruby had spotted him. A big smile was plastered all across her little face.

"Beau!" she screeched and started waving madly at him.

Shit! He sucked in a deep breath. Corinne had turned around. There went his chance to beat a hasty retreat! He fixed a smile on his face that felt more like a grimace and made his way over to them.

"Good afternoon, ladies."

"Hello, Beau! Are you going to have lunch with us? You can share my sandwich if you like!" She held up a grilled cheese sandwich that had been gnawed all around the edges.

He shook his head. "No!" Even he could hear how disgusted he sounded; he had a feeling he might have shuddered when he said it, too. He needed to make more of an effort. "No, thank you, Ruby. But it's very kind of you to offer."

Corinne caught his eye. He didn't even want to hazard a guess at what she was thinking.

"Sit down with us," said Ruby as she pulled out a chair.

He should make his excuses and make his escape while he still had a chance. He looked at Ruby who was smiling at him expectantly, then he looked back at Corinne. She raised an eyebrow. Damn! If that look was translated into words, it would say, I dare you. He didn't know how to refuse a dare. He was genetically incapable of refusing a dare. Dammit. He sat down, wondering as he did what the hell he was getting himself into.

Ruby grinned at him. Why the hell had he sat down? He smiled back uncertainly. So. This was awkward.

"I like Troy." Ruby grinned at him while he tried to catch up.

"He's a good horse." At least she wasn't demanding anything of him—yet!

Ruby's smile faded. "I don't think he likes me, though."

Beau didn't dare look at Corinne. "I'm sure he does."

Ruby shook her head. "No. He won't come when I call him."

"He doesn't come when anyone calls him."

"I bet he comes to you. He's your horse."

Beau nodded. "He does, but like you say, he's mine. We've been friends for a long time."

"Will you tell him that I'm your friend too and then maybe he'll like me?"

He could feel Corinne's gaze boring into him. He was in a total lose-lose situation here. Anything he said to appease the kid would just prove to her mom that he was a liar. Damn, he wished he hadn't sat down! He nodded. Hoping maybe they could move on.

"You are my friend, aren't you?"

Shit, shit, shit! He turned to look at her. She seemed so angelic. Big blue eyes, big blonde curls framing a sweet little face. He smiled.

"Aren't you?"

He nodded. "We haven't known each other very long though."

She grinned. "So we should do something together. Then we really will be friends and you can tell Troy we are and then he'll like me!"

Beau sighed. He didn't need to do this. He really didn't. He didn't need to impress her mother; she already knew the score, but looking at Ruby's hopeful little face he couldn't bring himself to turn her down. "What do you think we should do?" Damn! Why in hell's name had he asked?

She looked at Corinne. "You should give us riding lessons."

"I thought Mason was teaching you. He's the best teacher."

"Yes, but he's busy."

Beau pursed his lips. It wasn't something he wanted to get into, but he didn't know how to turn her down.

Corinne came to the rescue. "Mr. Mason is your teacher, Ruby. That's already decided."

Beau hoped his relief wasn't too obvious.

"You should come for dinner, then. Mommy likes to have people over for dinner and no one has been to our new house yet. You should be our first friend."

Beau froze. He slowly lifted his gaze to look at Corinne. She looked as frozen as he felt. Ruby grinned at them both.

"Tomorrow night is Friday night. You should come tomorrow."

He stared at Corinne. She stared back. Why did she have to be so damned beautiful? Why did that dimple on her cheek have to give away the hint of a smile? And why in the hell was he smiling back? And nodding? Oh, shit! He'd gone and done it now!

Ruby beamed at him. "Yay! And after we have dinner we can go and see Troy and you can tell him I'm your friend, so he can be my friend, too!"

Beau nodded. Then looked at his watch. "Okay, but I need to get going for now."

Corinne smiled. "Six o'clock tomorrow? We can't eat too late. Ruby needs to get to bed."

He nodded. Her voice was warm and soothing even in this situation that he'd walked himself into. All he'd wanted was to get Corinne into bed, not to have to worry about what time Ruby went. "Great. I'll see you then." He got up and made his way to the door. It was only once he was outside that he realized he was supposed to be getting lunch. No way was he going back inside though! He made his way back to the office, cursing himself as he went.

He stopped in the doorway when he got back. Wanda was sitting there eating a sandwich. A sandwich that had come from the coffee shop. He scowled at her. "Why did you let me go for your lunch when you already had it?"

She grinned. "I thought you might enjoy a visit to the coffee shop."

"You knew they were in there?"

He didn't think he'd ever seen a smile that big on her face. "How did it go?"

"How did it go?" he ran his hand through his hair. "I fucked up, Wanda. I well and truly fucked up."

"Oh, no! You blew it?"

He shook his head. "I'm having dinner at the cabin tomorrow night with both of them!"

Wanda laughed. "Good for you!"

"No. It is not good for me. It will be so bad for me. How can I spend an entire evening with that kid? She's a monster!"

"Now you stop that! She is not! You sound like a kid yourself. Waa, waa, waa. I don't like her! I don't want to play with her."

Beau had to laugh. "Seriously? I'm that bad?"

She nodded. "I'm afraid so."

"Well, shit! It's just that I thought I had this thing figured out. That I'd get to spend some time with Corinne—some adult time. And now I somehow roped myself into an evening with Ruby!"

"So make the most of it! Give the kid a chance. Stop thinking from your pants for a minute, and instead think with that big soft heart you keep hidden away. That poor little mite doesn't have a daddy. Her momma works a lot, she doesn't have any friends here yet. What would it cost you to show the little thing some kindness?"

Beau stared at her. "You're appealing to my better nature?"

Wanda made a face. "Sorry, I forgot you don't have one."

"Ouch. That hurts."

"So prove me wrong."

He pursed his lips. If he thought about Ruby in the way Wanda had just described her then he could feel a certain sneaking sympathy—until he remembered what she was like! "I suppose I could try to be nice to her. Just for one evening. It'd earn me some brownie points with Corinne." He shrugged. "And you're right, what would it cost me?"

Wanda laughed. "Only your reputation as an asshole, but don't worry I won't tell anyone."

"Well, thanks. I guess, since I got myself into it, I may as well try to make the most of it, huh?"

"See, there's the spirit! You can do it!"

Beau nodded. He was glad Wanda had faith in him—he wasn't so sure he did!

Chapter Nine

Ruby came out of her bedroom and did a twirl. She really did look cute in the purple dress.

"You look lovely, Ruby."

"I do, don't I? How long till Beau gets here?"

Corinne looked at the clock on the wall. "Fifteen minutes." And she needed to get ready herself. She wondered again why she'd agreed to this. She could have told Ruby no when she'd invited Beau to dinner. She could have let him off the hook when she'd seen the panic in his eyes. She wasn't stupid; she knew he didn't want to spend an evening with Ruby. She should have said no. But she hadn't. And she couldn't decide why.

She had two theories and she considered them both while she went to her room to change her shirt and freshen her makeup. She had to be honest, part of her hoped that Beau would like Ruby if he got to know her properly. And this was a chance for him to do so. She pursed her lips while she brushed her mascara on. Another part of her felt that if he really didn't like Ruby, then this was a chance to make him suffer! He was a guy, a guy who wanted sex. She wanted him, too, but it didn't seem right to go sneaking off to screw him! If he really couldn't stand Ruby, tonight would see him off altogether and she wouldn't have to wrestle with her own conscience. She probably shouldn't have to anyway, but she couldn't deny the internal battle that was raging: the battle between the devoted mother who put her daughter first in all things, and the young woman who might just occasionally want to put herself first. She felt guilty even thinking it, but it was true. It would be nice to have some fun, to feel attractive—and to have sex!

Ruby stood in the doorway. "You look pretty, Mommy."

"Thank you, sweetie. Not as pretty as you do."

Ruby smiled and twirled again. "Do you think Beau will like my dress?"

"I'm sure he will, but he might not say so."

"I'll ask him then."

"Ask him if you want to, but what matters most is if you like it."

"I do."

Corinne smiled. She wasn't going to tell her not to ask, and that wasn't about saving Beau. She'd grown up living by her own mother's rules. Believing that other people's opinions mattered more than her own. It'd taken her most of her life to step into her own confidence. Perhaps she was going too far in the other direction with the way she was raising Ruby, but she'd rather her daughter was outspoken, than crippled by fear of what people might think.

She started at the sound of a knock on the door. Oh, well. Here went nothing. Ruby ran to open it.

"Hello, Beau!"

Corinne smiled as she joined Ruby in the hallway.

Beau was gorgeous. He took her breath away. He was wearing black jeans and a black shirt and he had his hands behind his back. He caught her eye and winked before looking down at Ruby.

"Good evening, pretty lady. I have something for you."

"You do?"

He nodded and brought his hand around to present her with a little posy of flowers, pretty pinks and blues tied with a string.

Ruby's eyes were wide as she smiled and took them from him. "Thank you!" She turned to Corinne. "Look, Mommy. Beau gave me flowers!"

Corinne smiled. She didn't have any words right now, just a big lump in her throat. What a sweet thing for him to do! And the last thing she would have expected. She looked up to meet his gaze.

His smile was hesitant as he brought his other around from behind his back and presented her with a bunch of roses. She tried to swallow the lump in her throat, and nodded. She knew her smile would give him the answer he was looking for. Was this okay? Yes! Absolutely! He'd done right, gotten off on a good foot.

He smiled back and thrust them toward her, making her realize that she hadn't taken them from him, and also reminding her of their first encounter in the wine store when he'd given her that bottle. Finally she found her voice. "Thank you! They're beautiful. Why don't you come on in? We'll put them in water and get you a drink."

Ruby took hold of his hand and led him through to the kitchen. Corinne had to suppress a smile at the grimace on his face which he quickly and consciously transformed into a smile. He was making an effort. There was no mistaking it. Though how long he'd be able to keep it up remained to be seen.

"Would you like a glass of wine?"

"Yes, please."

She poured him a glass of the Cab and handed it over.

"Thank you."

Ruby picked up her glass of orange juice and held it up, forcing them to break eye contact. "We should do a toast, Mommy."

Corinne smiled. Ruby loved toasting to anything. "What do you want to toast to?"

Ruby looked from her to Beau and back again. "To making new friends!"

She raised an eyebrow at Beau and raised her glass. "What do you think?"

He nodded slowly and touched his glass against Ruby's and then hers. "I'll drink to that. Here's to making new friends."

Ruby smiled. "Shall we go and tell Troy that I'm your friend now?"

Beau laughed, but Corinne could tell it was forced and uncomfortable. He wanted to say no, but he either wasn't sure if he should, or didn't know how to.

"Not yet, Ruby," she said. "Perhaps later we'll walk down and see the horses."

From the look Beau gave her she could tell he was both grateful and concerned that he'd messed up somehow. She smiled reassuringly before she added. "By the time we've had dinner, Beau may not want to be our friend."

He narrowed his eyes at her, there was a smile lurking on his lips and questions lurking in his eyes.

Yes, she was teasing him! This wouldn't be worth doing if they couldn't have some fun with it.

He grinned and looked at Ruby. "And perhaps you ladies won't want to be friends with me."

"Don't worry. We will." Ruby patted his arm. "You gave me flowers. You're going to be my friend forever now."

Corinne couldn't hold back the little laugh that escaped.

To her surprise, Beau laughed with her. Ruby looked at them and joined in. Oh, well. They were off to a good start if they could laugh together.

"Do you like chicken?" asked Ruby. "We're having chicken."

"I do," said Beau and looked down at his glass.

Corinne knew what he was thinking. The Cab was hardly a traditional pairing with chicken. "I think you'll be surprised how well the Cab will taste with it, though I do have a whole selection of whites you can choose from if you prefer."

He met her gaze. "Of course, you used to work in wine country, right?"

She nodded. "And I know you don't tend to think much of us crazy Californians and our newfangled ways of doing things up here."

He held up a hand. "Hey, don't go tarring us all with the same brush. Yes, there is some resentment of the implants here, but most of us judge on a case by case basis."

"Implants? I thought people who came from a different state were known as transplants."

Beau laughed and let his gaze travel over her. Her entire body tingled in response and she felt her nipples tighten when he reached her breasts. "It's a California thing, isn't it?"

"Oh!" She crossed her arms over her chest. "Not in my case it isn't!"

"Like I said, it's a case by case basis, and in your case, I'm happy to say I wouldn't use the word implant." He lifted his gaze to meet hers. There was no mistaking the desire in his eyes, or denying that she felt it too. Part of her mind was screaming that she should be offended, but she couldn't bring herself to feel that way. She loved the way he'd looked at her, she loved feeling desirable, and some part of her felt as though she was being accepted into Montana. She knew some of the Californians that moved up here had earned themselves a bad reputation, she didn't want to be lumped in with them.

He shook his head as if to clear it, as if he were coming to his senses and realizing the exchange they'd just had. "Anyway. I'll be happy to try your recommendation. I'm always eager to try out new pairings."

Corinne had to wonder if he was still veiling one conversation with another. Was she a new pairing for him? The word coupling kept running through her mind, conjuring up images she shouldn't be thinking about in front of Ruby. "In that case I hope you have adventurous taste." She wanted to cover her mouth with her hand. Had she really just said that?

He smiled. "Oh, I do. In the meantime, is there anything I can do to help?"

Corinne shook her head. She shouldn't be playing with him like this. She hadn't even decided that she wanted to take him up on his offer yet. She was supposed to be seeing how he dealt with this evening before she'd entertain the idea of sleeping with him. At least that was what her head was saying. It seemed her body had already reached its decision and, left to its own devices, would be dragging him to the bedroom at the first opportunity. "Everything's ready, thank you. Just take a seat and we can eat."

Ruby tugged at his sleeve and led him to the table. "You get to sit next to me."

Corinne smiled as she turned to the fridge to get the salad out. She had to remember she might not get the opportunity to do anything at all with Beau—other than watch him ride off into the sunset at the end of the evening if he couldn't handle Ruby.

"So how do you like it here so far, Ruby?"

Corinne was curious as to what her answer would be. "I love it! I love our cabin, and I love the ranch, and I love the horses, and I love Miss Susie and I love that I get to see Summer Breese sometimes."

Beau laughed. "So lots of good things here for you then?"

Ruby nodded, as Corinne came back to the table and sat down. "And for Mommy too. Mommy deserves good things."

Beau smiled and met Corinne's gaze. "I'm sure there will be."

There went those tingles racing down her spine again. By the look on his face he was planning on being one of the good things that was about to happen to her. In the physical sense at least.

"Does your mommy get to go out and do good things?"

Ruby shook her head. "She always works too much."

Beau frowned. "But now that she's here she won't be working so much."

Ruby brightened at that. "No." She turned to Corinne. "You should go out. And if you do, I can go to Miss Susie's. She even said I can stay there sometimes if you don't mind."

"She did?" Corinne stopped with her fork midair. This almost felt as though there was some secret conspiracy that even Ruby was in on. Everything was being set up so she could spend time with Beau. Who was she kidding phrasing it like that? So she could sleep with Beau! It didn't feel right though. She'd never had that kind of relationship with a guy. Never been just a…a… what was the term? Fuck buddy? That sounded so crude. Because it was!

Ruby was nodding at her. "Can I? Can I go stay over with Tara and Josie?"

She realized that Beau was watching her, waiting for her reply almost as eagerly as Ruby was.

"We'll see." She wasn't sure she wanted to say yes to either of them yet.

After they'd eaten, Beau sat back. "That was wonderful, thank you."

"Yes, thank you, Mommy. Can we have the ice cream now?"

"I think we should wait a little while first."

Beau stood. "Can I get the dishes?" He started clearing plates.

"I'll help." Ruby jumped up to join him.

Corinne watched as Ruby bossed him around the kitchen. He was taking it well, getting a laugh where he could.

"Now we have to get my chair," she told him.

Beau gave her a puzzled look and looked to Corinne for help.

"It's okay, Ruby," she said. "I'll do the dishes later. I'll put them in the dishwasher."

"But I want to do them now. Beau's going to help." There was no mistaking the edge to her voice.

Beau sensed it too. "I can help. What do I need to do with your chair?"

Corinne smiled to herself as Ruby directed him until she was standing at the sink on her chair and he was beside her, towel in hand ready to dry the dishes. She was pretty sure this hadn't been in his picture of how this evening might go. He was doing really well, she had to give him that. He had Ruby laughing. He even dabbed some bubbles on the end of her nose when she handed him a plate that was still covered in them. She went to join them, realizing that, as Beau dried the plates, he had no idea where to put them and was piling them precariously on the countertop next to the drainer.

She took a plate from his hand, but he held on to it until she looked up into his eyes. His smile made her heart race. She got lost in his eyes wondering what was going on behind them.

"Are you two going to kiss now?"

"Ruby!" Corinne felt herself blush, which was pretty ridiculous since they were both just waiting for the time when they could sleep together, let alone kiss each other.

"What? Are you?"

"Not right now," said Beau.

"Soon though. You're going to. I can tell."

Corinne stared at Beau; he smiled and then gave a shrug. "Out of the mouths of babes…"

"What does that mean?" asked Ruby.

He shrugged again. "Do you want to go see Troy now?"

"Yesss!" Ruby climbed down from her chair, all thoughts of kissing and dishes forgotten. "Can we, Mommy?"

Corinne nodded. "Okay, but go and get your sweatshirt first, it's chilly outside."

Ruby ran to her bedroom.

Beau leaned toward Corinne, placing his hands on the counter on either side of her. "She's a smart kid."

Corinne nodded. She couldn't help it, she reached her hands up to his shoulders and looked up into his eyes. He smiled as his arms closed around her drawing her to him as his lips came down on hers.

It was a brief kiss, but it spoke of so much more to come. He stepped back at the sound of Ruby coming out of her room.

"Do you think I can ride Troy one day?" she asked Beau.

Corinne was grateful that she seemed oblivious to the fact that they'd just been fulfilling her prediction that they'd kiss each other soon.

"He's a bit big for you."

Corinne watched her daughter's eyebrows knit together and waited. She was relieved when Ruby smiled.

"We can wait till I'm taller then. You can ride Troy and I can ride Gypsy. But who can Mommy ride?"

Corinne deliberately avoided looking a Beau. She had a feeling she knew who he might suggest, and it wasn't one of the horses!

"How about we take a walk down to the barn and see," suggested Beau.

"Yes! Let's go."

Ruby took hold of Beau's hand as they walked down the path. He shot a glance at Corinne over her head. She had to give it to him, he seemed to be doing really well. She gave him a questioning look and he nodded. He did seem to have relaxed some. She was allowing herself to hope now, even though she knew she shouldn't. It would be so nice to think that she and Beau might start seeing each other—and that he might learn to enjoy Ruby's company as well.

When they reached the fence, Ruby leaned on the bottom rail and started calling Troy. He lifted his head and looked in their direction, but didn't come over.

Ruby looked up at Beau. "See, he doesn't like me."

Corinne couldn't have been more surprised when he picked Ruby up and sat her on the top rail, keeping his arm around her so she didn't fall. She could see that he was no longer trying to impress her, or Ruby. He was simply focused on what he was doing. He let out a long, low whistle.

Troy's head came up again and this time he trotted in their direction, tail lifted. He nickered and came close, but stopped a few feet away.

"Come here, buddy. Let's see you."

Troy took a step closer and stopped again, nodding his head and pawing at the ground.

Ruby grinned up at Beau. Corinne had to stop her mind from racing off in all kinds of ridiculous directions when she saw the way Beau smiled back. He put his hand in his pocket and pulled something out.

"I'm going to let you give him his favorite treat, and then it's guaranteed, he'll not only be your friend, but he'll love you."

Ruby's eyes were wide as he handed whatever it was to her.

"Now just hold your hand out flat."

Corinne was a little concerned. "He doesn't bite, does he?"

Beau shook his head.

"It's okay, Mommy. I just have to hold my hand flat and tuck my thumb out of the way so he doesn't think it's a carrot!"

Beau laughed. "I'm guessing Mason taught you that?"

She nodded and held her hand out. "Here, Troy. It's okay. Come here."

Corinne held her breath as the horse took two more steps. Ruby held her hand out, with what she could now see was a mint balanced on her little palm. The kid had no fear at all. "Come get it."

She giggled as Troy brushed his lips over her hand and took the mint. Both she and Corinne laughed when he lifted his head and peeled his lips back after he'd crunched it.

"He likes it!" cried Ruby. "Look, he's laughing!"

Beau grinned at her. "I told you, they're his very favorite."

"Can I give him another one?"

Beau shook his head. "No, they're a special treat. If he gets too many they won't be special anymore."

Corinne smiled, that was a line of reasoning she often used herself with Ruby, especially when it came to candies.

Troy stepped forward again and nosed at Ruby, making her giggle.

"See. He's your friend now," said Beau.

Ruby patted his nose. "Yes, now we're friends."

"Now we're all friends," said Beau.

Corinne gave him a questioning look. His nod was brief, but his smile seemed genuine.

Chapter Ten

Beau made his coffee strong and took it to sit out on the deck. It was a beautiful morning, promising a beautiful day ahead. He was heading back down to the ranch to ride Troy. And to see Corinne. Not that she knew it yet. After their walk down to the barn last night he'd made his excuses and left. He knew that had surprised her. She'd probably been expecting him to stick around until Ruby went to bed. Hell, that's what he'd been expecting to do, but somehow, at some point during the evening that had changed. He'd gone in expecting to have to endure Ruby for a couple of hours and then to get Corinne to himself for a little while afterwards. But seeing the way they were together, mother and daughter, he'd realized that they were a package.

He'd come to understand that his offer to Corinne, to meet up and sleep together whenever they got a chance, was pointless. If he just wanted sex, that was on offer anywhere. He could go to any bar in town, or to Chico, and find a girl willing to go home with him any night of the week. If that was all he wanted he didn't need to complicate his life, or Corinne's. He sighed and took a sip of his coffee. Maybe he was getting old, maybe it was watching his brothers find the women they were meant to be with and start settling down; he didn't know what it was, but he wanted more than just a body to warm his bed occasionally. He wanted…he didn't know what, but something, something more. It was crazy to think he might find it with Corinne. She definitely offered something more, but a five-year-old daughter hadn't been the kind of something he'd had in mind.

Crazy as it might seem though, he'd decided that he was going to give it a go. He was going to start seeing Corinne, and let the dice fall where they would regarding Ruby. So, this morning he was going to head down to the ranch to ride Troy, just like he'd planned. And he was going to go find Corinne and Ruby and see what their plans for the day were. See if they wanted to hang out, do something together. He chuckled to himself as he thought about calling Wanda to tell her what he was up to.

When he got to the ranch, he could see Ruby in the arena; she was riding Gypsy. Mason was standing in the middle calling instructions. Apparently, he'd decided she was ready to be off the lead rope. Beau wasn't sure he liked that idea. He shook his head as he closed the truck door and started down the path. What the hell was happening to him? He was protective of her all of a sudden? No, he was just being practical, that was all. He'd always been more cautious than Mason, in all things.

As he approached the arena, he spotted Corinne; she was perched up on the fence watching. She took his breath away. Her hair was tied in a ponytail, she wore a pink and blue checkered shirt, and jeans that hugged her figure in the most appealing way. She was even wearing boots, not something he'd seen her do before—but something he'd love to see her do again, minus the rest of her outfit. Damn! Where had that thought come from? He shoved his hands in his pockets to adjust his own jeans before he reached them. He didn't want her to notice just how pleased he was to see her, but thoughts of her in nothing but a pair of cowboy boots had him wishing Mason could make Ruby's lesson last at least a couple of hours.

She turned at the sound of his approach. Her smile was hesitant. He'd left in a hurry last night and it seemed she was thinking the worst. He needed to let her know as soon as he could that he was actually hoping for the best. He gave her what he hoped was a reassuring grin and went to lean on the fence beside her. Bad move. Now he was face to face with her breasts, that wasn't going to make for easy conversation, not while it sent his mind racing in another direction completely. He forced himself to lift his gaze and smile at her face. "Hi."

"Good morning. Are you here to take Troy out?"

He nodded. "You didn't believe me last night when I said I was leaving for the right reasons, did you?"

She held his gaze. "I think that depends on what each of us consider to be the right reasons."

He smiled. "That could get too complicated. What I meant was, I'd like us to start seeing each other, for real."

"Does for real mean not just for sex?"

That took him aback a little. He hadn't expected her to be so straightforward about it. He nodded. "It does."

She gave him a long measured look.

"What?" He'd been hoping, no, if he was honest, he'd been expecting her to be pleased. She didn't look it.

"So are you saying Ruby passed some kind of test last night and you're prepared to give us a go now?"

Ah. He guessed that might not feel too good looking at it from where she sat. "Honestly?"

"Yes, please. I tend to prefer the truth."

"Okay, honestly, when I came over last night, I came with that attitude—to see if Ruby could pass the test as you put it. But what I discovered, and what surprised me so much that I left in such a hurry, was that I passed the test. She's the first kid I've ever had to do deal with, I didn't know how to, and I didn't think I wanted to." He gave her a hopeful smile. "I guess we're all afraid of the unknown. Actually hanging out with Ruby made me see that there's nothing to be afraid of. She's just another person, only smaller."

Corinne smiled back. "And more opinionated, and more demanding."

He held a hand up. "I sure as hell wasn't going to go there!"

She laughed. "I know. But it's true. And if you really do want us to start seeing each other for real, there's no point in trying to gloss it over."

He nodded. "I know. And there's no saying how—or if—it will work out. I'm just saying I'd like to give it a go, if you're interested." He held her gaze. "Or did you like my first suggestion better?"

He could tell by the way her pupils dilated and that pulse started to flutter in her neck that she was more than interested in his first suggestion.

It was a long moment before she replied. "Since we're being honest about all this, I'd take you up on your original suggestion if it was all that was on offer, but I like the idea of us seeing each other for real better."

He couldn't help the smile that spread across his face.

She was no longer smiling back. "Seriously, Beau. I don't want you to feel you have to include Ruby, if it's not what you want. I'd rather not put her through that. If all you're after is no strings sex, be honest about it?"

He shook his head. "It's not. I'm not making any promises that I won't screw this up, but I'd like to give it a try."

"Okay, then. No promises, no expectations. Deal?" She held her hand out to him.

He shook it. "Deal," he replied, wondering as he did why her words bothered him. No promises, no expectations; he should feel relieved, but he didn't.

"Beau!" called Ruby. "Look at me! Mr. Mason says I don't need the lead rope anymore."

"Good job, Ruby. You're doing great." He really needed to come up with some other words of encouragement and stop borrowing Mason's.

"Soon me and Gypsy will be able to ride out with you and Troy, won't we?"

He pursed his lips, he didn't like the idea of being responsible for her out on the trails.

Mason saved him. "That won't be for a long while yet. Now you're off the lead rope we've got a lot of work to do."

Beau had to smile at the way Ruby nodded solemnly. "Yes, Mr. Mason. Sorry, Beau I have to go back to work now, I have a lot of work to do." She reined Gypsy around and headed back out into the center of the arena.

Mason grinned at them. "She's proving to be a star pupil."

Corinne laughed. "I think that's all down to her teacher. You've certainly got the hang of working with her; you bring out the best in her. I might be asking you for tips on how to handle her soon."

"Me too," said Beau. He didn't miss his brother's knowing look as he nodded and went after Ruby. He was surprised at himself. He didn't like feeling outdone by Mason. He wanted to know how to bring out the best in Ruby. He had to hope it was more than just the old sibling rivalry.

Corinne raised an eyebrow at him. "So where do we go from here?"

He smiled. "I guess we make it up as we go along?"

She nodded. "It's not my usual style, but I guess it's our only option."

"Believe me, it's not mine either, but since we're headed into unknown waters, all we can do is go with the flow."

"Okay then, but can I ask one thing of you, set one condition?"

Uh-oh. Women setting conditions—that usually spelled trouble. He nodded. "What?"

"Just be honest with me about Ruby? If she drives you nuts, say so? I know she's not easy; she's my whole world and she drives me nuts sometimes, but she doesn't deserve to be taken for a ride. Don't humor her just to get on my good side?"

"I won't." He gave her a wry smile. "I don't think I could. It's like you said, no promises no expectations?"

"Agreed."

"Okay, well I'm going to take Troy out. Can I stop to see you at the cabin when I get back?"

The way she hesitated made him wonder.

She shook her head. "Don't go thinking I'm backing out already. It's just that I agreed to go to Shane's cookout for the guests later. Would you want to come?"

He thought about it. It wasn't exactly what he'd had in mind, but why not. "Sure."

"Great." Her smile was back. "Just come on over whenever you're ready then."

"Will do."

It felt so weird to Beau walking up to the guest ranch holding Ruby's hand. He could just imagine Shane's face when he spotted them. He was going to give him so much grief! But what the hell, if he was going to do this, he was going to do it. Ruby squeezed his hand and smiled up at him. "Thank you for coming with us."

Damn! She was cute when she wanted to be! "Thank you for inviting me."

Corinne smiled at him. "Do you come out here much normally?"

He shook his head. "I come down to see my folks, I check in with Shane every now and then, or when it's Mason and Gina's turn to host dinner I come out to the cottage. Mostly I'm pretty busy up in town."

"Why did you move to town?" asked Ruby. "If I had my horse here I would never move away."

"I have my business in town. It's a long way to drive every day." Beau thought about his answer. Was that really why he'd moved to town? No, it wasn't. It was a practical consideration, but he'd moved up to town to make the break from his family. He'd needed to move out of his parents' place, they all had. Mason had taken the cabin, and, of course, Chance had gone in with him. It made sense since they were the two who worked the ranch. Shane had been away in the Navy at the time and he'd bunked in with them when he came back. He'd had to be out here too since he was building the guest ranch. Carter had moved out first—when he married Trisha, but even they had lived here, until Trisha cheated on him and it all went to hell. Carter had moved up to town to grow his landscaping business, but Beau had always believed that he'd moved away from bad memories as much as anything else. Now he lived just a few miles from the ranch, with Summer in the house that he'd sold them.

Beau himself had gone away to college, and by the time he came back, he'd felt like an outsider at the ranch. He had no reason to be here, and a lot of reasons to be in town. If he was honest he felt as though his place here and in the family had been usurped by Chance, so he'd gone his own way. Trying to prove that he didn't need them, he could do great by himself.

Corinne gave him a questioning look.

"Sorry. I'm just thinking that Ruby has a point. It'd be nice to live here."

He felt a hand come down on his shoulder. Shane had an annoying habit of appearing out of nowhere and doing that. "Did I just hear you right?"

Shit. Beau wished he hadn't heard him at all! "I don't know, what did you hear?" He wished that edge to his voice wasn't there, but he couldn't help it.

Shane surprised him by seeming to sense he shouldn't go there. "I dunno, I just thought for a moment I might get to have my other big brother back on my doorstep."

Beau gave him a hard stare.

Shane grinned, unperturbed. "I'd like that." He smiled down at Ruby. "I think it'd be awesome if Beau moved back down here, don't you?"

"Yes. Then we could see him every day!"

Beau didn't know what to say to either of them. He smiled at them both and left it at that.

"Anyway. I'm glad you're here," said Shane. "Would you mind if I steal Corinne for a minute? There are a couple of people I'd like to introduce her to."

Beau nodded. He hadn't expected to be left alone with Ruby, but he could hardly argue. Corinne shot him an apologetic look as Shane led her away. He looked down at Ruby, not sure what to do.

She was looking around, surveying the people gathering in front of the lodge. Her face broke into a big grin as she pointed. "Summer Breese!"

Beau cringed. He'd thought only dogs could hear such high frequencies, but his ears convinced him otherwise.

Ruby tugged at his hand. "Can we go see Summer? Pleeaase?"

He nodded, more than happy to oblige. He was happy to make an effort with the kid, but it sure would be easier if she were distracted by Summer.

Carter spotted them coming and put a protective arm around Summer's shoulders, making Beau smile. It reassured him that he wasn't the only one who was wary—or if he was honest, scared—of Ruby.

Summer, on the other hand, smiled when she saw them coming and held her arms out to Ruby who let go of Beau's hand and went running to her.

Carter raised an eyebrow as he joined them. "Hey. I didn't expect to see you here."

"He came with us," said Ruby.

Carter grinned. "I can see that."

Ruby wrapped her arms around Summer's neck as she lifted her up. "And where's your mom?"

Ruby looked around and pointed to where Corinne was standing talking with Shane and a group of guys Beau assumed were ranch guests. "There. She has to talk to people because this is her new job, but it's okay." She turned and reached her arms out to Beau. "I can stay with my Beau."

Beau felt a momentary panic. He was responsible for her? And she was reaching out for him to hold her? He took a deep breath and took hold of her. Summer smiled as she passed her over. Ruby wrapped her arms around his neck and took him totally by surprise by landing a kiss on his cheek. Carter and Summer both laughed at the look on his face.

"He is my Beau!" Ruby sounded hurt, as though their laughter was at her.

He wasn't sure who was most surprised when he planted a kiss on her cheek and said, "That's right, pumpkin." Where in the hell had that come from? Carter and Summer both looked stunned. Ruby looked as though she might float away on a happy cloud and he himself was left wondering what the hell he was playing at. He needed to get out of here! "Are the folks here?" he asked Carter.

Carter nodded. "They're around somewhere."

"Thanks. I wanted to have a word with them. Catch you later." He turned and walked away, smiling at the way Ruby was still clinging to his neck with a big silly grin on her face. He thought back to what Wanda had said about her. What would it cost him to show her some kindness? And just look at what happened when he did! He hugged her a little tighter as he walked. She could be sweet, there was no denying it.

He spotted his parents sitting under a big tree with a couple of the guests. He'd come looking for them without considering the implications of doing so while carrying Ruby around. He wondered if he should put her down before they saw him. The way she was still clinging to him, he didn't have the heart to. It was too late anyway. His mom had seen him, she tapped his dad who turned to look. Whatever expression he might have expected to see on their faces, it wasn't what he saw. They both smiled at him and then at each other, as if they knew something he didn't.

"Hey, Beau. I didn't expect to see you here," said his dad.

He nodded.

"But we're so glad you are," added his mom. How did she understand him so well? How did she know that he'd just been wondering why that was the first thing people would say to him. Why not, great to see you? Probably because they didn't understand how touchy he was. His mom obviously did though.

His dad grinned at him. "And in the company of such a beautiful young lady."

"Yeah, this is Ruby."

"We've met before, haven't we sweetie?" said his mom.

Ruby smiled. "Yes. Hello."

Beau started to put her down, but she wrapped her arms tighter around his neck and buried her face in his shoulder. She was going to act shy? Wow!

His dad laughed. "Want to tell us how this happened?"

Beau shrugged.

Ruby turned her head to peek out at them. "My mommy has to talk to work people, so my Beau is taking care of me."

His dad raised an eyebrow and his mom grinned at him.

He shrugged. There was no way this was going to be an easy conversation. "We should probably go find her."

"Okay, we'll catch up with you later." The look his mom gave him told him that she'd be asking all kinds of questions just as soon as she got a chance.

Chapter Eleven

Shane came and tapped Corinne's shoulder. "Can I borrow you for a minute?"

She made her excuses to the guests she'd been talking to and followed him away from them. "Is everything okay?"

"It sure is. I just figured you might need rescuing by now. This wasn't supposed to be an all work evening and they've been hogging you for ages. I thought you might want to check in with Ruby…and Beau."

"Oh, the poor guy. How's he doing with her? Have you seen him?"

Shane laughed. "They're doing just fine. In fact, judging from the reactions I've seen and heard, they are the golden couple of the party.

"Seriously?"

Shane nodded his head vigorously. "Seriously! I mean, c'mon, a tall dark handsome cowboy toting round a little blonde-haired, blue-eyed cutie pie. What's not to love about that picture?"

"Toting?" Corinne wasn't sure she understood. Well, she knew what it meant, but she couldn't quite believe it.

Shane nodded again. "Apparently Summer had her, she reached out for her Beau, and he hasn't put her down since."

Corinne shook her head. He was probably hating every second of it. "I'd better go rescue him."

Shane laughed. "That's not why I came for you; I just thought you'd like to see."

"Where are they?"

"Right over there."

Corinne's heart did an odd little flip in her chest when she saw them. Beau was indeed holding Ruby and she had her arms wrapped around his neck. He was chatting with a couple of guys she recognized, they worked at the ranch, though whether with the horses or the cattle she didn't know. As she watched, Ruby yawned and rested her head on his shoulder. Beau smiled and smoothed her hair away from her face. One of the guys said something and they all laughed, though Beau looked a little embarrassed. She realized Shane was watching her.

"He's a good guy, you know."

She sighed.

"I don't know what kind of first impression he's made with you, but he really is a good guy when you take the time to get to know him."

She turned to meet Shane's gaze. "I don't doubt it. It's not me I'm worried about, it's Ruby, and him."

"He did seem a bit scared of her at first, but hey so was I. We've never had any experience with little kids before, you can't hold that against us."

"I don't. It's just that I don't want him to try it out only to find that she drives him nuts, and I don't want her getting attached to him only to end up getting rejected. She doesn't need that."

Shane nodded. "He might not be used to little kids, but I do know he wouldn't intentionally hurt anyone."

"I don't think he would hurt her intentionally." Corinne couldn't bring herself to add what else she was thinking—but if he's got his head up his ass, would he even realize if he did hurt her.

"Come on. Let's go see them. This is so cute I may have to take pictures."

Beau looked up as they reached him. He looked almost apologetic when he met Corinne's gaze. "She says she's tired."

"Mommy!" Ruby lifted her head from Beau's shoulder and gave her a sleepy little smile. She looked worn out.

"Hey, sweetie. Are you being good?"

She nodded. "Yes, and my Beau is taking care of me." She laid her head back down and closed her eyes.

"I'm sorry, Beau. Let me take her."

He shook his head. "She's comfortable. We're fine."

"Don't feel you have to stick around," said Shane. "You've met everyone I wanted you to meet. Take her on home whenever you're ready."

Corinne would be more than happy to call it a night. She didn't want to make Beau leave though.

"Can we go home now?" asked Ruby.

"Sure thing, pumpkin," said Beau.

Corinne felt as though her mouth might have fallen open hearing him say that. She gave him a puzzled look.

He grinned back at her. "Hey, you're the one who left us to our own devices, this is what we came up with. I'm her Beau, she's my pumpkin. What can I say?"

Shane laughed. "I'm going to leave you guys to it."

"Okay, goodnight, Shane."

"See ya." Corinne didn't miss the look the brothers exchanged. She didn't understand the dynamics of the Remington family yet, but she could see that they truly cared for each other.

When Shane had gone they started up the path back to the cabin.

"How did you get on?" asked Beau.

She nodded. "It was a good chance to meet the guests before I start on Monday, and to see the atmosphere of the place in action. I'm sorry I just left you with Ruby like that."

"That's okay, we had fun."

"You did?"

He met her gaze. "We did. It gave us chance to spend a little time together."

Wow. He seemed to mean it.

"She's worn out now, though."

Ruby smiled at Corinne. "I'm not too tired for ice cream."

Corinne laughed. "We'll see." As she watched her daughter's eyes close again she knew she wouldn't be worried about ice cream by the time they got home.

~ ~ ~

Beau took a seat in the living room while Corinne put Ruby to bed. This was weird. He had to admit he'd had fun with the kid this evening. Wandering around chatting with friends and family, all the while carrying Ruby, had given him a different perspective on things. It certainly seemed to have made everyone look at him differently. They were so much friendlier. It was weird, but he liked it.

He'd chatted with Gina and Mason for a while. It made him smile that Ruby called him Mr. Mason, apparently that was because he was her teacher. When he'd first heard her call Mason that he'd thought she should call him Mr. Beau. That it was a respect thing and he deserved it, too. After tonight, when he'd become her Beau he couldn't imagine her ever calling him Mr. at all. He wouldn't want her to. He shook his head with a rueful smile, she was his pumpkin after all! Where the hell had that come from? He had no idea, but he knew she loved it, and that was all that mattered.

Corinne popped her head around the living room door. "She's fast asleep, do you want a glass of wine?"

"Yes, please."

She was back in a couple of minutes and handed him a glass. "Thanks again for tonight. You were wonderful with her."

He smiled. "She made it easy, she was wonderful with me!"

"I'm glad, but don't get carried away. She can be so sweet sometimes, but you weren't calling her a monster without reason."

Beau frowned. He's hoped she'd forgotten that. "My only reason was that I didn't understand. I didn't know how to take her, or how to talk to her."

Corinne smiled, "I know. All I'm saying is that tonight you saw the sweet, tired Ruby. She won't always be like that. She's still going to argue with you and boss you around."

He nodded. "I get it, but now I think I understand her a bit better, I'm better prepared to deal with it."

"Okay, sorry."

He held up a hand. "There's nothing to be sorry for."

"There is. I'm sorry that so far everything we've talked about has revolved around Ruby."

"It has to, doesn't it?"

"Not always. I just need for us to be straight about it in the beginning."

"And now that we are…" He put his glass down and went to sit beside her on the sofa. "How about we talk about you and me?" He took her glass from her hand and set it down on the coffee table. "Or better still how about we quit talking altogether?"

As he leaned toward her, her arms came up around his neck, pulling his head down to her. He loved the way she kissed him, she opened up to him, allowing him in, welcoming him. He closed his arms around her and held her to him, loving the feel of her warm soft breasts against his chest. She surprised him by lying back on the sofa, taking him with her so he was lying on top of her. He'd have to slow down in a minute. This was way too tempting, and he couldn't go where temptation led him, not with Ruby asleep in the next room. He lifted his head and gave her a questioning look.

She shook her head. "We can't."

"No! I know. That's not what I was asking. I just wanted to make sure you're okay."

She sat back up. Dammit. Why hadn't he just rolled with where they were going?

She ran her fingers through her hair looking embarrassed. "I'm sorry. I was getting a bit carried away."

He smiled. "That's what I thought. That's why I wanted to make sure you were okay. I didn't want to take advantage and go where we both know we shouldn't."

Her next words took his breath away. "But I want to."

Damn! Temptation was a bitch! He eyed the door as though Ruby might come walking through it at any moment, and knowing his luck she probably would. "Well, don't think I'm the kind of guy who's going to say no."

Corinne let out a big sigh that only turned him on more as he watched her breasts heave. He forced himself to look back up at her face.

"We both have to say no. If one of us crumbles we'll take the other down with us."

He nodded, it was true. "So how about we figure out what we can do?"

She gave him a puzzled look.

"I mean when we can get together and…" Hmm, maybe he should rephrase what he'd been about to say. "And not have to worry about her?"

Corinne nodded. "Let me work on it?"

He smiled. "Can I work on it, too?"

"What do you mean?"

He shrugged. "I don't know yet, but I might be able to come up with something."

She nodded. "We'll work something out."

He leaned back toward her, hoping that just because they were being responsible didn't mean he couldn't at least keep kissing her. She leaned in toward him, too, her pupils wide in the moment before her eyelids closed over them and her lips met his.

"Mommy!"

Beau recoiled as if he'd heard gunshot.

Corinne stifled a giggle. "Coming, sweetie." She didn't get chance to go check on her before the living room door opened.

Beau had to question whether he'd ever seen anything cuter than her standing there in her blue pajamas, looking bleary eyed and dragging a bear by one paw. "Are you okay, pumpkin?"

She smiled and nodded. "I didn't get a goodnight kiss." She came to him and wrapped her arms around his neck, a feeling he was pretty used to after this evening. Then she planted a sloppy kiss on his cheek. "Goodnight, Beau."

He hugged her to his chest for a moment and kissed the top of her head. "Goodnight, pumpkin."

She smiled and took hold of Corinne's hand as she led her back to bed. Once the living room door had closed behind them he heard her say. "You should kiss him too, Mommy."

If only she knew.

Corinne was back in another few minutes. "Sorry."

"I think we already did this. There's no need."

"Okay, thanks. Where were we?"

He raised an eyebrow. "About to get it on, on the sofa until I had an attack of conscience, if I remember rightly."

She laughed. "You do. I was wishing you hadn't, but I'm so grateful now!"

He nodded. His own desire dried up at the thought of Ruby walking in and finding them naked on the sofa together. That would no doubt traumatize the kid. Hell, it'd traumatize him!

"You know, we've established that we want to sleep with each other, we've both done an awful lot of thinking and talking about how your daughter and I might or might not get along, do you think we maybe jumped the gun somewhere down the line?"

"What do you mean?"

He shrugged. "I mean how about we go all the way back to the beginning and just talk. Get to know each other."

She nodded.

"I was so bowled over by you the very first time I heard your voice, I…" he hesitated, but decided to say it anyway. "I didn't give much thought to who you are as a person, I just knew I liked the way you sounded, and looked. Then when we met, I knew I liked the way you make me feel." She smiled as he brushed a stray strand of hair away from her face. "I may be going in reverse order of what's really important, but now I want to know who you are."

She smiled. "I guess I'm guilty of the same thing. From when I first saw you in the wine store, I saw a gorgeous guy."

He grinned. "Keep talking. I like this."

She pushed at his arm. "Like you need your ego feeding!"

"I do. My poor ego is starved, it never gets fed."

"Bullshit!"

That made him laugh. "It's true! Why don't you believe me?"

"I don't know you Remingtons very well yet, but even I can see that it's a family trait, you're all well-endowed in the ego department, except maybe Carter."

"That's not the only department," he couldn't resist saying.

She laughed. "All I can do is take your word on that for now."

He nodded. "We'll get there." He wished they could get there right now, but it wouldn't be right, and this was fun. They did need to get to know each other better.

Corinne smiled back at him. The more time she spent with him the more she liked him. She was a little surprised at herself that she'd been so eager to pull him down on the sofa with her when he'd kissed her. Was it just that it had been such a long time, or was it that he had some strong pull on her? She knew it was the latter. He was gorgeous, but it was more than that. Whenever he came close her insides melted, she started to forget everything, her inhibitions, her responsibilities, everything except the way he made her feel and her need for more. She didn't want to have to just take his word for it for too long.

"What are you doing tomorrow?"

"Nothing exciting. Getting everything ready for Ruby to start school and me to start work on Monday."

"What about tomorrow evening?"

She shook her head sadly. "We both need to get an early night. I want Ruby home."

Beau laughed. "I thought we were talking about spending time together."

She felt her cheeks color. She was still focused on how and when they could get time alone together. She laughed it off. "What can I say? I'm not normally this brazen. I blame you."

"I take it as a compliment." He smiled. "Unless you're only after me for my body?"

"I'm not that kind of girl."

His face was serious. "I didn't think so. Do you mind if I ask you something?"

"What's that?"

"Is Ruby's dad in the picture at all?"

She shook her head. "No. He was, for a short time. But…" How to explain it? "David and I dated for a couple of years before I got pregnant. We knew we weren't forever, but it was comfortable. When Ruby was born, we tried to make a go of it, but we were both miserable. We went our separate ways quite amicably. He used to see Ruby on the weekends when she was a baby. Then he met someone and got married, they had a baby of their own and that was it. We don't hear from him anymore."

Beau frowned. "Does he help financially?"

Corinne let out a short laugh. "Do you think I would have been working three jobs if he did? No. And don't look at me like that. I know I could try to make him, but I don't want to."

"Why not?"

She shrugged. "As far as I'm concerned it's me and Ruby against the world. I can take care of her. She doesn't go short of anything. If he doesn't want to contribute or be part of her life then I don't want him to." She ran a hand through her hair. "My family thinks I'm stupid. Carly's husband James gets after me all the time. Things have been tight, but I just prefer it this way." She looked at him. "Don't worry, I don't expect you to understand. It's not a pride thing, it's about Ruby and me and how we make our way in the world."

Beau nodded. "I'm not going to claim to understand, but I think I'd feel the same way if I were you."

"You would?"

"Yeah. I mean if the guy doesn't want to be a part of her life then she's better off that he's out of it completely. What would you do if he did come around though? If he wanted to start seeing her?"

"I doubt that would ever happen. But if he did, I wouldn't stop him. He's a decent enough person and he is her father. I don't believe you should ever stop a child from knowing their parents—if they want to." She shrugged. "I don't like the idea, but it's not about what I want. It's about doing what's right for Ruby. Luckily, as I said, I don't think it would ever happen. But you just never know."

"And what if Ruby wants to see him?"

"Then I'll ask him." She frowned, wondering how it would feel if the day came when Ruby wanted to get to know her father. She knew it would hurt, but she also knew that she would do what was right for her daughter.

"Sorry, I sound like I'm interrogating you. I guess I'm just curious, I've never thought about that kind of situation before."

"It's okay. I try not to think about it most of the time. If it does ever happen I'll deal with it. And the one thing you learn very quickly when you have kids is that you have to set aside what you want in order to do what's best for them."

"But so many people don't seem to learn that. Your ex didn't. He set aside what was best for Ruby in order to do what he wants."

"I choose to believe that he has done what's best for Ruby. He removed himself from her life."

Beau smiled. "I guess so. You like to turn things around and see them in the best light possible, don't you?"

"I do. Always. If you don't, you just end up miserable over things you can't change."

"I admire that. I think I might need to take lessons from you."

"Why's that?"

He shrugged. "I will admit that I tend to get hung up on things I don't like. I want to change them. To make them better."

"Well, that's a good thing. If you're talking about things that you can change, it's just knowing the difference. If you can't make something better, then all you can do is find a better way to look at it and move on. If you can make it better, then you should."

He smiled. "I feel as though I should write that down."

She laughed. "Sorry I didn't mean to get all philosophical on you."

"I'm glad you did." He checked his watch. "I should probably get going."

"Oh. Okay." She had to wonder if she'd said something wrong.

He smiled. "Can I see you tomorrow?"

"I'd like that."

"Me, too. I'll call you in the morning." He leaned in to kiss her, making her want to ask him to stay. She didn't, but she wanted to. Instead she walked him to the door.

"Drive safely."

"I will."

Once he'd gone she went to check on Ruby. She was fast asleep, her bear clutched tight to her chest. She smiled. Glad that she and Beau had hit it off so well. Maybe things were starting to go right now. She could only hope so.

Chapter Twelve

The next morning Beau decided to stop in to see his folks. He'd said he'd call Corinne, but thought he may as well call her once he was already out at the ranch.

His dad was sitting at the big table in the kitchen when he walked in.

"Morning, son. It's good to see you back down here again."

He smiled. "It's good to be here."

His dad grinned. "You don't know how good it is to hear you say that."

He smiled and took a seat at the table. "Things seem to be changing, or maybe it's me. I don't know. Maybe I'm hitting an early midlife crisis or something…"

"Or maybe you've just been working too hard for too many years." His mom appeared at the top of the stairs from the basement and smiled at him. "And now you've found a reason to relax a little and have some fun."

He shrugged. He didn't know what to say, and he knew she would have a lot more to add.

"Are you back to ride Troy, or to see Corinne?"

He smiled. "I came to see you guys."

His dad laughed, "Since we're right next door to Corinne?"

"Well, it helps, but I've been meaning to come see you anyway. There's something I want to talk to you both about." He felt bad that his dad looked wary. "Am I really that bad?"

His dad shrugged. "You're not bad at all, son. I just know how you get about the division of the ranch. I don't want to hurt your feelings, I really don't. But at the same time, I have to do what I believe is right."

Beau nodded. "I know that, Dad. I think I'm starting to see where I've been going wrong."

"Oh, Beau!" His mom was smiling.

He held up a hand with a rueful smile. "I only said I'm starting to see. I'm not quite there yet. So if you don't mind I'd rather avoid that subject for a while longer."

His mom's face fell, but his dad nodded his understanding. "I'd call that progress, at least."

"Thanks, Dad. Me too."

"So if that wasn't what you wanted to talk about, what was?"

Beau couldn't help the big smile that spread across his face. "Well, it's kind of to do with all that."

"Just tell us," said his mom.

"Okay. Since Mason and Gina are going to be moving in here after the wedding. What are you guys planning to do?"

"We're going to Arizona for the winter. You know that." His dad had that wary look again. Beau just wanted to see him smile, to look happy.

"I do, but what about when you come back in the spring?"

"We're going to look into getting a place up in town." His mom smiled, but it didn't reach her eyes.

His dad looked away. Beau knew that he didn't like the idea at all. "We'll figure something out."

"Well, I have a suggestion."

His mom laughed. "Are you going to sell us a house?"

He shook his head. Was he really that bad that his own parents thought he wanted to make a profit on them?

"Go on, son," said his dad.

"I don't want to sell you a house, no. What I'd like to do is give you the cottage."

They both stared at him. His mom recovered first. She pointed out across the creek to where the roof of the cottage was just visible. "That cottage? The cottage. And you want to give it to us?"

He nodded.

His dad grinned. "Are you serious?"

He nodded again. "I thought you might like the idea. I know you don't want to be up in town. This way you'd still be right here, but not in the middle of everything. You can be as involved as you want to be, or not if you don't."

His dad reached across the table and gripped his arm. "Thank you! That is best solution possible!" He sighed. "You have no idea how happy that makes me."

Beau had to swallow the lump in his throat. He hadn't had any idea that it would mean so much. He could see his dad's eyes were shining. His mom had tears rolling down her face. She came and hugged him. "Oh, Beau. That's a lovely idea. We must buy it from you though."

He shook his head. "Nope. It's my gift. You guys have always done so much for me, this is finally something I can do for you."

"But…"

"Monique." His dad gave her a stern look. "I'm so proud of my boy that he's able to do something like this and more so that he wants to. We need to accept in the spirit that's it's given."

His mom smiled through her tears. "Thank you, Beau."

Beau had to blink away tears of his own. To hear his dad say that he was proud of him meant the world. That was all he'd ever wanted; to make them proud of him.

The back door opened and Mason came in. He stopped when he saw all the tears and smiles.

"Is everything okay in here?"

Beau smiled at him. "Everything's just great."

"Good. In that case I'm not even going to ask."

Beau was grateful for that; this was a moment he wanted to share with his parents, just him and them for once. He knew Mason didn't mean it, but he always seemed to walk in and steal the limelight. His dad smiled at him and nodded; it seemed he understood.

"Let's just say that today is a great day. Your brother just made it one."

Mason grinned. Beau was pretty sure he knew what was going on. "Beau seems to be going from strength to strength at the moment."

That took him by surprise, and put him immediately on the defensive. "What do you mean?"

"Just that you've made Mom and Dad's day today. I think it's fair to say that you made Ruby's night last night. You seem to be a little ray of sunshine these days, spreading joy and happiness wherever you go."

Beau had to laugh at the way he put it. He shrugged. "What can I say?"

"Don't say a thing," said his dad. "Just keep at it. It suits you."

"It does?"

His mom nodded and came to hug him again. "It really does. It's so nice to see you starting to relax and enjoy life." She gave him a sly smile. "And I have to tell you how cute it was to see you with Ruby last night. You're a natural."

Beau swallowed. "I'd hardly say that. We got off to a pretty rocky start."

"Yeah, but you're making up for it fast. The kid adores you!"

"And her mom does."

Beau turned to look at Mason. He didn't know what to say. He wasn't used to opening up to anyone. He'd been getting a bit better lately, but opening up to the three of them at once seemed a bit overwhelming.

His mom smiled and came to the rescue. "And who can blame them. Would you like to bring them up here this afternoon?" She rubbed her hands together. "I'd love to get to play with the little one. I've been wanting to invite them up here, but your father says I need to give them time to settle in."

His dad laughed. "Corinne needed a little time to find her feet and get settled in, that's all." He looked at Beau. "Maybe your mom could spend some time with Ruby this afternoon and you could spend some time with Corinne?"

Beau couldn't believe that he felt heat in his cheeks. He didn't think he'd ever blushed in his life! But it felt as though they all must know that he'd been hoping to get Corinne to himself, and the thought of them all knowing why was just a little embarrassing.

His mom clapped her hands together. "Oh, say you'll ask her, Beau! That would be wonderful! I've been getting all broody with your brothers settling down." She shot a look at Mason. "But since they don't seem in any hurry to provide me with grandbabies you might just beat them all to it."

He stared at her.

His dad laughed. "Don't worry, son. Your mom just wants a kiddy to play with. Don't take her words too seriously, just make the most of the offer."

He couldn't take her words too seriously. He couldn't even contemplate them right now. That he could provide her with a grandchild? In the form of Ruby? That would mean…He shook his head. Nope. Not going there. Better to do as his dad said and focus on the possibility of getting Corinne to himself for a few hours this afternoon. He smiled. "Thanks. I'll ask Corinne."

~ ~ ~

Ruby squealed when she saw the truck pull up outside. "My Beau's here!"

Corinne took a look through the window. He'd said he'd call, she hadn't expected him to just show up. She was glad he had. Her cell phone rang and she picked it up from the table.

"Hello?"

"Hi, it's me."

She had to laugh. He mustn't realize that they could see him. He would do in a moment though. Ruby was opening the front door.

"Oh!"

Corinne laughed again. "I thought you were going to call first."

He laughed with her. "That's what I am doing. I came by to see my folks and then came straight over. I realized when I pulled up that I hadn't called first."

"Well how about we hang up and you come on in?"

"Yeah. See you in a minute."

She watched as he climbed out of the truck and Ruby ran up the path to meet him. Her heart did that weird little flip as she watched him pick her up and swing her around. She clasped her arms around his neck and kissed his cheek. Corinne sighed. She knew most relationships went through a honeymoon stage. She could only hope that Ruby and Beau weren't riding for a fall. And what about her and Beau?

She smiled as he came in. "Does this little creature belong to you?" he asked. "I found it wandering around in your front yard."

Ruby giggled. "I am not a creature! I'm a Ruby."

Beau looked at her. "The creature talks and everything."

Corinne laughed. "I've never seen one of those before, where do you think it came from?"

Beau shrugged. "Maybe we should take it up to the big house and see if it's theirs?"

Corinne gave him a puzzled look, but Ruby was happy to play along. "To see your mommy and daddy?" she asked.

Beau nodded. "They have all kinds of creatures at their house. They might like to play with a new one."

Ruby looked at Corinne. "Can we? Can we go play with them? They're nice. I saw them last night."

"I don't know." Corinne looked at Beau, trying to figure out what he was up to.

"I was just over there and my mom was asking after Ruby. She said she'd love to meet her properly sometime and have her over to play."

Corinne's heart raced. He had said he'd see what he could do to get them some alone time, but she hadn't expected it to be today, and she certainly hadn't expected his mom to mind her daughter so that they could sleep together! She wasn't sure how she felt about that at all!

"Pleeasse, can we?" begged Ruby. "I want to go see them."

Corinne nodded slowly. "Okay." They didn't have to stay for long and she didn't have to leave Ruby with them. But it would be rude not to go if they were asking.

Beau caught her eye. "Are you sure? It was just an idea."

She nodded. "No, it's fine. It'd be nice to meet them properly."

He grinned. "Okay. Let's go."

When they got to the ranch house they found Mrs. Remington in the kitchen. Whatever she was baking smelled delicious.

Ruby sniffed the air. "Yummy! Apple pie."

Mrs. Remington turned and smiled at her. "Well, hello, Miss Ruby. Do you want to come help?"

Ruby looked at Corinne. She nodded and let go of her hand making straight for the kitchen table to get one of the chairs. They were big old wooden chairs, and heavy.

Corinne smiled to herself as Beau went to help. "Here, let me get it, pumpkin."

He carried it over to the counter where his mom was rolling dough. "Thank you, Beau. Are you going to help too?"

He shook his head. "You know better than that. I'm good at eating it, not so much at making it."

"I'm good at making it," said Ruby. "I can help."

"Yes, you can," said Mrs. Remington. She looked at Corinne, "As long as your mommy says it's okay you can help with another apple pie and a couple of batches of cookies."

"Can I, Mommy?"

Corinne nodded slowly. This wasn't what she'd expected. She'd thought they were going to visit for a while, not just drop Ruby off.

Mrs. Remington smiled at her, sensing her unease. "I'm sorry. I'm busy getting these done. If you don't mind letting Ruby stay to help, I'd love to catch up with you later."

"Okay. Thank you."

"No, thank you! I need an extra pair of hands. Ruby, could you pass me the flour please?"

Ruby grinned and handed it over.

"You two run along," said Mrs. Remington. "Go have some fun. We'll be busy here until at least five o'clock, if that's okay?"

Corinne looked at her watch. It was only eleven! She and Ruby had to get ready for their new starts tomorrow. But what could she say? She smiled. "Thank you. Can I leave you my number in case you need me?"

"Of course you can."

As she wrote it down on a piece of paper she felt a little silly, realizing that Beau's mom would know how to get hold of him if she needed them for anything. She gave her an apologetic smile as she handed it over.

Mrs. Remington smiled back. "We don't have to do this, if you're not comfortable."

For a moment she hesitated. She wanted to take Ruby, go home and close the door behind them. Keep the two of them safe in their own little world and not let anyone else in. She looked at Ruby. She was happily rolling dough. It made her understand that it was herself she was trying to protect, not her daughter. She smiled. "This is wonderful, thank you. I guess I'm just not used to it, that's all."

Mrs. Remington gave her a kind smile. "I know, but I think it might do you good to get used to it." She looked at Beau. "At least I hope so."

"See you later, Mommy!" called Ruby.

Corinne laughed. "I guess that's me dismissed." She went and kissed Ruby's cheek. "You be good. I'll see you later."

"Bye."

Ruby looked at Beau expectantly and Corinne exchanged a smile with Mrs. Remington when he, too, went and kissed her cheek. "See you later."

Beau looked at her as she climbed into his truck. "Are you okay with this?"

"Yeah. It just caught me off guard."

"Sorry, it did me too. Mom suggested I should bring you both over and said she'd love to play with Ruby. I thought it would be a good chance to…"

She raised an eyebrow at him.

He laughed. "I know. It all seems kind of premeditated and weird, doesn't it?"

She nodded, relieved he felt that way, too. "It does."

"So what do you want to do?"

"I don't know. What are you thinking?" They finally had some time alone together, but he was right; it did feel weird to think that they would just go back to her place and jump into bed together.

"I think you know what I was thinking. But how about we go up to town? I can show you around. If you're hungry we can get some lunch at the Mustang."

"I'd like that." That felt much more comfortable and natural.

He started up the truck. "Let's go then."

Chapter Thirteen

When they got to town Beau pulled up outside the Mustang. "If you're hungry we can eat now and then go for a walk. It's a neat little town really, there's a lot to see."

"That sounds great," said Corinne. "I haven't had a chance to look around yet, and I am hungry, if you are."

"Yep, that works for me. I didn't get breakfast this morning and it can get busy in here if we leave it too late."

Beau held the door for her and followed her inside. As the hostess showed them to their table he wondered if this hadn't been a bad idea—a really bad idea. It seemed the whole town had decided to come out for lunch. Angie shot him an evil glance as they passed the table where she was sitting with her friend, Katie. And shit, shit, shit! Wanda! She was sitting in a corner booth with her husband, Terry, and what looked like their whole clan. At least she hadn't seen him—yet. And as they reached their table he spotted Guy Preston sitting with one of his drinking buddies. He hadn't realized that lowlife like him ventured out in daylight hours. He sighed as he took his seat. Hopefully they would be able to ignore their fellow diners and just enjoy lunch.

"Are you okay?"

He nodded. "I'm fine. Sorry. Just a few too many familiar faces in here for my liking."

"Do you want to leave?"

He smiled. "No. It's all good. I wanted you all to myself. I can just forget they're here."

"Beau Remington!" The sound of Wanda's not so dulcet tones echoing across the restaurant proved him wrong about that as soon as the words were out of his mouth.

He gave Corinne a rueful smile. "Okay, so maybe not. You're about to meet my assistant, Wanda. I can't tell you what to expect, she's a law unto herself."

Corinne looked scared to death as Wanda bore down on them.

"Well, hello, hello and how are you?"

Beau smiled. "I was doing just great, enjoying my Sunday, until I heard my name being bellowed across the room."

Corinne's eyes widened, but Wanda laughed. "Don't mind him, hon. He loves me really, he's just got a funny way of showing it." She thrust her hand out. "I'm Wanda. I work for him, and you must be Corinne."

Corinne nodded and smiled. "Nice to meet you."

"I'm sure you don't think it is right now." Wanda smiled warmly at her. "And I'm sorry for that, I don't mean to spoil your lunch, but I just couldn't resist the temptation to come over and make him squirm."

Corinne laughed.

Beau narrowed his eyes at Wanda. "Okay, well you succeeded. You can go and sit back down now."

"Oh, no. My fun is just getting started." She winked at Corinne and leaned her hip on the edge of the table. "I think I should let Corinne here know what she's in for."

Beau rolled his eyes. Wanda was fun, but she really did have him squirming in his seat wondering what she might be about to say. "And what, in your not-so-humble opinion, is she in for?" He caught Corinne's eye, she was enjoying this.

Wanda bent down and lowered her voice. "Well, Corinne, honey. Our Beau has quite a reputation in this town."

Corinne looked more wary than amused now and Beau had to wonder where Wanda was going with this.

"You see," she continued, "people think he can be an asshole, and he does nothing to disabuse them of that belief." She grinned at him. "And I just can't understand why. Because when you get to know him, when you get past the tough outer shell, he's an absolute sweetheart underneath. So give him a chance, and if he seems like an idiot sometimes, just remember he can't help it, he's a man, they all are."

Corinne burst out laughing. "Good to know. Thank you."

Wanda nodded. "I also wanted to say thank you. You bring out the best in him. He's been a different guy since he met you. And I think, if you give him a bit of time to get used to it, I think he'll do great with your daughter, as well." She looked back to where her family was sitting. "And if your daughter needs some playmates, get Beau here to give me a shout. I've got a whole herd of grandkids she can come play with."

"Don't you think you should be getting back to them?" asked Beau.

She laughed. "You mean would I please go away and stop embarrassing you now? Sure. I can do that. I'll see you in the office tomorrow." She looked at Corinne. "If I still have a job! It was a pleasure to meet you."

"You too."

Corinne smiled as she watched her go. Beau was glad for a moment to recover and to try to figure out what he could say to explain Wanda.

"She's awesome! I bet she keeps you in your place."

He laughed. "She gives me enough shit, I can tell you that. I don't know why I keep her around."

"Because she adores you."

"You reckon?"

Corinne laughed. "She does and you know it. And if you weren't trying to keep up that tough shell she was just talking about you'd admit that you adore her, too!"

"Adore her? More like I endure her. She's good at her job, but she's a pain in the ass."

Corinne shook her head. "Is it that you won't admit it or that you can't see it? That woman is like a second mother to you and you love it!"

Beau chuckled. "I suppose, but my mom would never talk to me like that."

"It's my guess that no one talks to you like that, and that's why Wanda gets away with it, and also why you love her for it."

He nodded. "I guess so. You're pretty good at figuring people out, aren't you?"

"Yep, I have to be. I'm not as good as Ruby though."

"I noticed that last night. She seemed to have these instincts, she lights up around good people and shuts down around assholes. And she just instantly knew who was which. It was amazing, people who it took me years to figure out, she just knew and she was spot on every time."

Corinne smiled. "She does seem to have a sixth sense, and…" She kept on smiling but didn't finish her sentence.

"And what?"

"And she likes you. She more than likes you. You've been her favorite ever since she came up here with Carly and James."

Beau thought about the first few times he'd met her. She'd seemed like a bossy, demanding little creature, but thinking about it with the perspective he had now, she'd just been craving his attention. "I don't think she liked me the first few times she met me."

"No?"

"No. I remember seeing her with Summer and Carter when we were going to look at houses. She didn't want to go with me. She wanted to stay with Summer. Summer had to convince her I was her friend before she'd even consider it."

"Ah, but that's different. Summer is her idol; she wouldn't want to leave Summer to go with me."

"I suppose."

"And you can't argue that she adores you now. And anyway, why are we talking about Ruby again? I thought this afternoon was about the two of us."

He nodded. "It is. And hopefully, now the intrusions are over with, and we can enjoy it." He thought about it. "But I don't think there's anything wrong with us talking about Ruby. She's important."

The way she smiled at him told him how much his words meant to her. He hadn't said them for her sake though, it was just that he was figuring out how important she really was.

They managed to get through lunch without any further interruptions. Beau was shocked when he called for the check and looked at his watch. They'd been sitting there chatting and laughing for two hours.

"Do you want to go take a walk?"

She nodded. "I'd love to, and if we sit here much longer, we'll end up having to go straight back."

She was right and he did want to enjoy their time while they could.

They walked down Main toward the park. He wanted to take her down the trail that followed the river. A car honked as it passed them. Beau looked up and waved; it was a couple whose house he'd finally closed the sale on last week.

"Does everyone know everyone around here?"

He smiled. "It feels that way most of the time."

"That must be weird."

He shrugged. "You get used to it. You can ignore the ones you don't want to be involved with." He reached out and took hold of her hand as they walked. "And you just focus on the ones you are interested in."

She smiled up at him. "There has to be a lot of women who are interested in you."

"What makes you say that?" He already thought he knew.

"The girl who gave you a dirty look when we went into the restaurant. The one who kept looking over the whole time."

"Angie."

"An old girlfriend?"

"Does it matter?"

She shrugged a little too hurriedly, making it seem that it did. He felt bad, but he liked it. "I just like to know what I'm dealing with. I mean for all I know she could still be a girlfriend."

He frowned. "She's not. We went out a couple of times that's all. I only have one girlfriend at a time, and most of the time I don't have one at all."

She looked up into his eyes.

He smiled. "I'd like to say that right now I have one."

She smiled. "You would?"

He nodded. "What do you say? Do you want to be my girl?" He knew it was a cheesy old line, but it felt right.

She smiled. "We may have a problem there."

His smile faded. What did she mean?

"You said you only have one girlfriend at a time. If you took me on, you'd have two."

He laughed. "In your case I could handle two. And besides, it'd be one girlfriend and one pumpkin."

"Have you seen her face whenever you call her that? She looks like the cat that got the cream!"

"I know. The first time I said that I had no idea where it came from, but seeing the way she reacted I just had to keep going with it. And now it's our thing." He shook his head.

"What?"

"Nothing. If you'd have told me, even a week ago, that Ruby and I would have a thing, any kind of thing at all, I would have laughed in your face and told you you were crazy."

"What changed though? I'll be honest, it worries me a little that you went so fast from calling her a monster to calling her pumpkin."

"In part it's just that I didn't know her, or want to know her before." He smiled. "I guess in part I have Wanda to thank, too."

"How's that?"

He realized that in order to explain he'd have to admit that he'd talked to Wanda about her and Ruby. Why not though? For once he didn't want to hide what he'd been thinking, didn't want to keep his inner processes secret. He wanted her to know and hopefully to understand. "Well, I may have mentioned you to Wanda a time or two."

She raised an eyebrow. "And?"

"And I may have mentioned that I like you."

Her smile grew wider.

"And I may also have mentioned that I didn't know how to handle Ruby."

She laughed. "Do you mean you might have said that she was a monster?"

"Maybe, but as you noticed just now, Wanda has a way of setting me straight. She made me see Ruby in a different light."

"How?"

"She told me to think how it must feel for her. That she's in a new place, she hasn't had a chance to make any friends yet, and that she doesn't have a daddy of her own. That it wouldn't cost me anything to show her some kindness. I don't know, she made me think of Ruby as someone I could help. That changed everything."

Corinne didn't look too thrilled with his explanation.

"Did I say something wrong?"

She shook her head. "No. It's nice that you feel that way." She looked up at him. "I just don't want you to think of Ruby, or me, as an underdog. We don't need someone to look out for us. We're not helpless."

He stopped walking and looked down into her eyes. "That's not how I think of you. Either of you. I think you're both strong and perfectly capable of surviving by yourselves. It's more that I was building Ruby up as the enemy and Wanda made me see how stupid that was."

She smiled. "Okay. I can see that, but how are we back to talking about Ruby again?"

He didn't even know. "I guess it's necessary and natural that she's going to come up a lot, isn't it."

"I suppose so. I just don't want you to think that everything has to revolve around her."

"It kind of does though, and I'm okay with that."

"I am too, as long as we get to be just us sometimes."

He smiled. They were down by the river now and he started walking again. "So how about we do something that's just about us right now?"

"What?"

He smiled and tugged her hand to make her walk faster. "It's a surprise. Do you trust me?"

Chapter Fourteen

Corinne nodded. She did trust him. He was trying to be completely open with her and she appreciated that. She almost had to trot to keep up with him as he strode along the path by the river. "Where are we going?"

"I told you it's a surprise."

She hoped wherever it was wasn't too far or she'd be too worn out to enjoy it by the time they got there. He took a smaller path that led away from the river and back toward the houses. These houses were bigger and much grander than the ones they'd passed earlier. This was the upscale end of town by the looks of it. He left the path and walked across the grass toward the backyard of one house. She was surprised when he took his keys out of his pocket and unlocked the gate in the tall fence. She stepped through and waited while he locked it behind them. When he had, he took her hand and led her through a beautifully manicured garden with lawns and flower beds.

"This is your place?" Her heart was hammering. He'd said they were going to do something that was just about them. Then he'd brought her here. The tingly shivers were running down her spine again.

He nodded. His eyes were even darker than usual and there was no mistaking the desire in them. He started to unlock the back door. "Do you want to?"

"Yes."

He held the door open for her, and she stepped inside. It was a lovely house, but she didn't get a chance to admire it. He came to stand behind her and slid his arms around her waist. She sagged back against him as his hot, wet mouth came down on her neck. She pressed her ass back against him. The way his hard cock pushed at her told her that he wanted her badly. She gasped as one hand came up to close around her breast while the other slid down inside the waistband of her skirt. It felt as though he was everywhere.

She turned around to face him, sad to feel his hands move away. But it wasn't his hands she wanted most. His mouth came down on hers as he pinned her against the wall with his weight. His hands were busy lifting her skirt pushing it up around her waist and then finding their way inside her panties. She moaned when his fingertips brushed over her clit. Oh God! That felt so good. She scrabbled at his belt buckle, then his zipper. She was desperate now, to get him out of his jeans. He didn't make it easy, continuing to taunt her with his fingertips while he took her bottom lip inside his mouth and sucked. It took every scrap of concentration she could muster to get his jeans undone and push them down past his hips. She took hold of him with both hands and was rewarded when he let out a low moan. He hadn't been joking about being well-endowed. He felt huge, so hard and hot in her hands. But that wasn't where she wanted to feel him.

He pressed his knee between her thighs making her open them. She gasped when he thrust two fingers deep inside her. Then somehow his fingers were gone and the throbbing head of his cock had taken their place. He was spreading her legs wider, opening her up as he pressed at her entrance. She braced herself for the thrust, but instead let out a long deep sigh as he slowly slid inside. He grasped her hips tight and slowly but surely rocked his hips against her. It was like some kind of exquisite torture. He was stretching her to the point she didn't think she could take any more, but he kept coming, ever so slowly until his self-control was gone and he thrust deep and hard making her scream and clutch at his back. He hooked his arm behind one of her legs lifting it up to wrap around his waist. Now she was completely at his mercy. She had to cling to him to stay upright and he was pounding into her, his hips thrusting wildly. His hands found their way around her ass and held her open. That was more than she could take. The pressure began to build and build until she couldn't hold it back. Her orgasm erupted like a dam breaking. She screamed as it swept through her, then screamed again as she felt him stiffen and gasp. His release intensified her own, their bodies straining together as the waves of intense pleasure swept through them. By the time they were both still she felt as though her legs were about to give out under her.

Beau lifted his head and smiled. She smiled back. It seemed neither of them had any words just yet. He took her hand and led her upstairs where he showed her to the guest bathroom. While she was in there she started to wonder. That had hardly been romantic, had it? They hadn't even made it two feet past the back door. She sighed. And now he'd shoved her into the guest bathroom and was no doubt cleaning himself up ready to take her home. She sighed. Oh well at least she'd ended her dry spell! And what a way to end it!

She peeked around the door wondering where he was.

"In here," he called.

She followed the sound of his voice and found him in the master bedroom, lying on the bed with a towel around his waist. He patted the bed beside him, but she hesitated, not sure that she wanted to join him.

"I'm sorry, sweetheart. I wanted to make it up here, I wanted to do it right, but something about you just brings out the need in me. I needed you, right there, right then." When he smiled like that he looked almost boyish, he was so open, vulnerable almost. He sat up and held his arms out to her. "Please?"

She went to him and sat on the edge of the bed.

"Are you mad at me?"

She shook her head. "No, if anything I'm mad at me. You bring out the worst in me. You make me lose track of everything but lust."

He smiled and lifted her chin with his thumb, making her look up at him. "And that's a bad thing?"

Looking into his handsome face and his big brown eyes, she knew it was a dangerous thing. She shrugged. "It depends."

"On what?"

"Nothing. I'm sorry, it's a good thing."

"Good. I'm glad you see it that way, because I plan on doing it again."

Her body was already reacting to him. "Doing what?" she asked, as if she didn't know.

"On making you lose track of everything but lust." He traced his fingers down her cheek and on down over her throat. He traced each breast in turn then started to unfasten her top. "Your lust, my lust, our lust. They are the only things you're going to be aware of."

They already were! This didn't feel right any more though. She wasn't sure why, but it just didn't. She knew she felt stiff as he closed his arms around her.

"What's the matter?"

She shook her head. "Nothing. Everything. I don't know."

He hugged her to his chest. "I screwed up, didn't I?"

"No, you didn't do anything wrong. I was right there with you. I wanted it as much as you did, but it feels weird now. I've gone back to thinking about the time and wondering if Ruby's okay. It's not you, it's me. I put myself and what I wanted first and I guess now I'm feeling guilty." She looked up at him. How could she expect him to understand? He wasn't a parent, he was a guy who was used to going after what he wanted and getting it.

His expression was gentle, concerned. "I don't want you to have to feel that way. You should be able to do what you want. But I don't want you to feel bad about it. How can we turn it around?"

She shrugged. "I don't know. I wish I did."

Beau nodded. "We'll figure it out." He planted a kiss on the top of her head. "Do you want to get going?"

Her heart sank. He'd been hoping for more sex and she'd gone and spoiled it. Now he just wanted to get rid of her.

Once they were back in the truck and on the way back down the valley he looked over at her. "You've hardly said a word. I'm starting to feel as though I really screwed up here."

She smiled sadly. "I think we both know that it's me who screwed up. I just don't want this good-bye to be awkward. And I don't want things to be awkward when we run into each other in future."

"Are you saying you don't want to see me again?"

"No, I'm assuming you don't want to see me again. Come on, Beau. I'm sure you can have your pick of the ladies around town. You're better off with someone who can jump into bed with you whenever you both feel like it."

His face turned stony at that. "That's not fair. You were just as up for it as I was. And don't make out that's all I want. I thought you knew better than that. If it was, why wouldn't I have stuck to my original offer? Why would I have enjoyed so much time with Ruby?" He glared at her, waiting for her answer.

She shrugged. "I don't know. I'm sorry. I'm feeling guilty, I'm realizing how difficult this could be and I suppose I'm deciding for you that it's not worth your time."

"Well, do me a favor and let me make my own decisions?"

She stole a glance at him. "Okay."

He turned and smiled. "Thank you. You're right, this is kind of tricky, but if we want it enough, I don't see why we can't make it work."

Wow! "Are you saying that you want it enough?"

"I am. I do. Do you?"

She nodded. "I'd like to try."

He smiled. "Then how about we both try to relax a bit?"

"Easier said than done I think."

"Yeah, which is why we'll both need to make an effort. And most importantly we'll need to keep talking. You can't go clamming up on me like that."

"I'll try not to, but I will warn you, it's a defense mechanism."

"I can see that. We all have them, but we don't have to let them override everything."

"Okay, I'll try not to."

"Me too."

When they were almost back to the ranch, Beau stopped the truck in one of the pull outs by the river. He reached over and took her hand. "What are you going to do when we pick Ruby up?"

"We need to get everything ready for tomorrow. For her first day at school and my first day at work."

"Can I come hang out and help?"

She smiled. "I don't know what you can do to help."

"So how about I hang out and make a nuisance of myself?"

She laughed. "That's more like it, and yes, I'd love you to. And I know Ruby would."

"Thanks. See, I've been thinking on the drive back and it strikes me that you're not going to be able to relax with me until we're used to being around each other."

She nodded.

"So I'd like to be around each other as much as we can."

Wow. She hadn't expected that, but she did like the idea. "So, come spend the evening with us."

~ ~ ~

Beau smiled as Ruby climbed onto his lap. "I like your mommy."

"I like your mommy, too." They were back at the cabin after picking up a tired but happy Ruby from his folks' place.

"I know. She likes you. Are you going to be girlfriend and boyfriend now?"

He smiled. "I hope so."

Ruby smiled. "You should ask her. She'll say yes."

Corinne came back into the living room. "What am I going to say yes to?"

Ruby smiled up at him. "Go on then," she urged.

What the hell, he'd asked her once, but that was before she'd weirded out on him this afternoon. It wouldn't do any harm to ask again. "To being my girlfriend."

She smiled.

"Say yes, Mommy!"

"Yes, I'd like that."

"Yay!" Ruby bounced up and down on Beau's lap. "Are you going to kiss each other?"

Corinne laughed. "Not right now. No. We're supposed to be getting you ready for your big day tomorrow."

Ruby smiled at Beau. "I'm going to school tomorrow with Josie and Tara."

"I know. You're going to have fun."

"Can you come pick me up?"

Beau frowned. He could, but he didn't think that was part of the plan.

"You know Miss Susie is going to pick you up," said Corinne.

"Yes, but I mean from her house."

"I'm going to pick you up when I finish work."

"But my Beau could come with you." She looked up at him with her big blue eyes. "Pleeasse?"

He looked at Corinne. He didn't know how he could say no to that little face, but he didn't see how he could say yes either. It'd be up to Corinne.

"You want to?"

He nodded. "I'd love to see how you both enjoyed your first day. I could come meet you when you finish work?"

She smiled. "That'd be lovely."

"Okay. I'll be here then."

Ruby flung her arms around his neck and kissed his cheek. "I can't wait!"

He laughed. "You just make sure you're a good girl and have fun, then you'll have lots to tell me about."

"I will. I'm already good at letters and I'm going to make lots of friends, too."

"I'm sure you are."

"And you need to get a good night's sleep first, so it's time for bed for you, madam."

Beau was surprised to see her eyebrows knit together. She'd been so sweet the last few days, he'd already forgotten about the other side of Ruby. The side he feared was about to surface again now.

"I don't want to!"

"Well, want to or not, you have to."

"But I want to stay up with my Beau!"

"You need to go bed, pumpkin." He was hoping that by now he had some influence over her. He was thrilled to see that apparently he did.

"Do I have to go now?"

He nodded. "Yeah, you've got a big day tomorrow. And I'll see you when you're done."

"Okay. Will you read me a story?"

He looked at Corinne uncertainly. She smiled. "That's a great idea. Beau can read us a story and then you go straight to sleep."

Ruby scrambled down from his lap and ran to her bedroom. Beau stood to follow her.

Corinne caught his arm. "Are you sure you don't mind?"

"Not at all."

It was weird, but weird in a good way to sit on Ruby's bed and have her and her bear snuggle against him. Corinne sat on the other side of her and smiled at him over her head. She handed him a book. "This is what we've been reading."

Not ten minutes later, Corinne touched his arm. He was getting into the story of the two kittens who were trying to find their way home. Ruby, on the other hand was fast asleep. He gave Corinne a sheepish grin.

She motioned toward the door with her head and they slipped out as quietly as they could. Corinne closed the bedroom door and led him back to the living room. "I'm supposed to pick her up from Susie's at six-fifteen. Are you going to be able to come?"

He nodded. "I've already figured one thing out, and that's that I'm not going to tell her I can do something unless I'm one hundred percent sure I can. I'm showing a house over in Emigrant at four-thirty, so I'll just stick around after that. I won't head back up to town."

"You can stay for dinner with us if you like?"

"That sounds great." He closed his arms around her waist and drew her closer, loving the way she sagged against him as she looked up into his eyes. "I should probably get going."

Her smile faded. "Do you have to?"

"No. Nor do I want to. I just wanted to give you the option to kick me out if you still have stuff you need to get done."

"I think I've got it all covered, and right now I'd like nothing more than to just curl up with you and a glass of wine and enjoy what's left of the evening."

He smiled. He couldn't think of anything he'd like more either, at least not while Ruby was asleep next door. "Let's do that then."

Chapter Fifteen

Corinne shifted, trying to get comfortable. She couldn't, her neck ached and she couldn't bend her knees up, there was something in the way. She opened her eyes and realized that the something was Beau. She wasn't in bed, they were on the sofa. They'd sat down there last night with a glass of wine, then they'd lain down to watch a movie. She sat up in a panic and looked at the clock, hoping to goodness she hadn't overslept today of all days. She heaved a sigh of relief when she saw it was only six-thirty.

Beau opened his eyes and looked up at her. "Oh, shit!"

That made her laugh. "Thanks! Good morning to you, too!"

He smiled blearily. "I didn't mean it like that. We fell asleep, didn't we?"

She nodded. "It's not late though."

He looked at the clock. "Maybe not for you, but I need to get up to town and get showered. I've got meetings this morning." He sprang up from the sofa. "I should get going."

"Mommy!" Oh, no. Ruby was awake.

Beau looked at her. "Should I sneak out?"

Corinne sucked in a deep breath and made a decision. "Not if you've got time to say a quick hello before you leave?"

He grinned. "It'll have to be quick."

"Okay. I'll go get her."

She came back a couple of minutes later with a sleepy Ruby in her arms. Beau was sitting at the kitchen table putting his shoes on.

"Beau!" squealed Ruby.

He looked up at her with a smile. "Morning, Ruby. Are you ready for your big day?"

She nodded. "Did you come to take me?"

"No, sweetie," said Corinne.

Ruby's eyes grew wide. "Did you sleep here?"

Beau gave Corinne a panicky look.

"Yes, Beau and I fell asleep watching a movie."

"Did you sleep in Mommy's bed?" she asked Beau.

"No. We fell asleep on the sofa."

Ruby smiled. "You should sleep in Mommy's bed tonight it's more comfy. I sleep there sometimes, if I get scared."

Beau smiled. "I'll have to try it out. For now though, I have to go to work. I just wanted to wish you good luck for today."

Ruby held her arms out to him. Corinne's heart did that odd little flip again as she watched him take her daughter and hug her. She planted a kiss on his cheek and he smiled, planting one on top of her head before he handed her back. "You have a good day, pumpkin. I'll see you later." He turned to Corinne. "You have a good day, too."

She reached up and pecked his cheek. "Thank you."

Just as he'd done with Ruby he planted a kiss on top of her head. It was sweet of him, but it wasn't what she wanted. She knew she surprised him by pecking his lips. He grinned first at her then at Ruby. "See you later."

"Bye," called Ruby as they watched him let himself out.

When he'd gone Ruby wriggled to get down. "I hope he can stay again tonight."

Corinne was going to give it some thought. In the normal run of things it would have been a long while before she would have considered having him stay over, but since they'd accidentally crossed that bridge by falling asleep on the sofa, she might as well make the most of it.

~ ~ ~

Beau didn't make it to the office until lunchtime. Wanda looked up and grinned at him when he walked in.

"Greetings, boss man. I trust you had a good weekend?"

"It was great. Apart from running into a busybody when I took Corinne out for Sunday lunch."

Wanda laughed. "She's beautiful. And don't give me your crap about ruining your lunch. I helped you out and you know it. You can thank me any time, and a raise would be a nice way to show your gratitude."

"Ha! Dream on."

"I know, I know, but maybe someday I'll break through and that big heart of yours will overflow."

He smiled. "You'd have been proud of me if you'd seen me and Ruby this weekend."

Her expression softened. "Really?"

"Yep. I hate to give you the satisfaction, but I remembered what you said about her being just a poor little mite. When I looked at her like that everything turned around pretty fast."

"Aww, ain't that sweet!"

Beau rolled his eyes. "It is actually. You have no idea what it's like to have a little person look up at you and know they trust you, that they've put their faith in you."

Wanda laughed. "I have no idea, no. I haven't raised three of my own, I don't have a flock of grandbabies around every weekend. I'm just glad you can see it now. It changes everything, doesn't it?"

He nodded. "It really does. It's her first day at school today and she wanted me to go see her afterwards."

"And you're going?"

"I am."

"You're in deep then?"

He shrugged. "I wouldn't say that. I mean we've only known each other a couple of weeks. It's a bit soon to talk like that, isn't it?"

Wanda shook her head. "Either you're bullshitting me because you don't want to admit it, or you need to slow down. You don't want to let that little girl think you're going to be a part of her life if you're not."

Beau stared at her. He'd thought he was making pretty big strides. He was getting into a real relationship with Corinne, he was opening up to Ruby. That was huge to him. But saying he was going to be a part of their life? That was even bigger, that was enormous. Was that really what he was getting into? Was it what he wanted?

Wanda held his gaze. "Think about it. Anyway, here are the files you're going to need this afternoon. I've emailed you everything that's come in on the house on Convict Ridge. Oh, and a guy called to see if you could show him the one on Second Street this evening."

"No. I can't. See what time he can do tomorrow instead?"

Wanda raised an eyebrow. "I thought you were free after the showing down in Emigrant at four-thirty? That should give you plenty of time to get back up to town."

He shook his head. "I'm not coming back up. I told you, I'm going to see Ruby after her first day."

Wanda grinned. "Ah, I see."

"What?" That look she was giving him said she saw a whole lot, but he didn't know what it meant.

"Nothing. Nothing at all. I'll call him back and set something up for tomorrow." Beau stared at her, but she just smiled innocently. "Anything else, boss?"

He had to laugh. "No. That's all."

"Okay, well I'll get back to work then, and I suggest you do the same."

He laughed and picked up the files and took them into his office.

He'd just got settled down when his cell phone rang. It was Shane.

"What's up, bro?"

"Hey. Just checking in with you. Dinner's at our house this week and we're aiming for Thursday. Will that work for you?"

"Sure."

"Okay…"

"And what?"

"Well, we're going for Thursday because Chance is getting back Wednesday night."

"Ah."

Shane didn't say anything for a long moment.

"I hope that means his dad's doing okay?"

"Yeah, from what he said he's getting a bit better every day and it sounds as though he's hitting it off pretty well with the woman who's come to live in while he recovers from his stroke. Chance said he's starting to feel like a spare part so it's time to come on home."

"Good. I'm glad everything's going well."

"Do you think you could bring yourself to tell him that? It'd be nice if you two could finally bury the hatchet."

Beau sighed. "There is no hatchet."

"So why can't you just accept him as another brother?"

"Because he's not, and… You know what. Let's not go there."

"More than happy to oblige," said Shane. "All I really wanted was to make sure that you were still going to come to dinner once you knew Chance is going to be there."

"It never stopped me before, did it?"

"No. I just didn't want to spring it on you."

"Thanks. I appreciate it."

"He's going to get part of the ranch you know."

"I know. Don't push it, Shane. I'm coming around on a lot of things, but that one will take me a while. You can't hurry me, you'll just piss me off and there's no reason for you and I to fall out over it is there?"

"Hell, no. I'm amazed that we're even having this conversation! So, no I'm not going to push it. I'll see you Thursday."

"If not before."

Shane laughed. "Was I seeing things or was that your truck leaving the ranch as I was getting there this morning?"

Beau smiled to himself. There was no point lying. "You weren't seeing things."

"I didn't think so. Then I hope you'll be pleased to know that we asked Corinne to come out on Thursday as well."

"More than pleased. If you hadn't asked her, I would have."

"Like that, is it?"

"Yep."

"Good for you."

"It is. I don't know about you though, but I've got work to do."

"Yeah, okay. See ya."

"See ya, and Shane?"

"Yeah?"

"Thanks."

Beau hung up and stared at the wall for a few minutes. So Chance was on his way back. That would no doubt mean that his dad would finally get around to telling them all his plans for the ranch. Beau knew that Chance would be included. No matter how much that bothered him. He'd told Shane that it would take him a long time to come around to accepting it. He didn't know that he'd ever be able to. Corinne's words came back to him. If you can't make something better, then all you can do is find a better way to look at it and move on. He knew he couldn't change the fact that his dad was going to give Chance part of the ranch. He couldn't change it, but was it possible that he might be able to find a better way to look at it? He didn't see how, but it would be nice to let it go and move on. So much had changed over the last few months. Seeing his brothers settle down, feeling the family dynamic shift as they all found their feet and were being drawn closer to each other again had changed the way he felt about a lot of things. He'd changed. And he had a feeling that being around Corinne and Ruby would change him even more if he let it. He shrugged. He didn't have time to figure it all out right now, but he did know that his ill-feelings toward Chance were the one downer in his life at the moment. And he was the only one responsible for them. He knew it wasn't Chance's fault; hell, he liked the guy. He just resented the way he'd come into the family and been given a place in it that he hadn't earned.

He flipped open the file in front of him. It was time to get down to work, not to dwell on all of that.

~ ~ ~

Cassidy grinned as she came striding through the lobby of the lodge. "So how was your first day, girlfriend?"

Corinne smiled. "It was great, thanks. I'm so glad Shane had us come out on Saturday night to mingle with the guests. It made things so much easier today."

Cassidy raised an eyebrow. "And from what I saw you were doing some mingling with a certain Remington brother, too. How's that going?"

Corinne looked over her shoulder. She didn't feel as though she should be talking about her personal life at work. Especially since her personal life involved her boss's brother.

Cassidy laughed. "Don't worry. No one's listening. And besides everyone saw the two of you, or should I say the three of you together on Saturday night. It was adorable! You should have seen Ruby snuggling up on her Beau while you were busy."

Corinne smiled. "I did see, they carried on like that even after we left."

"And you were worried about whether he hated her. I guess you know the answer to that now."

"Yeah. It was like you said, he just didn't know how to handle her. Apparently he got some help from his assistant at work; she gave him a good talking to about how he might need to just show Ruby a little kindness."

Cassidy laughed. "You met Wanda? Isn't she awesome? She's in my seniors' art class. She's a hoot."

"She seemed it. And she obviously adores Beau." She didn't miss the look of distaste that crossed Cassidy's face before she managed to hide it. "You don't like him though, do you?"

"I wouldn't say anything against him. I mean he does seem to be coming around more and more lately, but…" she sighed. "I can't lie. He's not my favorite."

"Why?"

Cassidy thought about it. "I guess he's not my kind of person. No, that's not fair, he is fun when you get him talking, but he's just that much more aloof than the others. The rest of them are open books. What you see is what you get, and they're all…they're kindhearted."

"And you don't think Beau is?"

Cassidy frowned. "I'm not saying that. At least I don't think so. He might be. It's just that with the others you know right off the bat that they've got great big hearts. Beau may have one too, but if he does, he keeps it hidden." She shrugged apologetically. "You'd probably be better off talking to Summer or Gina, they're more diplomatic than I am."

Corinne smiled. "No, I like hearing it straight up. And I think he really does have a big heart. That's what Wanda said, too. That you just have to break through the tough outer shell before you see it."

Cassidy smiled. "Well, if Wanda says so, then I'm buying it. That woman takes no prisoners, if she thought he was an asshole she'd tell you straight up."

"I very much got that impression, but she really seems to adore him. Do you mind if I ask you though, is there any particular reason that you don't like him?"

Cassidy sighed. "I suppose if I'm honest it's because he's mean to Chance."

"He's mean?"

"No, that's not fair. He's not mean. Ugh, I don't know how to put it. Has Shane asked you about dinner on Thursday?"

"Yes."

"And you are coming, right?"

"I think so. If I can work something out for Ruby."

"Just bring her if you can't that's fine. My point is Chance will be there, so you'll get to see how Beau is with him. He's not mean, but he resents him. I don't know why, I don't know what the history is. I don't even think there is a history. From what I've gathered Beau just feels as though Chance came into the family and stole his place."

"Stole his place?" Corinne had heard talk of Chance. She knew he ran the cattle side of the ranch and that the guys considered him another brother, but that was about it. Other than the fact that he'd been in California for a little while, where his sister had got married and his dad had had a stroke.

"He didn't," said Cassidy. "But he and Mason are really close."

"Mason's the eldest, right?"

"Yep, and Beau is the second and I think he feels as though Chance pushed him down the list."

"Hey, princess. I didn't realize you were here." Shane came in through the back door and grinned at them.

"Yeah, I came down a little early so I thought I'd stop in and see how Corinne's doing."

Shane smiled. "She's doing awesome. You might have to get used to me being around more at home. The way she's knocking things into shape around here, I'm going to be superfluous to requirements within a week or two."

Corinne smiled. She was pleased that Shane saw it that way. The guest ranch was a great business, and he had a wonderful marketing system in place, but she'd already seen lots of areas that could be improved, lots of ways to make the place run more efficiently, and at the same time, provide the guests with an even better experience.

Cassidy grinned at her. "Do me a favor and keep some menial tasks that he can still be involved in? I couldn't stand to have him under my feet all day."

"Don't worry, we'll keep him around as a figure head, just wheel him out to smile and chat to the guests now and then."

"Sounds good to me," said Shane.

"Come on, you," said Cassidy. "Let's go saddle up. You promised me a ride."

"Okay." He turned to Corinne. "You may as well head out, too. Go see how Ruby did on her first day. The night staff are here."

Corinne smiled. "Thanks. I will do. I'm sure Ruby did fine, but I can't wait to see her, and to hear all about it."

"See you tomorrow then."

"And I'll see you Thursday, if not before," added Cassidy.

Chapter Sixteen

Beau figured he was early when he pulled up outside the cabin. Corinne didn't finish work until six and it was a few minutes before that. He was surprised when the front door opened and she came out to meet him.

"Do you want me to drive?" he asked.

She nodded and climbed into the passenger seat. "Thanks."

He didn't start the engine up straight away, but just looked at her for a moment. She was so beautiful, he just wanted to appreciate it for a moment.

She gave him a shy smile. "Is everything okay?"

"More than okay. I was just thinking how lucky I am."

"Lucky?"

He smiled. "Lucky that you decided to give me a chance."

She laughed. "It was you that decided to give Ruby a chance. I was always a sure thing."

He raised an eyebrow. "A guy could take that the wrong way."

She laughed. "You know what I mean. I mean I feel like I'm the lucky one."

He shook his head. "Nope, that'd be me." He leaned over and she leaned in to kiss him. He'd only meant it to be quick, but somehow they lost a few minutes as their tongues tangled. Her arms came up around his neck and he drew her closer. Eventually he pulled back. The way she kissed him made him want more. He'd spent way too much time this afternoon thinking about yesterday. He wouldn't argue that taking her against the wall like that had been great, and sure he'd do it again given half a chance, but part of him regretted it too. He should have taken her to bed, taken their time. Explored each other. Held each other afterward. He hoped they'd be able to do all of that soon. For now though they needed to go get Ruby.

He smiled, and from the way she smiled back he'd guess that she was having at least some of the same thoughts he was. "So how was your first day?"

"It was great. I'm going to love this job, I can tell. If Ruby's day was anywhere near as good as mine was, then I'll be relieved."

"I'm betting she's had a great day." He started up the truck. "We should get going and see."

"I can't wait to see her. It's been weird today. I mean I've always worked, but I've gotten used to being with her all the time since we moved."

"Well, this will probably make you laugh, but I know exactly what you mean. I missed her today, too. I kept wondering how she was getting on."

"Aww." Corinne laughed. "I'll have to ask her what her secret is."

"You don't need to. I kept thinking about her today, but I don't think I've stopped thinking about you since I first saw you in the wine store."

Her eyes widened in surprise. What the hell had he gone and said that for? It might be true, but he didn't need to go blurting it out like that! He shrugged and pulled out onto East River Road. "Sorry, but it's true."

"Please don't say sorry. I'm surprised, but very pleasantly so."

"Good."

They rode on in silence for a few minutes before she spoke again. "Since it seems I spend a lot of time in your head, and I admit that you spend a lot of time in my head, how would you feel about staying tonight?"

He shot a quick look at her. She looked nervous, her cheeks were slightly flushed, as if she were embarrassed to ask. "I'd love to," he answered quickly, hoping to reassure her that she wasn't going out on a limb for no reason. "Are you okay with it, though? I mean, for Ruby and everything?"

She nodded. "You stayed last night, and she was so happy that you were there this morning. I think I build it up in my head more than she does."

He smiled. "Because you know better what it involves than she does."

Her cheeks turned red at that, then she laughed. "Yep, I know I'm asking you to sleep with me—in every sense. She just thinks it's about sleeping over."

Beau reached across and took hold of her hand. "And I know that I would love to sleep over and to sleep with you." He decided it was only fair that he should lay himself open, as she just had. "I've been trying to figure out how I could get you into bed." He laughed at the look on her face. "Let me finish. I know how wrong that sounds. I mean to spend some time in bed with you. After yesterday. Yes, I want more, but I just want to lie with you, hold you, spend some time together." He shrugged, feeling embarrassed and wishing he hadn't started this. He looked over at her.

She smiled. "That sounds very different from the guy who was offering just sex less than a week ago."

He nodded. "It feels very different, too." Jesus! What was he getting himself into here? It was bad enough that all these feelings kept ambushing him, but did he have to let them escape through his mouth every time?

The way she smiled, he didn't feel so bad about it. Still he was grateful when the turn for Susie's place came into view.

"It's just up here," said Corinne.

"I know."

"Of course, I forget that everyone knows everyone up here."

He smiled. "It's hard not to, when you grow up here. I mean there aren't that many people around, so those that are tend to get to know each other."

"I read before I came up here that there are six point eight people per square mile in Montana."

"Yeah, but that includes the cities as well."

She laughed. "Your cities are tiny compared to ours though. It got me curious so I had to look it up. For California, they reckon there are two hundred and thirty-nine people per square mile, and that includes all the open space and national parks. If you take just the big cities, it's unbelievable. Los Angeles is up to ten thousand people per square mile and San Francisco is over six thousand."

Beau shook his head. He couldn't even comprehend that. Of all his brothers, he was the one who'd gone out into the world most, both for college and to real estate conventions. He also liked to travel for fun, and had seen quite a few parts of the country. But to think about living crammed in with thousands of other people? It just didn't bear thinking about. "When you put it like that, I'm glad that I know all my neighbors, and where they live. And that I consider everyone who lives in a valley that's fifty miles long and twenty miles wide to be my neighbor! Though I may change my mind about that if I ever run into that point eight of a person roaming the back country on a dark night."

She laughed as he pulled up in front of Susie's. "I'll be honest, the thought of it being so empty freaked me out at first, but now I'm here, I love it. It doesn't feel lonely."

"You don't ever have to feel lonely." He smiled. What did he even mean by that? If he didn't know himself, then there wasn't much chance Corinne would figure it out, though she looked as though she was trying to. "Do you want me to wait here?" he asked.

"Yes, if you don't mind. I want to have a quick word with Susie, see how they got on. That might be tough to do if Ruby's fawning all over you."

He laughed. "No problem. Take your time."

~ ~ ~

Corinne paused in the doorway to the living room. Beau was sitting on the sofa with Ruby snuggled into his side. They were watching a show on TV while she made dinner. Ruby was pointing at the guy singing, telling Beau she'd seen him sing with Summer. She was getting used to the way her heart flipped every time she saw them together. She mustn't get carried away though. Beau had come a long way with Ruby in a very short time, there was no saying he'd want to go where her heart hoped whenever she saw them like that. And there were no guarantees that he wouldn't do a one eighty just as fast and want out. She had to be realistic. She wondered again whether she was taking too much of a risk, having him over like this, letting Ruby get so attached to him. She'd even asked him to stay the night. She sighed. All she could do was roll with it and hope for the best. If it all went wrong, she'd get over it, and so would Ruby. She'd have to.

Beau smiled when he saw her standing there. "Can I do anything to help?"

She shook her head. "It's almost ready."

"We can do dishes afterwards!" said Ruby with a big smile. "That's how I help Mommy."

Beau smiled at Corinne. "Maybe this weekend we should take your mommy out for dinner so she doesn't have to cook."

"Yay!" cried Ruby. "I like going out to dinner. Can we go to Chico with the warm water?"

She meant the hot springs, and from the look on Beau's face it wasn't an idea that appealed to him.

"We'll have to see, at the weekend," she said. "For now you need to go and wash your hands and get ready for dinner."

Ruby got up and tugged at Beau's hand. "Come on. You need to wash yours too."

Beau rolled his eyes at Corinne as Ruby dragged him into the bathroom. She had to laugh. He was going along with everything so well, and really did seem to be enjoying himself. "Come on through when you're ready," she called after them.

After dinner they went through the same routine as they had before. Ruby took up her position on her chair at the sink and bossed Beau around the kitchen while they did the dishes. Corinne hovered and made sure that nothing got broken. It was fun. Beau seemed to be enjoying himself, which was a relief. And there was no question that Ruby was enjoying herself.

She wanted Beau to read to her, so once again the three of them sat on her bed while he read the story about the two kittens. Ruby's eyes closed almost immediately. She'd enjoyed her day immensely from what she'd told them, and it had obviously worn her out.

Beau smiled. "She may need to start going to bed earlier. I need to find out what happens with the kittens."

She chuckled and got up from the bed. "Come on, you can bring the book with you and read to the end if you want. I won't tell her."

He put it down and came out, closing the door gently behind them. "It wouldn't be right to read it without her. I'll just have to come back tomorrow."

She raised an eyebrow. He'd said he'd like them to spend more time together, that that was the only way they'd get to be relaxed around each other, but she hadn't expected him to want to be around every night.

"Would you mind that?"

"Mind? I'd love it. You surprised me, that's all."

He shrugged and gave her the smile that made her want to grab him and drag him into the bedroom. "You can't get too much of a good thing. And this…" He put his hands on her hips and pulled her toward him. "You and me. We're a good thing."

She rested her head against his shoulder. It felt like a good thing, a very good thing indeed. She just hoped that it might last. In her experience, no good thing ever did.

He took her hand and led her back into the living room, sitting down and patting the sofa beside him. She sat down and turned to smile up at him. "So what are you thinking you'd like to do this weekend?"

"I dunno, I just wanted to make sure that I was part of your plans. It would be nice to go out to dinner if you'd like. I'm not much use in the kitchen, or I'd offer to cook for you."

"You don't like the idea of Chico, though?"

He smiled. "The restaurant's good. And you'd love their wine cellar. But I'm not big on the hot springs. I don't enjoy sitting in a steaming pool with a bunch of other people." He gave her a wry smile. "No offense or anything, but especially small people."

She had to laugh. "You don't trust them not to pee?"

He made a face. "Do you?"

She shook her head. "We don't have to decide now; we can see how we feel when the time comes. Oh, and Shane and Cassidy invited me to dinner on Thursday."

He nodded. "Shane told me. I hope you said yes?"

"I said I would if I could figure something out for Ruby."

"We could take her?"

Corinne had to smile at that. He really had come a long way in a short time.

It wasn't too long before she could feel her own eyes drooping. They were sitting on the sofa, watching a movie, but apparently her first day had taken more of a toll than she'd realized.

Beau leaned over and swept the hair off her face. "Come on sleepy, you should get to bed. Another night on the sofa isn't going to do you any good. I can go home."

She sat up at that and shook her head. "No! Don't go. I want you to stay."

"Okay."

It was strange to take turns in the bathroom and get ready for bed. It was so very different from the time they'd spent at his house. There, it was in through the door and up against the wall. Now they were more like an old married couple, each getting themselves undressed and sliding into bed.

He rolled on his side and smiled at her. She smiled back, he was so gorgeous! He put an arm across her. "Goodnight, sweet lady. Get yourself some rest."

Oh! This wasn't right! She finally had this gorgeous man in her bed and they were just going to roll over and go to sleep!

"Goodnight, Beau." She reached up and pecked his lips, then turned over. She smiled as she felt him edge closer and spoon her. "Don't worry, I'm not going to molest you. I just want to hold you."

She smiled and snuggled into him. She was glad he couldn't see the big silly grin on her face. He felt so good with his big strong arm wrapped around her, his body pressed against hers. For the first time in a long time she really did feel totally relaxed and somehow safe.

She woke with a start. It was still dark. And Beau was still holding her close. She smiled and relaxed again, grateful to whatever had woken her. She got to lie here and enjoy this while she tried to get back to sleep. She couldn't, though. Her brain was wide awake and so was her body. And they were both acutely aware of Beau lying beside her, of his arms around her. She shifted a little and confirmed it. At least one part of him was very much awake and pressing into her. She leaned back into him and felt his arm tighten around her. Her body was humming with anticipation now.

She let out a sigh when his warm lips brushed over her neck and his hand came up to close around her breast. She pressed her ass back against him and felt his cock respond.

"I take it you're not asleep then?" he murmured.

"No."

She turned over to face him and pressed the full length of her body against his. His hard naked chest felt so good against her bare breasts. His hand closed around her ass and pulled her to him. He was still wearing his boxers, but she could feel the heat of him through them. His mouth came down on hers and she kissed him back hungrily. She wasn't aware how, but within seconds she was on her back, her panties were gone and so were his boxers.

He propped himself up on his elbows and smiled down at her in the darkness.

She smiled back and ran her hands down his back, closing them around his firm butt cheeks and rocking him against her. He held her gaze as he spread her legs wider and then he was there, pushing at her entrance. She stared back into his eyes as he gave the slightest nod and thrust his hips hard, plunging deep inside her. They began to move together. He was driving her crazy, taking it so slowly that the pressure built and built. He took her right to the very edge and kept her there, refusing to take her over. Every time she tried to pick up the pace, desperate for release he slowed his thrusts and made her wait. She was panting, grasping his ass, holding on for dear life as the sensations rolled through her. She needed him to finish her off.

He smiled and let himself go, thrusting deep and hard, finally sending her hurtling away on the waves of an orgasm that tore through her. She clung to him as she felt him get closer and then with a gasp he came with her, their bodies straining together as they rode the waves.

He collapsed on her shoulder breathing hard, she clung to him, feeling as though she might dissolve if she didn't hold onto something solid. A tremor ran through her, making her hold on tighter.

He lifted his head. "Are you okay?"

"Couldn't be better," she breathed.

He smiled. "Me neither." He dropped his head to kiss her again. This time it was slow and soft and gentle. It was a kiss that made promises, or maybe she was just imagining it.

Chapter Seventeen

"Hey," called Summer as she came jogging down the path from the barn to the lodge. "I was hoping I might catch you."

"Well, this is the place to find me," said Corinne with a smile. "How are you?"

"I'm great, thanks. We're going to take Jake and Lola out for a while, but Carter's gone up to see his mom and dad first. I just wanted to see how you're settling in. How do you like the job? How's Ruby doing at school?"

"So far, so good. With everything. Ruby loves school and she loves Susie's girls. She's really settling in well. And I love the job. Shane's set up a great business here."

"And from what I hear, you've got all kinds of ideas on how to make it even greater."

She nodded. "I have plans. There's so much potential."

"That's great. Just don't get carried away and work too much, will you? We live in a beautiful place, you need to get out and make the most of it."

Corinne smiled. "You're right. We were talking about taking Ruby down to the park this weekend."

"And by we I'm guessing you mean you and Beau?"

"Yeah."

"Have you been seeing a lot of each other?"

She wasn't about to admit that Beau hadn't spent a night at home this week. The way things were going it seemed that he always just came down after work and stayed the night. "Yeah." was all she felt safe admitting.

Summer gave her a knowing smile. "Good for you. He's a good guy."

"He is. I know some people don't seem to think so, but I believe you take as you find. And he's been amazing with me and with Ruby."

Summer laughed. "That first time he picked her up and called her pumpkin I knew they were made for each other. I know you had your doubts, but he seems to be learning fast."

"He is. Sometimes I feel as though I'm the spare part. The two of them get along so well."

"Is she coming tonight?"

"No, I was going to bring her, but Susie asked if she wanted to stay over there with Josie and Tara."

"Perfect!"

Corinne nodded. She knew the timing was perfect, but she felt a little uncomfortable about it.

Summer smiled reassuringly. "She'll be fine. And so will you, if you just relax and enjoy yourself."

"I know, I guess I just need a bit of practice at that."

Summer looked up at the sound of a truck approaching. She waved as it drove on by toward the cabin by the ranch. "Have you met Chance?" she asked.

Corinne shook her head. "Not yet."

"Well, you'll meet him tonight. I don't know him that well, but he seems awesome and the others all love him."

"Not all of them, from what I can gather."

Summer's face fell. "Oh, of course. I don't know what Beau's problem with him is. I mean. I know about them dividing up the ranch and everything, but I don't know why Beau minds Chance being a part of it."

"Neither do I." Corinne had heard enough snippets to piece together the fact that Beau had a problem with Chance, but he'd never talked about it, and she didn't feel she should ask. She would like to be aware of any sources of tension between them before tonight though.

Summer shrugged. "Hopefully it won't be a big deal."

"Hopefully."

Summer looked up again. This time there was a green truck coming down from the big house. "Here comes Carter. I'd better get going, I said I'd meet him at the barn."

Corinne nodded. "See you later then."

"Yep, see you later. You should get out and ride yourself. It's so much fun."

Corinne smiled. She'd like to, but finding the time was another matter. Even Ruby hadn't managed to ride again yet. They'd been so busy, but then so had Mason. Maybe next weekend, they'd get around to it. For now, she had some time to kill before she needed to get ready. Beau was coming over to pick her up to take her to Shane and Cassidy's for dinner.

Beau pulled into the driveway at Shane and Cassidy's place and smiled at Corinne. "Have I told you how beautiful you look?"

She laughed. "Only about seventeen times since you arrived."

"Sorry, but you do."

"Thank you."

She'd taken his breath away when he pulled up at the cabin earlier. She was wearing a dress and boy did it show off her figure. He'd wondered if they could get away with not going to dinner, because all he really wanted to do was stay home with her—and get her out of the dress!

He pulled up outside the house and frowned when he saw that Chance's truck was already there. Oh, well. His plan was to smile and be cordial, ask Chance about his family and stay away from anything that might cause friction between them.

"Are you okay?" asked Corinne.

He put a smile back on his face. "I sure am. Are you ready?" He started to open the truck door, but she put a hand on his arm.

"Do you mind if I ask you something before we go in?"

He nodded, wondering what it might be.

"What's the story with you and Chance?"

He stared at her. How the hell could he even start to explain that one? Especially sitting outside the house like this when they were about to go in and meet him.

"I'm sorry. Never mind. I shouldn't have asked."

He held up a hand. "No, don't take my silence as anything bad. It's not that I don't want to tell you. It's just that I don't know how."

"Okay. I shouldn't have asked. I'm not trying to be nosey. I just don't want to inadvertently put my foot in it."

He smiled. "There's nothing to worry about. There's no big deal, or horrible secret or anything. If I'm honest, it's just me. Something about the whole situation rubs me the wrong way. That's all."

She nodded slowly. He wasn't at all sure she was convinced.

"How about I try to explain it to you later, when we go home?"

She smiled and he had to wonder if it wasn't at least in part because she liked the way that sounded. Home, the place where they would go together later. He sure as hell liked it—a whole lot! Which left him wondering what the hell he was playing at.

"Come on, let's get in there for now."

When they reached the top of the steps, the front door swung open and Shane stood there grinning at them. "Greetings. Welcome to our humble abode."

Beau laughed. "Humble my ass! How you doing?"

"Yep, doing great. Come on in. Everyone's here, except Carter and Summer. They went out for a ride and got back a little later than they planned."

Beau took hold of Corinne's hand and they went through to the living room. He tensed instinctively at the sight of Mason and Chance standing by the windows, deep in conversation. It took him all the way back to high school. He'd been a bit of nerd in those days. All his brothers had a very strong sense of who they were. Shane had always been the golden boy. He was big and lovable and fun. Carter was quiet and kept to himself, but he had his world all mapped out, he was all caught up in Trisha and their plans to get married and live happily ever after. Mason was Mr. Popular. He was smart and he was tough, he'd played football, all the girls loved him. And Beau had wanted to be like him. But he wasn't. He wasn't comfortable in his own skin. He wasn't comfortable in his own life. He wasn't as anything as the others. They all knew their place in the world, in the family. He hadn't. He used to tag along with Mason and his buddies. Mason was okay with him, but the buddies used to run him off sometimes. Then Chance had come along, and he'd immediately fit in with everyone—in the way Beau had always wanted to, but never been able to.

Corinne squeezed his hand. "Are you okay?"

She noticed! She realized he was uncomfortable and she cared enough to check in with him. He felt his heart pounding in his chest, and it had nothing to do with Chance and everything to do with the beautiful woman standing beside him. He smiled. "I am now."

She raised an eyebrow.

"Now that you're with me," he clarified.

She was even more beautiful when she smiled like that.

"Hey, guys!" Cassidy called from the kitchen. "Come get a drink. I've got a couple of new reds from Deb's store for you to try."

They walked into the kitchen and Cassidy grinned at them. "It's not that fancy stuff you buy, Beau. That's a bit expensive for my taste."

He laughed. "It's my one indulgence, so shoot me."

"Don't tempt me. I might."

Gina smiled at them from her perch at the island. "Hey, Corinne. I'm going to ask you about your new job in just a second." She turned to Beau, "But first I want to ask you about Guy Preston."

Beau frowned. "Why me? I can't stand that asshole either."

"I heard he wants to buy a little house on Second Street in town. And if anyone knows about house sales around here, it's you."

Beau thought about it. Wanda had mentioned Second Street at the beginning of the week, but he'd said no because he was going to see Ruby, but she hadn't told him about another appointment. "You know what, Wanda did mention a guy wanting to see that place, but I assumed it was some generic guy, not the Guy Preston. And he never did set up an appointment. "Why, what's the problem?"

Gina made a face. "I think he's up to no good again."

"He always is. That's nothing new."

"I know, but…never mind. It's probably just me. Forget it."

"Are you sure?" Beau had known Gina pretty much all his life, when she got an idea about something she was usually right. He didn't want to brush her off if she was serious.

She shook her head rapidly and gave him a meaningful look. "No, it's nothing."

"Okay." Beau had a feeling she did want to talk to him, but she'd do it in her own time.

Cassidy thrust a glass of wine into his hand. "There you go, now if you've got any sense you'll go find your brothers. It's not safe for a man to be alone in the kitchen with us!"

He laughed and looked around. "Yeah. I'm outnumbered here, I'm off." He leaned in and kissed Corinne's cheek.

"Aww!" said Cassidy. "Isn't that sweet."

Beau gave her a sheepish grin and made his way back to the living room. Though if he was honest, he'd rather have stayed in the kitchen with the girls. It would have been easier. No. He sucked in a deep breath. He was changing in so many ways, this was just one more. It was time to get over it. He walked straight up to where Chance was standing talking to Mason and slapped him on the back.

"Hey, Chance. It's good to see you back. How's your dad doing?" He smiled, hoping that Chance would accept his attempt to make a fresh start and move things forward between them.

For a moment he held Beau's gaze, his light blue eyes narrowed, his lips pressed into a thin line. He was suspicious and who could blame him? Beau stared back at him, he wasn't backing down, for better or for worse.

It was a long few moments before Chance gave the slightest nod and smiled. "Hey, Beau. He's doing a lot better, thanks. He was lucky, my sister found him and got him straight to the hospital. Plus, he's a stubborn old bastard. He's determined to make a full recovery and when he gets like that, there's no stopping him."

Beau smiled. "That's good news." He didn't know what else to say. He'd made his big effort and now he wasn't sure where to take it.

He needn't have worried, Shane stepped in as if to help him out. It seemed he wasn't the only one who was changing lately, Shane seemed to have become a lot more perceptive and willing to act on it. He grinned at Chance. "Have you met Corinne yet? Our Beau's been a busy boy while you were away. He's gone and found himself a girlfriend, and one with a little kid, no less!"

Chance raised an eyebrow at him. He jerked his head toward the kitchen. "She's with you? Nice."

Beau smiled. "She is, she's good people. I'll introduce you in bit. I'm not risking going into the kitchen right now, though."

Chance laughed. "That's okay. I wouldn't venture into a group of gossiping women if you dragged me. And she's got a kid, too?"

Beau nodded. He felt defensive all of a sudden. "Ruby, she's only five. I was scared shitless of her at first, but I think we're figuring things out as we go."

Chance nodded and grasped his shoulder. "Good for you. You know I was just at my sister's wedding? Well, the guy she married, Dan, is the best thing that could have happened to her son, Scot. It's amazing to see how good they are for each other." He smiled. "I'll keep my fingers crossed for you and this little Ruby. But I'll tell you, it can work, I've seen it."

Wow! Encouragement from Chance was the last thing he'd expected. "Thanks, Chance."

Mason grinned at them both. Beau knew he was enjoying this. He'd tried so many times over the years to talk him around into giving Chance a chance, so to speak.

Shane grinned. "And what about you? Is there any possibility that you're going to find yourself a good woman and settle down?"

Beau was surprised at that. It was an unspoken rule that none of them bugged Chance about women. His girlfriend had died in an accident before he ever came to Montana. It was just known, if never stated, that he still loved her, he wasn't looking for someone new. He was even more surprised that Chance smiled at the question.

"These last couple of trips back to Summer Lake have done me a lot of good, Shane, but I've still got a long way to go."

Shane nodded. "Did you see April?"

"Yeah, I did. She's doing great." He turned to Beau. "She might even turn out to be another success story of a single mom who meets a good guy who's good for both her and her kid."

"That's good to hear," said Mason. "So, she's met someone?"

Chance smiled. "She's met him, but I don't think either of them know that it's going to go anywhere yet. It's obvious to everyone else though."

Mason nodded. "He'd better be a good guy. I'll go down there and kick his ass if he hurts her."

Shane laughed. "Don't let G hear you talking like that!"

Mason shook his head. "Gina gets it. I still feel kind of responsible for April."

Beau nodded. There was a lot of history between Gina, Mason, April and her ex-husband, Guy Preston. Even Chance had been in on helping April leave the valley and move to the little town in California where his sister lived. It made him wonder why Gina had been curious about Guy earlier. He thought better of mentioning it now though. Gina had said to leave it, so he'd wait and see.

They all looked up at the sound of the doorbell ringing.

"Dammit!" said Shane. "It must be Big C and Summer and I missed them." He went to let them in.

Mason laughed. "He's like a big kid with that video monitor. As soon as he sees a car coming up the driveway he goes and waits to open the door just as people get to it."

Beau laughed. "That's how he does it! I didn't even think. He surprises me every time."

Shane came back in with Carter and Summer.

"Hey guys," Cassidy called from the kitchen. "Can you all come through now?"

Chance walked by Beau's side as they made their way to the dining room. "Whatever's changed. I'm glad. Thank you. And if there's anything I can do to make things better, you tell me," he said in a low voice.

Beau nodded at him. This was one of those situations that didn't need too many words. Words only tended to get in the way. He smiled. "Can I introduce you to Corinne?"

Chance smiled back. "Lead on."

Beau made his way to Corinne and took her hand when he reached her. Maybe he was being too hands on with her, he didn't know. But he didn't care either, he was going with what felt right and screw the rest.

She smiled up at him.

"Sweetheart, I'd like you to meet Chance."

"Chance, this is Corinne."

"It's a pleasure to meet you, I've heard a lot about you," said Corinne.

Chance grinned at Beau. "I'm not that bad, I promise."

Beau laughed. "Whatever she's heard, it wasn't from me."

"Good." Chance slapped him on the back before turning to Corinne. "And you're managing the guest ranch for this guy?" He jerked his head toward Shane.

"I am, and so far I'm loving it."

"She's going to run me out of my own business," said Shane with a forlorn look. "They don't need me anymore, now Corinne's come to the rescue."

"Well, I already told you," said Cassidy. "I don't want you under my feet all day."

"Aww, you can come work the cattle with me, if you like," said Chance.

Shane laughed. "No thanks. I'll stick to resting on my laurels, while Corinne runs the place. The cattle are the real hard work. I'm too soft for it these days."

Beau tensed slightly as he listened. The other guys had all worked the cattle or the horses at some point. He never had. It bothered him that they might think he was too soft. He wasn't. It wasn't that he didn't have the brawn, he just preferred to use his brain. He made a damned sight more money than the rest of them, too.

Corinne was watching him again. She really wanted to make sure he was okay. He wasn't used to having someone care. He smiled and squeezed her hand, letting her know he was fine. How could he explain that he was simply feeling defensive against perceived criticism that probably didn't even exist?

Chance surprised him with his next words. "Nah, my work's at the bottom of the totem pole. It's hard physical work, but that's all. The rest of you have moved up and on by using your brains." He grinned at Beau. "None of us could keep up with this guy, though. He figured out how to have the best of all worlds. Build himself a business empire by using his brains and he still gets to come down and ride and enjoy the ranch, when he wants to, not because he has to."

Beau stared at him for a moment, not sure how to take that. He wanted to take the compliment he believed was intended, but he was so used to defending himself he had to wonder if it wasn't somehow a dig that he wasn't smart enough to see.

Carter grinned. "Yep, Beau is definitely the smart one."

Everyone was smiling at him. He smiled back feeling incredibly self-conscious. "Thanks, guys."

As he took his seat at the table he found himself between Chance and Corinne. Chance raised his glass to the two of them. "Here's to new beginnings."

Beau smiled. He was more than happy to drink to that, with both of them.

Chapter Eighteen

Corinne opened her eyes on Saturday morning and smiled. She didn't have to rush to get up this morning and she was so glad of it. Her first week at the guest ranch had been great, but it was tiring. She'd expected that she would work Saturdays, it was one of the busiest days, being changeover day for the guests, but Shane had insisted that she didn't need to. She knew he was looking out for her and Ruby and she appreciated it. At some point she would want to work and see how he had check-ins and checkouts set up. She was sure she'd find ways to streamline the process, but for today she was glad that she could enjoy the day with Ruby and Beau.

She turned onto her side and watched him. He was still sleeping, his handsome face relaxed. Looking at him, you'd never guess he worked a desk job. His broad shoulders and hard chest over a narrow waist spoke of a guy who worked the outdoors like his brothers. She felt as though she got the best of all worlds. She had a cowboy on the weekends and a businessman during the week. He opened his eyes and smiled.

"Good morning," he murmured.

"Good morning."

He reached out to draw her closer to him. She loved the way he held her. He made her feel so safe. He'd been right that spending more time together would help them relax around each other. She felt totally comfortable with him now, and for the last week they'd been together all the time that they weren't working—including every night. He read Ruby her story each night and had made sure he was up before she was each morning. Corinne wasn't sure why, but that had seemed the right way to do things. Ruby knew he was staying with them, but they'd avoided the topic of him sleeping in Mommy's bed.

Until now. The bedroom door creaked as it opened and Ruby stood there, dragging her bear by one paw. Her eyes widened when she saw Beau.

"My Beau!" she said with a smile and came and climbed onto the bed.

Corinne wanted to laugh at the way Beau sat up and pulled the covers up to his chin. "Good morning, pumpkin."

She grinned at him and wrapped her arms around his neck. "Good morning. Isn't Mommy's bed comfy?"

He nodded and gave Corinne a panicky look. "Yes, it is."

Corinne smiled. "But it's time to get out of it, now. Do you want some juice?"

Ruby shook her head and snuggled against Beau. "No. I want Sunday morning cuddles."

It was a tradition they had back in California. Sunday had been the one morning when Corinne didn't have to get up and go until ten. She was usually exhausted and both she and Ruby had loved their time just cuddling up in bed for an extra hour.

"Maybe we can do that tomorrow. Today's Saturday and we want to go out and have fun, don't we?"

Ruby nodded reluctantly, but didn't let go of her stranglehold on Beau.

Beau smiled and wrapped his arms around her. "Come on, let's get up and see what mischief we can get into today."

"Okay."

Corinne took her hand. "Will you come help me get the coffee started?"

"Yes. Can I squish the oranges?"

"You can help." Corinne led her out of the room, knowing that Beau would want her to leave before he got out of bed. He'd slept in his boxers the first few nights, but since then she'd learned that he preferred to sleep naked. She winked at him over her shoulder before she closed the door after them.

~ ~ ~

Beau smiled as he watched them go. It was hard to believe how much his world was changing. How much he was changing—and how much he loved it. Ruby was cute as a button and he loved her to pieces. He wanted to get up and go help her squish oranges.

He got out of bed and went through to the bathroom. When he came out he went to rummage in his holdall for clean clothes. He hadn't spent a night at home all week, but he kept having to go back for clean clothes and other odds and ends that he needed.

He jumped at the sound of the door opening. He was still buck naked. "Ooh, I see my Beau's butt!" squealed Ruby.

Beau grabbed a pair of jeans from his bag and covered himself with them as he fled back to the safety of the bathroom.

"Ruby!" He could hear Corinne call from the kitchen. "Come back in here. Leave Beau alone!"

He heaved a sigh of relief as he heard the bedroom door close and only then did he realize that he had his back pressed against the bathroom door. He chuckled to himself and headed for the shower, then stopped and went back to lock the door. He didn't need another shock like that!

They were sitting at the table when he joined them in the kitchen. Corinne gave him an apologetic look.

Ruby giggled. "I saw my Beau's butt."

"Ruby!"

"What? I did!"

Beau smiled. He felt a little embarrassed, but he was glad that Ruby found it amusing, at least she wasn't traumatized. Though he might be.

"Sorry," said Corinne. "Do you want some coffee?"

"I'll get it," he said as she went to get up. It made him realize that though he'd been staying here and they were getting more relaxed around each other, she was treating him as if he were a guest. "Can I get you anything?"

She shook her head. "I'm fine, thanks.

Ruby held her glass up. "More juice."

"Please," added Corinne.

Ruby smiled and nodded.

Beau laughed and took her glass. When he handed it back to her he held on to it until she said. "Thank you."

Corinne caught his eye and gave him a grateful smile. See, he could get the hang of this!

Ruby clung to Beau's hand as they walked down the path to the barn. He'd promised he'd take her to see Gypsy and Troy before they headed down to the park for the afternoon.

Corinne smiled to herself as she watched them. They made quite a pair! As they reached the barn doors, Chance came out and greeted them with a smile.

"Hey guys! Are you coming to ride?"

"No, just to see the horses," said Beau. "Gypsy is Ruby's new best friend."

"Ah, I wondered what she was doing up in the stalls. I almost turned her out." He smiled at Ruby. "It's nice to meet you." He bent down and held his hand out to her.

Corinne was surprised to see Ruby turn suddenly shy. She wrapped her arms around Beau's legs and hid her face against him.

Chance straightened up and shrugged.

"Come on, pumpkin," said Beau. "Say hello. Chance is my friend."

Ruby peeped out at him from behind Beau's legs.

He smiled and winked at her.

"Is that true?" she asked.

Corinne noticed the look the two men exchanged. She knew it hadn't really been true until Thursday night at dinner, and she wasn't sure it was entirely true now.

Chance nodded, but didn't actually say yes.

Beau did. "Yep, it's true."

Corinne wasn't sure whether he was confirming it for Ruby or for Chance.

It did the trick for Ruby. She came out from behind Beau's legs. "Do you have a horse?"

Chance nodded.

"Which one?"

"I like them all, but the one I ride the most is Maverick."

"Which one's he?"

Chance turned and pointed toward a big sleek-looking black horse grazing in the pasture behind the barn.

"He's pretty."

"Thank you."

"Do you want to come to the park with us?" she asked.

Chance smiled. "Thank you, but I can't. You have fun though."

She nodded. "We will." With that it seemed she considered the conversation to be over and took hold of Beau's hand again. "Let's go find Gypsy."

Beau shrugged at Chance. "Good to see you."

"You, too." He smiled and tipped his hat at Corinne. "Have a great day."

"Thanks, Chance, you too." He seemed like a good guy. Corinne still didn't know what Beau's problem with him was, or had been. They hadn't gotten around to talking about it when they got home on Thursday—they'd both had other things on their mind.

After they'd visited with Gypsy and Troy and shared way too many mints with them, they made their way out of the barn and back into the sunlight.

"Hello!" Corinne was surprised to see Monique Remington coming down the lawn from the big house, waving at them as she came.

"Hey, Mom," called Beau.

"Hello, darlings," she said when she reached them. "I'm so glad I spotted you. Can you spare a little while to come up to the house?"

Beau looked at Corinne. "We're just leaving. We're headed down to the park."

Monique gave Corinne an apologetic look. "I'm sorry. It won't take long. It's just that, by some miracle, everyone is around this morning." She turned back to Beau. "Your dad wants to make the most of the opportunity to tell you all what his plans are."

Corinne's heart sank when she saw the way Beau's expression changed. His jaw was set, his face turned stony. She knew this wasn't something he'd been looking forward to.

She wanted to soothe him, to make him feel better, but he didn't look as though he'd be interested right now. She gave his hand a little squeeze anyway, wanting him to know that she was there, and sympathized with whatever he was feeling. Even if she didn't understand it. She hated to see him hurting, and she'd come to realize that that was what it was. Whenever he looked hard, or angry, or intimidating, he was usually hurt or afraid.

He gave her a grateful smile. "Do you mind?"

"Of course not. Ruby and I can wait at the cabin."

"No, I want you to come with me."

"Oh, do come," said Monique. "Everyone is up there. I wouldn't want you to be left out."

Corinne didn't know what to make of that. She wasn't part of the family and this was family business.

Beau wrapped his arm around her shoulders. "Please?"

She nodded.

"I want to come," Ruby piped up.

"Well, come on then," said Monique taking hold of her hand. "Let's go and see everyone."

When they reached the big house the kitchen was crowded, everyone was in there. Mason and Shane were talking with their dad. Gina and Cassidy were sitting at the kitchen table. Carter and Summer were chatting with Chance. Corinne felt like an intruder. She shouldn't be here. All eyes turned toward them, making her feel even more uncomfortable. Their smiles were friendly enough, and she knew that if there was any tension it was more likely about Beau than her.

Dave Remington wasted no time. "Okay, now we're all here, let's sit down." He gestured toward the big kitchen table.

Corinne wondered what these guys had been like growing up. The four of them and later Chance had all eaten at this table for years. They were all so different. All good-looking, especially Beau.

He waited until the others had chosen their seats and then pulled a chair out for her, sitting down at the one beside her. Ruby scrambled into his lap and smiled around at everyone. For once though she wasn't getting much attention. There was serious business at hand.

"Okay," said Dave. "I think you all know what's coming."

"You've gathered us all together to tell us you're taking us to Disney Land?" Shane had everyone laughing and managed to break the tension.

"No, sorry. You're going to have to take yourself, Shane." He turned to Cassidy "Good luck with that! In the meantime, it's time to tell you what I've decided to do with the ranch. As you know, Mason and Gina are going to be moving in here after they get married. And your mom and I are leaving for Arizona after the wedding. Things are going to be different around here when we come back, and I want to make sure that you all have your own stake in the place. I know you'd like to think we can just leave the place as it is and share it, but you're all going to be starting families of your own at some point. You need a place that's yours, to do with as you see fit, without it affecting your brothers."

The guys nodded their agreement, but no one spoke. Dave pulled a sheet of paper out of his pocket and unfolded it. "So this is what I'm thinking."

Everyone crowded in to see a rough hand-drawn map of the ranch. It was divided into five parcels. It looked pretty logical to Corinne. Mason's share included the big house and the barn. Shane's included the guest ranch and the acreage surrounding it. Carter's was the northernmost portion of land. Chance got the cattle buildings and the cabin on his portion. She looked up to check Beau's face. The part that was marked with his name was the southern end of the ranch. It bordered the land where the cottage sat. She knew that was land that he already owned, so it made sense.

He didn't look angry or like he was about to argue. He simply nodded and looked up.

All eyes were on him now. She knew they'd be expecting to hear his anger or disagreement or something. He smiled. "It looks good to me."

"It does?" Dave sounded incredulous.

Beau nodded. "Don't worry. I'm not going to kick up a fuss. I appreciate that I get the tract adjoining the land I own down there."

His mom smiled at him. "We thought that made most sense."

She shot a quick smile at Corinne. "And if you ever build a house down there, we'll be right there on your doorstep."

Corinne wondered what she meant, but it made Beau smile and that was all that mattered to her.

"Awesome."

Chance was watching him closely. He looked wary, almost as though he wondered if he was walking into some kind of trap. The tension in the air was tangible.

Beau stood up. "Stop looking at me like that, would you, guys? There are no surprises here. It's what we all expected. It's all good. And if you don't mind, we were on our way to the park."

Ruby stood up to join him. She held her arms up to him and he scooped her up. Corinne scrambled to follow them.

When Beau reached the door. Ruby waved over his shoulder. "Bye! We're going to see the buffaloes!"

No one said anything for a few moments after they'd gone. Chance wasn't sure what to think, or what to say. He'd always felt a little guilty that he would become a part owner of the ranch. If anything, he agreed with Beau. He didn't feel he was entitled to a share, and certainly not an equal share.

Dave caught his eye. "Don't you go feeling bad. This is my decision. You're respecting my wishes."

Chance shrugged. "I know, but it's hard not to feel guilty about it."

Mason shook his head. "What's to feel guilty about? And besides, Beau just said he didn't have a problem with it. I say we should just take him at his word and let it go. The big bust up we all feared doesn't look like it's going to happen."

Shane smiled. "It might sound strange coming from me, but I've gotta say, I'm proud of him."

"Me, too," added Carter. "He's changed so much just in the last few weeks. He's never been as bad as he liked to make out, but just lately, he's come a long way."

Monique smiled. "And we all know why."

Chance smiled. "Ruby's got him wrapped around her little finger."

"And Corinne does, too," added Dave. "I'm relieved he's okay with it, but even more than that, I'm happy for him."

Everyone nodded their agreement. Chance looked around, grateful that he'd become a member of this family. He did have his own family back in California: his sister, Missy, and their dad. But he hadn't thought of Summer Lake as home for years. Montana was his home, this was the place where he belonged, and these were his people.

Shane punched his arm. "I know the cabin is yours now, but can I still have a claim on my old room?"

Chance raised an eyebrow at him.

He laughed. "For the times when Princess here gets mad and kicks me out for the night."

Everyone laughed.

Cassidy grinned at him. "I wouldn't do it if I were you Chance. I might just send him back to you permanently."

He smiled. "Uh-oh. Don't drag me into this one guys?"

"Okay," said Cassidy. "But remember, it was your friend here that dragged you in, and me that let you off the hook."

Shane laughed. "Yeah, so remember who you have to suck up to!"

"Anyway," Dave cut across the banter. "Is everyone happy? Anyone got any questions, comments, or reservations?"

Chance looked him in the eye. "My only reservation is about what you two are going to do. I think you should keep the cabin. I can bunk in with the hands. It wouldn't feel right, me living in there while you guys find a place in town."

Dave smiled at him. "You keep the cabin, Chance. It's yours." He took hold of Monique's hand. "We've been given a perfect solution."

Chance noticed that some of the others nodded, while some looked puzzled.

Monique smiled. "Beau has given us the cottage. As a gift."

Chance grinned. That really was perfect. It made him happy; he'd hated the thought of Dave and Monique living away from the ranch.

"Wow!" said Cassidy. "He really has turned a corner, hasn't he?"

Carter grinned. "He's never been as bad as he made out. I've known about the cottage for ages. I was dying to see all your faces when you found out. I just wish he was here to see it."

Whatever Beau's reasons were, Chance was happy. He hoped this was the end of any tension between them. And the beginning of a new era.

Chapter Nineteen

Beau drove most of the way down the valley in silence. He was grateful that both Corinne and Ruby seemed to pick up on his need for quiet. He needed time to think. The day that he'd been dreading for months had come and gone. No big fuss, no big fight, no falling out, nothing. He'd expected to feel hurt and angry. But all he felt was relieved. So Chance was going to own a part of the ranch. What did it matter? It had never been about how much land they all got. It had been the principle that bothered him. He didn't understand why his dad loved Chance as much as he loved Beau and his brothers. He wasn't his flesh and blood. But what did it really matter?

They reached the entrance to the park and Beau handed his pass over to the ranger working the gate.

Ruby smiled and waved at him. "We're going to see the buffaloes," she told him.

The guy smiled. "There are plenty of them to see. And don't forget to look out for the elk too. They're hanging out by the Visitor Center at Mammoth."

"Thanks," said Beau. He really needed to wrestle his head around and get back to the present. He wanted to make sure Ruby and Corinne enjoyed this. It was the first time they'd come to the park and he wanted to make it a memorable visit.

He turned to smile at them. "What do you think, shall we get an ice cream first?"

"Yesss!" cried Ruby. "Yes, please," she corrected herself as Corinne looked at her.

"Is that okay with you?"

Corinne smiled. "Sounds great. Are you okay?"

He nodded and reached for her hand. "I am. Sorry I've been quiet."

"Don't apologize. I understand. This morning was a big deal."

"But it turned out not be." He held her gaze, hoping that she might understand. "All this time, I've been making it a big deal in my head, but it didn't have to be. So I didn't make it one. And I've got you to thank for that."

"Me? How?"

"Remember what you told me about if you can't change something? If you can't make it better you just have to find a better way to look at it and move on? What you said really stuck with me. I couldn't change the fact that my dad wanted Chance to have a share of the ranch. I've been hung up for so long on how it just wasn't right. But then I realized, right or wrong, I couldn't change it. So I had to find a better way to look at it and move on. It's like you set me free by saying that. I decided to just look at it how it is. Chance was going to get a share whether I liked it or not. I decided to just accept it. I decided it's more important to be close with my family than stand up against something I believed to be wrong. And in the process I discovered that I really don't mind. It's none of my business. And when I choose to look at it that way all the stress and tension is gone—for me and for everyone else."

Corinne smiled. "I'm glad you feel that way. I've been worried about you. I thought you were accepting something that you were unhappy about. I'm glad that it doesn't bother you."

He nodded. "Me, too. Thank you."

Once he'd parked the car they went inside the gift store and each got an ice cream. They ate them as they walked up the path toward Mammoth Hot Springs.

Ruby looked up at him, making him smile. She had sticky ice cream remains all around her mouth. "I like Chance."

He realized that nothing they said went unheard by little ears. "So do I."

"Do you? You said he was your friend, but you didn't want to share with him."

He thought about it. He nodded. Not sure what to say, or how to explain it. He figured it was probably best left alone.

Apparently Ruby didn't. "I share with my friends." She made a face at Corinne. "Even when I don't want to, Mommy makes me sometimes. Because it's kind."

Beau smiled at Corinne. He hoped she didn't think he was unkind because he hadn't wanted to share with Chance.

"Why didn't you want to share with him?"

He sighed, while he thought about how to explain it. "Because this wasn't just sharing a toy. It was about dividing up our ranch."

Ruby nodded. "But you didn't mind sharing with Mr. Mason or Shane or Carter?"

"No, because they're my brothers. I used to think it wasn't right that my dad should treat Chance the same as the rest of us."

"Because he isn't Chance's daddy?"

Beau nodded, hoping that was the end of it. "Look, can you see the elk over there?"

Ruby looked toward where he was pointing. She gave the slightest nod and then turned back to look up at him.

"You're not my daddy."

That stopped him in his tracks. He stared down at her, not sure where she was going with this. To his horror, she burst into tears.

"What is it, pumpkin?" He tried to pick her up, but she pushed him away. He looked to Corinne for help, but she looked as perplexed as he felt. She picked Ruby up and soothed her. "What's the matter, sweetie?"

"Beau doesn't love me!" she wailed.

"Yes, I do! Come here." He tried to pry her away from Corinne, but she clung tight to her mom's neck and refused to look at him.

He walked around behind Corinne so he could see her face. "Listen, Ruby, I do love you. And I love your mom. You're my little pumpkin and she's my lady. Just because I'm not your daddy, doesn't mean we can't be a family."

Corinne spun around to face to him, forcing Ruby to turn back around. He had both their attention in a big way. He swallowed. He hadn't known he felt that way, but now the words were out, he knew he meant them.

Ruby was the first to break the stunned silence. She reached her little arms out to him and he took hold of her. "I love you! You're better than a daddy, you're my Beau."

He smiled at Corinne as Ruby buried her face in his neck. She still looked stunned. He reached for her hand. "I'm sorry, sweetheart. I could have found a better time and a better way to say it for the first time, but I do love you."

She was smiling, she looked happy, but he could tell there was a certain hesitation in her eyes. And who could blame her? They hadn't known each other that long, and words were cheap. He knew he'd have to prove his love with actions over the long term for Corinne. His heart almost stopped beating. Unless she didn't want him? That thought hadn't even occurred to him until that moment. Maybe she didn't feel the same way? He held her gaze, willing her to tell him that she loved him, too.

She didn't.

The silence lengthened until Ruby looked up at him. "Will you still love me when you have babies?"

"Of course I will."

"But not as much as them?"

"I love you just as much as if I were your daddy, Ruby." As he spoke the words he knew they were true. And he finally understood how his dad might feel. He would never be able to treat Ruby any differently than his own kids, if he ever had them. How could he expect his dad to differentiate between Chance and the rest of them? He turned to look at Corinne. Here he was telling Ruby that they were a family and he would always love her, yet Corinne hadn't said a word. She hadn't said she loved him.

She smiled, but there was still that fear in her eyes. And it was fear, he could see it now.

He wanted to ask her what was wrong, ask her if she loved him, too. But how could he do that in front of Ruby? He wasn't sure that he wanted to hear her answer. What if she said no? Where would that leave them? He felt frozen and helpless.

Corinne took a tissue from her pocket and wiped Ruby's face, cleaning up the tears and ice cream. "Come on, let's walk up to the top, shall we?"

Beau nodded and started walking again. What else could he do?

It was late by the time they got back to the cabin. They'd gone all the way down to see Old Faithful and it was a long drive home from there. Corinne lifted a sleeping Ruby out of her seat, but Beau took her and carried her inside.

"I'll put her straight to bed," she said.

He nodded and retreated to the living room.

Corinne's mind was racing as she got Ruby undressed and tucked her in. It had been quite a day. She knew that when she went back out there, Beau would want to talk. She wanted to talk to him, too. She'd managed to avoid it all day.

Her heart had leapt in her chest when he'd told her that he loved her. She knew he wanted to hear her say the same, but she couldn't. She wasn't even sure she knew why. She did love him. She'd realized over the last few days that she was in love with him. But that didn't mean they had to act on it. Hearing him tell Ruby that just because he wasn't her daddy didn't mean that they couldn't be a family, had melted her heart. She'd love nothing more than for that to happen. But this was all moving so fast. They'd only known each other a few weeks. He was doing wonderfully with Ruby. He was proving to be everything she herself could want in a guy, but she needed more time. She couldn't just throw caution to the wind, there was too much at stake. Not only her heart, but Ruby's.

He was sitting perched on the edge of the sofa when she went in to join him. He looked nervous as hell. Poor guy, it must have been awful for him to have been left wondering all day. She felt bad. She went straight to him and sat down beside him.

He took hold of her hands. "I screwed up, didn't I?"

She shook her head. "No, it's okay."

"But I shouldn't have said all that to Ruby without running it by you first. I should have talked to you, found out how you felt. It just came out when she thought I didn't love her."

"I know, and it was so sweet of you. You hated to see her hurt and you said what you needed to make her feel better. But Beau, I don't want you to feel trapped into loving her, or me. I don't want you to feel sorry for her."

"No. That's not why I said it. I said it because it's true. I do love her. I know it's not that long since I said she was a monster who gave kids a bad name, but I had no clue. Now I do. It's only been a short time, but I'm a fast learner. I've learned who she is, how she works and why she does what she does. And I've learned a lot about myself, too. You've played a huge part in that. And…" he stopped and looked deep into her eyes. "I love you. I don't want to put you under pressure to say it back to me. I just need you to know. Whether you feel the same way or not, I love you. I'm the guy who has always hedged, played things close to my chest and assessed the consequences before I say or do anything. But this, us, you and me…the way I feel about you is more important than that. I love you, plain and simple. I want us to be a family, I want us to have a life together." He stopped again. "And here I am running my mouth and just making it more difficult for you to tell me that you don't feel the same way."

She shook her head. He was making it more difficult, but not in the way he thought. He was making it more difficult to hold on to her fear, more difficult to remain cautious. "I do love you, Beau."

A huge smile spread across his face.

"But…"

His smile faded. "I had a feeling there was a but coming."

"It's not a big one, it's just that I need more time. We've pretty much been living together for the last few weeks, and it's been wonderful. It's so easy and we gel so well. But before that we'd only known each other a couple of days. There's so much we don't know about each other. This is like the honeymoon stage; what will happen when real life sets in? How do we know if we'll be able to handle the tough times together? If we'll even be able to put up with each other when the going gets rough?"

He shook his head. "We don't, but does anyone ever know?"

She shook her head. "I suppose not, but they date for a while before they jump into things. And it's not just me, it's Ruby I'm worried about. What happens to her if she gets more and more used to having you around and then we break up?"

Beau shook his head. "I'm saying I don't want us to break up. Ever."

She stared at him.

He nodded. "You know what I mean, but I'm not going to say the words yet. It wouldn't be fair. But I need you to know that's what I want. And I'm prepared to wait however long you need me to."

She didn't know what to say. He squeezed her hand. "I forced things to move faster than either of us expected by saying what I did today. We don't have to keep racing forward, nothing needs to change from where we were this morning. Nothing other than the fact that you know where I want us to go. Is that okay?"

She smiled. "That's more than okay. It's wonderful. And Beau?" She cupped his face between her hands and kissed him. "I need you to know that I want to go there too. I'm just scared to rush into it."

He nodded. "I know, and there's no rush." He closed his arms around her and she rested her head against his shoulder.

He was such a solid, reassuring presence. She held him tighter. It would be wonderful to think that this was it, that they'd found each other and he really was her future. Hers and Ruby's.

"You know what I think I'd like to do?"

"About what?" she wasn't sure what he was talking about.

He leaned back so he could look her in the eye. "About a place for us to live."

"What do you mean?"

"I mean, I want us to live together, properly."

"And you don't like this place?"

He smiled through pursed lips. "It's not exactly my style, no. But apart from that, it belongs to Shane. It's on his part of the ranch. He stood up and led her to the window where he pointed over toward the creek. "Just beyond that line of trees there's a clearing, I always thought it would be a great place for a house. I want to build one. For us."

She didn't know what to say. "But what about your house up in town?"

He shrugged. "It's a nice house, but I can hardly ask you to move up there when you work down here. And Ruby's at school down here; she won't need to go up to town until high school."

"I couldn't ask you to build a house here just to suit us."

He smiled. "It'd suit me. I want to be wherever the two of you are. And besides, you're giving me a reason to come home. I never thought I'd have a reason, but I love the idea."

"Wow. I don't know what to say."

He smiled. "Then don't say anything yet, but I will tell you one more thing. I'm thinking if I have a house here, then even if you decide you don't want me, Ruby and I will still be able to hang out sometimes and it won't be weird."

She swallowed and tried to blink away the tears.

He smiled. "Don't say anything."

She couldn't if she tried.

Chapter Twenty

Wanda poked her head around the office door. "Hey, boss. You've got a visitor."

"Who is it?" Beau could do without the interruption right now. He was pulling together all the files for a closing.

Wanda's eyes were wide. "It's Chance!"

"Great. Send him through."

"Really?"

He laughed. "Yeah, at some point I need to catch you up on all kinds of things that have been going on."

"It sounds like it! I'm free for lunch, if you're buying?"

"Maybe tomorrow."

"I'm not sure I'll be able to keep my questions to myself till then, but I can try."

He shook his head at her. "Go tell Chance to come in, would you?"

"Okay."

Beau had to wonder what he wanted. This was the first time he'd ever come in to see him. But then it seemed there were a lot of firsts happening lately. Most of them good, very good indeed.

Chance tapped on the door.

"Come on in, take a seat. What can I do for you?"

Chance looked ill at ease, but then Beau always thought he did whenever he was indoors. He was just one of those guys who was born to be outside, riding, working cattle. Right now he was holding his hat in one hand and running the other through his unruly black hair. He gave Beau a sheepish grin. "Nothing you can do for me. Don't laugh, but I came to see if you wanted to go grab some lunch. I had to come up to town to go to the bank and…well…I thought. You know. Since we're buddies now."

Beau smiled. This was Chance making an effort. And no way was he going to mess it up. "That'd be great." He stood up, almost toppling the pile of folders in front of him. The folders that he'd thought were so urgent were going to have to wait. Solidifying his new relationship with Chance was way more important. "Where do you want to go?"

Chance grinned. "I was thinking the Mint. I've had a hankering for one of their burgers for a while now, but I never have reason to come up here anymore."

"Well, you do now. I'll always come for a burger with you if you're passing through town." A thought struck him and he decided to go with it. "And if ever you want a night out up here you can stay over at my place. It's not like I'm ever there these days."

Chance grinned. "Thanks. I might take you up on that. It'd be good to come up and have a few beers."

Beau nodded. "Any time you want. In fact, I'll get you a key made." He led Chance back out through the reception area. He knew Wanda had been eavesdropping by the stunned expression on her face which she quickly tried to cover with a smile.

"I'll be back in a while, Wanda."

She simply nodded, apparently lost for words for what must be the first time in her life. Beau grinned to himself as Chance put his hat back on and tipped it at her. "Have a great day."

Once they got to the Mint they settled into one of the booths at the back of the bar. After the server had brought their drinks and taken their order, Chance raised his glass. "Cheers."

Beau smiled. "Cheers." He realized he didn't know what to talk about with Chance. He didn't want to talk about the ranch, he hoped that they could just leave well enough alone on that score.

Apparently Chance felt differently. He held Beau's gaze. "Listen, I wanted to say thank you…"

Beau held a hand up. "There's no need. I wanted to say I'm sorry…"

Chance shook his head rapidly. "No! I get it. I felt the same way you did."

Beau nodded. "Okay so how about we close that chapter and move on?"

"Sure."

Beau knew they'd said all they needed to, more words wouldn't make things any clearer. He smiled, but he wasn't sure what else the two of them might have to talk about. He went for the only thing he could think of. "What's the news on your dad?"

Chance nodded. "He's doing well by all accounts. I talk to him on the phone every night." He stared off into the distance for a moment before turning back to Beau. "I've never done that in my life till now."

Beau nodded. He didn't know much about Chance's family or his history with them, but he'd always figured it must be pretty bad. He couldn't imagine living so far away from his own family.

Chance's smiled disappeared in a hurry, his eyes narrowed and his lips pressed into a thin line. "That's enough to put me off my burger."

Beau looked over his shoulder. Shit! Guy Preston had just walked in with a very young looking blonde. Beau turned back around, hoping that Guy might not see them. Of course that was too much to hope for.

"Well, if it isn't my old friend Beau." Guy came to stand over their table.

Chance looked like a wild animal about to attack. Beau could only hope that he wouldn't.

"What do you want, Guy? We're having lunch."

"I can see that. What I can't figure out is why. I thought you were the only Remington who had any sense. At least enough sense not to hang out with lowlife like that." He jerked his head toward Chance, who Beau could see had his fists clenched and looked about ready to pounce.

"That is my brother. So fuck off, Guy."

He didn't know who looked more surprised at his words, but it felt good saying them. Guy sneered. "I really thought you were smarter than the rest of 'em, Beau. But you're just the same. Well, you listen and you listen good. I'm going to take him down, I know what he did. And he isn't going to get away with it. You get in my way, I'll take you down with him."

Chance stood up. "Do not threaten me or him or anyone else, unless you're prepared to get into it right here, right now."

Guy took a step back with an ugly smirk on his face. "I'll say when and I'll say where. This was just a warning. You won't see it coming." He turned on his heel and left.

Chance started to go after him, but Beau caught his arm. "Leave it, Chance. He's not worth it."

For a moment he thought Chance might punch him. He was so wound up. Thankfully the wild look faded from his eyes and he nodded and sat back down. "Sorry."

"No worries. I get it, but he's just not worth it."

"You didn't see April, you didn't see her little kid, Marcus, when we left here. They were both scared of their own shadows. I don't know what that bastard did to them, but I do know he needs to pay for it."

Beau nodded. He'd known that April had had a rough time being married to Guy, but he had a whole new perspective on it now. He thought about Corinne and Ruby in that situation and it made him almost as mad as Chance. "He does, but beating the crap out of him in here wouldn't make him pay. It'd only land you in trouble. There has to be a smarter way to do something."

One side of Chance's mouth lifted in a wry smile. "We should have teamed up sooner, you and me. With your brains and my brawn we'd be a force to be reckoned with."

Beau liked the sound of that. All he'd ever really wanted was to be included. He'd always seen Chance as the one who pushed him out, but it wasn't really true. The thought of the two of them being a team made him smile.

"Anyway. You're right. We shouldn't waste our time on him. Tell me what's going on with you? How are things with Corinne and the kid? She's a real cutie."

Beau smiled. "She is. Things are going great. In fact, things are going really great. I…" Was he really going to tell Chance before he told his brothers? He knew he was as he mentally corrected himself—his other brothers. "I'm going to build us a house down at the ranch."

"Wow!" Chance raised his eyebrows. "It's serious then?"

"It is. She just needs some time. It's hard for her to jump in because she's got Ruby to think about."

Chance smiled. "I understand how that goes. It was the same for Missy with Dan."

"Do you know what Dan did to convince her?"

Chance smiled a very genuine smile. "It was awesome. His ex showed up at Missy's birthday party. She was trying to cause trouble and he put her down in front of everyone. Then he made this big whole speech about how he knew what love meant, and how much he loved Missy and Scot. And he went down on one knee, right there with everyone watching, and asked her to marry him."

Beau shuddered. He couldn't imagine doing something like that. "I'm guessing he's the outgoing type?"

Chance laughed. "He couldn't be less outgoing if he tried. He's a geek, a bit of a nerd. He's awesome! That was what made it so special. He went so far outside his comfort zone, there was no way she, or anyone else, couldn't see not only that he meant it, but that he wanted it with all his heart and soul."

Beau nodded. It did sound great, but he had no idea what he could do to show Corinne that was how he felt.

Chance smiled at him. "You'll figure it out."

"I hope so."

~ ~ ~

Corinne parked the car in the only space she could find on Main Street. She'd come up to town on her lunch break to get some supplies for the ranch and now she just needed to stop into the post office. There was quite a line and she checked her watch as she joined it. She didn't want to take too long. She had a lot to do this afternoon. She thought she recognized the girl at the head of the line, but she couldn't place her. It seemed the girl recognized her, though. She was making her way back out when she stopped. "Are you still here then?"

"Excuse me?"

"Don't think Beau will waste too much time on you. He can't stand kids, you know."

Corinne watched her leave. She did recognize her now. She'd been the one at the Mustang when they'd had lunch there. The one Beau had said he'd dated. Apparently she wasn't too happy that he'd moved on. She sighed.

The guy in front of her turned around and gave her a friendly smile. "Don't worry about Angie. She can be like that. And I mean, you can't really blame her after what Beau did, can you?"

Corinne had no clue what to say, she just stared at him.

"Oh, shit. Did I just put my foot in it? You didn't know?" They'd reached the head of the line now. "Sorry," he said before going to the counter.

Corinne's mind was reeling. What on earth was he talking about? What had Beau done? She took her turn at the other counter and watched the guy while she did.

They ended up being finished at the same time and he walked out beside her. She didn't want to ask him what he meant, even though part of her was dying to. It was Beau she needed to ask, not some stranger.

Once they were outside he put a hand on her arm. "Just forget I said anything." He smiled and Corinne wanted to pull her arm away, there was something creepy about him. His smile made her think of a wolf. "I'm sure you'll be fine."

What the hell did he mean by that? She didn't get a chance to ask even if she'd wanted to. He was already walking away and she sure as hell wasn't going to run after him. She hurried back to her car, just wanting to get out of here and back to the ranch. As she was opening the car door a truck honked its horn and she looked up to see Chance raise his hand as he drove by. She was starting to understand how everyone knew each other's business in this place. Everywhere you went someone saw what you were doing!

She couldn't help wondering all afternoon what the guy had been talking about. She tried to put it out of her mind, but it kept gnawing at her. What might Beau have done that would warrant Angie being so mad at him? By the time she was done with her day, she'd determined that she needed to ask Beau as soon as she saw him.

His truck was already parked outside the cabin when she got home with Ruby.

"My Beau's here!" she squealed.

On the one hand, Corinne was thrilled that Ruby adored Beau. On the other, and especially with the doubts that had been seeded in her mind this afternoon, she had to wonder whether it was wise to let her get so attached. The last thing she wanted was her daughter getting her heart broken if things went wrong between them. She daren't even think about her own heart. She knew now that she'd given it to Beau somewhere down the line without even realizing it.

He greeted them at the door with a smile. "There are my two favorite ladies."

Ruby ran to him and he swung her up into the air, making her giggle. "How was your day, pumpkin?"

"It was good. How was your day?"

Beau nodded. "Mine was good too. And how about you?" he asked Corinne.

She smiled. "It was okay." She just couldn't fake jolly and happy. That man's comments were gnawing at her. She had to know. "Ruby. You go and get changed."

Once she'd gone Beau came to close his arms around her. "I made us dinner." He looked so proud of himself.

She wanted to just relax and enjoy the evening with him, but she couldn't yet. Not until he put her mind at rest. She pecked his lips and pulled away.

"What's up?"

"Nothing." She sighed. "Well, something. And I feel bad about it."

He looked concerned. "What? Tell me."

"I ran into Angie in the post office today."

"Oh. What did she have to say?"

Corinne made a face. "She said you wouldn't be with me for long because you can't stand kids!"

He laughed. "Well, you know you've got no worries there."

She nodded. She did. It made her realize how far they'd come that she had no doubts about his feelings for Ruby. "It wasn't what she said that bothered me. After she'd gone a guy told me I shouldn't mind her, but that I couldn't really blame her after what you'd done."

His smile was gone. "Why, what am I supposed to have done?"

She shrugged. "I was hoping you'd tell me."

"I have no idea."

"Don't, Beau. Please just tell me. Whatever it is, I don't think I'd care. I just don't like the feeling that you have some horrible secret."

He shook his head. "I would tell you, if I knew what I was supposed to have done."

She sighed. "Okay then."

"No. It's not okay. You obviously don't believe me. I promise you, sweetheart. I'm not hiding anything. Angie and I went out a few times. Then she messed things up for Carter and Summer and I just didn't ask her out again. She asked me a few times, and I said no and I've tried to avoid her ever since. That's the entire history."

"Okay." Corinne didn't want to force him to explain anything. She shrugged. "Maybe it was just gossip."

He put a hand on her shoulder. "If there's gossip about me, I want to know about it."

She shrugged again. "Well, I can't help you. I don't even know what it is."

"Please don't." His eyes were pleading with her.

She nodded. "I'm sorry."

He closed his arms around her. "So am I, but I don't even know what for."

She hugged him tight. "Don't worry about it."

"I do, though. I worry about you. I worry about what you think. I worry about how I can prove to you that I'm for real. And then something like this happens and there's nothing I can do or say to prove anything to you."

She sighed. "I'm sorry. All I can do is believe you."

"I hope you can."

So did she.

~ ~ ~

After they'd put Ruby to bed, they sat on the sofa. It had become something of a routine that by the end of the evening they both just needed to veg out for a while. Beau had his arm around her shoulders. He wanted to feel close to her, but she still felt a little distant. He stared at the TV, but wasn't really watching the show. His mind was still caught up in what Corinne had asked him about. What the hell was he supposed to have done? And who had said something like that anyway. Then it dawned on him.

"You know the guy who spoke to you in the post office?"

"I thought we were going to leave that alone."

"I can't sweetheart—any more than you can. So what did this guy look like?"

She shrugged. "He was tall. Brown hair."

Beau nodded. For the second time in a couple of weeks, he realized it wasn't just a guy, it was the Guy. Guy fucking Preston. He'd made all his brothers' lives hell at one point or another. Now it seemed Beau himself was his latest target. It made sense, too, especially after their little encounter at lunchtime.

Corinne looked up at him. "What is it?"

"I think I know who it was. Guy Preston has had it in for all of us since we were kids. He's the reason Mason and Gina broke up for nearly ten years. He tried messing with Shane and Cassidy. Now it looks like it's our turn. If I know him he's just trying to mess with your head to cause trouble between us."

"Why would he do that?"

"Because he's a Grade A asshole. That's why."

Corinne didn't look convinced.

"I know it sounds like schoolyard stuff, but that's the way he operates. Don't buy into it, sweetheart, please. We can talk to Gina and she'll tell you just how much damage he can do."

"Okay."

Beau smiled. Although he was pissed that Guy was trying to mess with them, he was at least relieved that now he knew what he was dealing with. He squeezed his arm around her shoulders. "This is going to be like a test for us."

She looked puzzled. "What do you mean?"

"I mean, I'm going to need you to trust me. You said you need to know that we can get through life's bumps in the road together. Well, if I know anything about Guy it's that he's going to throw us some bumps. We're going to have to be strong together to get through it."

She nodded uncertainly. "I'm not sure I understand, but if we're going to grow stronger and closer for it, then bring it on, I guess."

Beau hugged her a little tighter. He could only hope that they would grow stronger and closer.

Chapter Twenty-One

Corinne looked up at the sound of a knock on the door. She been working on the staff roster all morning and was glad of the interruption.

"Hi, I hope you don't me dropping in," said Gina.

Corinne smiled. "Not at all. It's good to see you, and I could use a break."

"Can you take long enough to come outside for a while?"

Corinne got up, she didn't need asking twice. It was a beautiful day.

They walked down toward the barn. "I just wanted to come see you while I had chance," said Gina. "We never get to hang out, and I'd like to."

That made Corinne smile. "I'd like that, too. I'm still finding my feet here, and between work and Ruby I haven't done much of anything else yet."

"Other than Beau," said Gina with a smile.

Corinne giggled at the implication. "Well, yes, I have been doing Beau rather a lot."

Gina laughed. "Good for you. That's probably what's managed to loosen him up."

Corinne nodded, surprised not to feel embarrassed. She didn't know Gina that well and here they were talking about her sleeping with Beau, but it felt right. She chuckled. "You mean helped him get his head out of his ass?"

"I wouldn't have put it quite like that, but since you did. Yes! You've done him the world of good. And Ruby, too. Watching the two of them together is just so cute."

"It is, isn't it? They seem to bring out the best in each other."

Gina nodded. "Do you mind if I ask you something?"

"What?"

"I know it's none of my business, but how serious is it?"

Corinne sighed. "It's serious. I guess I'm just a little cautious."

"Which is understandable, in your position."

Corinne nodded. "Why do you ask?"

Gina gave her a rueful smile. "I don't know. Maybe spending so much time with these Montana men has rubbed off on me. I guess I'm trying to look out for him. I worry about him. I'd hate to see him get hurt. He seems as though he's all in. And, the old Beau, at least…well, I don't think he'd realize if you didn't feel the same way. He's always been one to go after what he wants and not necessarily see that other people might want something different. Like I said, I know it's none of my business, but I just had to know. I wouldn't want either of you getting hurt."

Corinne nodded. She was glad Beau had someone who cared enough to look out for him and she knew Gina was trying to look out for her too. "No, I do feel the same way. And he is being understanding of me and what I need. You're right, he'd like to go after what he wants, but he's prepared to go more slowly because he knows it's what I need."

Gina grinned. "Good. I hope you don't think I'm being a busybody. I almost didn't say anything, but a helping hand from someone who cares, can save a lot of misunderstandings."

Corinne looked at her. "Did he ask you to talk to me?"

Gina shook her head rapidly. "God, no. I'm sure he'd be pissed at me, but it was worth risking it. Why do you ask?"

"The other day I apparently had a run in with Guy Preston. Not that I knew it at the time. He said some things that made me wonder about Beau."

Gina blew out a big sigh. "That man is trouble."

"That's what Beau told me. He said if I didn't believe that he was just trying to cause problems for us, I should ask you about him."

"Yep. I can tell you just how much trouble that man can cause. And I'll also tell you that if he's got his sights set on you and Beau, you're going to have to hang in tight. He's the reason Mason and I didn't speak for ten years. And even after we got back together he was still messing with my head. He tried to do the same with Shane and Cassidy, but they had enough sense to trust each other and keep talking."

Corinne nodded. "That's what Beau said. But why would this Guy do it?"

"It goes all the way back to grade school. It was kids' stuff to start with, but it came back to the surface earlier this year."

"Why?"

"Because Mason and Chance helped Guy's wife, April, to leave town."

"Wow!"

"Yeah. He is not a nice man. And she had the bruises to prove it."

"Oh, no!"

"Yeah. She's safe now though."

"Good."

"It is, but you watch your back and if he says anything to you, don't let him get inside your head. In fact, if he says anything that makes you wonder about Beau, you come to me, okay? Beau's the one you need to talk to, but I know how hard it can be to trust after Guy gets to you."

"Thanks, Gina."

She nodded. "No worries at all. I want to see the two of you make it, and if I can help in any way, I will. And you can bet any of the others will, too."

Corinne smiled. "I love the way their family works. They all want to see him happy."

"And they know you're the one who can make him happy."

Corinne loved to think that Beau's family thought she was good for him. She already knew that he was good for her and Ruby.

They walked in silence for a few minutes. "Oh, I also wanted to ask you about dinner this week. We're having it at the cottage on Wednesday, if that works for you."

"It does. I might need to bring Ruby."

"You know she's more than welcome."

"Thanks."

"Okay, well I should probably get going. I need to get to the gallery and meet with Cassidy."

"Say hi to her for me."

"Will do. I think she's your biggest fan. She didn't think much of Beau until he met you. You should have heard her on Saturday after you guys left. She was so impressed with the way he handled the dividing of the ranch."

"I can't take any credit for that. Beau's making a lot of progress all by himself."

Gina gave her a knowing smile. "He's not by himself, though, is he? Not anymore."

Corinne nodded. No matter what reservations she might have about taking things slowly, it seemed they really were in it together. Beau was stepping up and growing, Ruby was blossoming, and she herself was feeling more relaxed and settled than…well, than she ever had now she thought about it. That was quite a realization.

Gina raised an eyebrow. "Penny for them?"

"I'm just realizing how good we are together."

"You are. I understand your wanting not to rush, but if I were you, I wouldn't take it too slowly either. Take it from one who knows, when you know you've found the right man, all the time in the world won't change it." She looked at her watch. "And now I really need to get a move on. See you soon."

"Yep, see you, and thanks for coming by."

Beau decided he may as well walk to Second Street, it was such a beautiful day and it seemed he rarely got the chance to get outside. He smiled. They should change that this weekend and take Ruby out for a picnic or something. His smile faded when he turned onto Second and saw Guy's truck parked up outside the house. He had to wonder if he was doing the right thing. After their run in the other day, he'd been surprised when Wanda had handed him the appointment slip. Guy still wanted to see the little house and Beau had to wonder why. He lived down the valley, his ranch was one of the largest in the county. He wished now that he'd gotten around to talking to Gina. She knew something was up.

There was no time now, though. He nodded when Guy climbed out of his truck and grinned at him. "Beau."

"Guy."

"I hope we can put recent events aside? I can't say I'm impressed with your change of attitude toward Chance, but I do know you're a man who will always put business ahead of other considerations."

Beau nodded, even though he wasn't sure he agreed with that assessment. He would have until not so long ago, but these day he knew he'd put Corinne and Ruby ahead of anything else. He made his way up the path to the front door. "Let's get on with business then." He opened the lockbox and let them in. "I'm sure you don't need the realtor spiel, so I'll let you look around."

Guy smiled and wandered into the kitchen.

"How are your folks doing?" he called.

"Good, thank you." Beau had to wonder where in the hell he was going with that.

"Are they all set to head for warmer climes this winter?"

"They are."

"It'll be strange for them not to live at the ranch when they come back, won't it?"

"I guess." He knew Guy was fishing, but he didn't know what for. He didn't intend to give anything away.

Guy wandered around the house and then came back to join him in the living room. "It's great. I want it."

"What for?" Beau let his curiosity get the better of him.

Guy shrugged. "I don't know. I just figure it'd be good to have a little place in town."

Beau shrugged. He didn't need to know. "Okay. What kind of offer do you want to make?"

"Five grand more than any other."

"What?" That was crazy. As far as he knew there hadn't been any other offers on the place.

Guy gave him a condescending smile. "You just run along and write it up for me, okay?"

Beau shrugged. "Okay."

When he got back to the office he decided to call Gina. Maybe she had some insight on what Guy was up to.

"Hey, Beau!" she answered.

"Hi, Gina. Can I ask you what you were worried about when you mentioned Guy Preston being interested in the place on Second Street?"

"Sure. It was ages ago that your mom had mentioned she wanted to look at it. You know, when they were thinking they were going to move up there. It struck me as odd that Guy then started showing an interest. I guess I'm just paranoid about him, but I thought maybe he'd got wind and was trying to make sure your folks couldn't buy it. It was probably silly of me. And it doesn't make any difference now, does it? Not since their wonderful son gave them a cottage right there on the ranch."

He had to smile at that last part. His mind was working overtime though. "I guess Guy doesn't know about the cottage."

"Why's that?"

"Well, why would he? Unless any of you have talked about it. And I just showed him the house on Second. I knew he had to be up to no good and the offer he wants me to write up doesn't make any sense."

"Why?"

"He's wants to beat out any other offers, and he's willing to pay over the odds to do it."

Gina laughed. "Well, I hope you're going to let him. It'd serve him right."

Beau thought about it. It would. "I dunno, G. It'd hardly be ethical, would it?"

"No, you're right. But it would be fun!"

He chuckled. "True. Anyway, I'll let you go. Thanks for the info."

"No worries. Oh, and I saw Corinne this morning."

"You did?"

"Yeah. I like her Beau, she's the best thing that's ever happened to you."

"Tell me something I don't know."

She laughed. "Okay, I will. You don't yet know that there are going to be four Remington weddings this year, but I'd put money on it."

He had to smile. "Damn, I hope you're right."

"Me too."

He didn't know what else to say. He felt as though he might have opened up too much. "Well, I'll see ya."

"Bye, Beau."

He hung up and stared at the wall for a moment. He would love to think that he and Corinne might get married before the year was out, but he could hardly see it. She wanted to take things slowly and he understood that.

While he still had his phone in his hand, he decided to give her a call.

"Hey," she sounded pleased to hear from him.

"Hey. I just wanted to check in with you. How's your day going?"

"Okay. Busy. And I saw Gina this morning. Dinner is at their house this week."

Beau smiled to himself. He loved the idea that they were now one of the couples. Gina hadn't mentioned dinner to him, but she hadn't needed to. She'd already spoken to Corinne. "Great."

"I was wondering if you think we should offer to host next week?"

He grinned. "I'd love to. I'd thought about it, but I wasn't sure."

"Well, I like the idea if you do."

"I love it. It gives me hope."

"Hope?"

"That we're getting closer. That you're starting to trust that we're for keeps."

She was quiet for a moment. He had to hope he hadn't pushed it.

"Are you still there?"

"Yeah. Sorry."

"Did I screw up?"

"No. I did. I was just wondering how to tell you that I think we are getting closer."

He smiled. "To each other, or to the point when you'll say yes?"

She was quiet again, but this time he waited.

"Both."

Wow! "You have no idea how happy that makes me, sweetheart."

"Well, touché, because you have no idea how happy you make me."

She was right, he didn't! But hearing her say that gave him hope for the future—and hope that the future might come sooner than he'd thought. "I want to make you happy for the rest of your life, Corinne."

She was quiet again before she said. "I know."

That answer was the best gift she could have given him. She believed him!

"I need to get back to work. I'll see you tonight."

"Okay. See you later."

"I do love you, Beau."

"And I love you. More than you know."

That evening they decided to grill out on the deck. It was a lovely evening and Corinne loved being outside here. It was so beautiful. The horses grazed in the pasture nearby. The mountains loomed above them, finally green, though some still had white peaks. Corinne smiled at Beau as he cut Ruby's steak into little pieces for her. He almost caught her finger with the knife as she swiped a piece before he was finished.

"Ruby!" she admonished.

"Sorry." Her bottom lip slid out and she looked close to tears.

Corinne felt bad. Ruby had been cranky since she'd come home. She was tired.

"I just don't want you to get hurt, sweetie."

Ruby nodded, then she smiled up at Beau. "My Beau would never hurt me."

Corinne had to swallow the lump in her throat as she nodded. She knew it was true now. She hadn't forgotten what he'd said about building a house down here so he could still see Ruby even if they weren't together. At one point she might have thought they were just words. But she knew that Beau and Ruby had their own thing. He really loved her, there was no doubting it as she watched them together.

Beau smiled. "You know it, pumpkin, but it's still not a good idea to stick your fingers near a sharp knife."

Ruby leaned against him and smiled up at him. "I love you."

Corinne's heart overflowed as she watched him wrap his arm around her daughter. "And I love you. More than you know."

"This much?" Ruby held her hands up about six inches apart.

Beau shook his head. "More."

"This much?" She held them a little wider.

"Nope. Much more than that."

"How much?"

"Come here."

She leaned in closer and he held his arms out wide as he said, "As much as the whole wide world." And then he closed them around her and hugged her tight. "And back again."

She giggled. "When are you going to marry my mommy?"

Beau looked up and met Corinne's gaze. She didn't know what to say. She hadn't expected to be put on the spot like that.

"Someday." Beau saved her from having to say anything.

"When you do, will you be my daddy?"

Corinne didn't understand the look on his face. She waited to see what he'd say.

"I'm your Beau. Beaus are better than daddies."

Ruby nodded and snuggled against him. "You're the best Beau in the world."

He chuckled. "Thank you."

"I hope you marry my mommy soon."

"Why?"

"Because I want you to. I don't want to wait."

Beau met Corinne's gaze. "Neither do I."

Corinne smiled back at him; she was starting to wonder why she had wanted to wait. She wasn't sure she did any more.

She turned to Ruby who was giving her a meaningful look as she said, "Sometimes people say they're going to do something then they don't."

"Not when it's something important," said Corinne.

Ruby didn't look convinced. "Will you get married soon then, please?"

Corinne smiled, first at Ruby then at Beau. "I hope so."

When they went to bed, Beau drew her to him and nuzzled his face into her neck. "Did you mean what you said earlier?"

"Yes."

He raised his head to look into her eyes. She hadn't hesitated. Hadn't asked him what he meant.

He smiled, but it was his turn to feel hesitant. He wanted to understand what had changed. What had taken her from wanting to take their time to saying she hoped they would get married soon?

He raised an eyebrow.

She smiled and shrugged. "You're dispelling all my fears. All the time. Every day you do something else that proves it to me. You're in this for the long haul. We work well together, and even when things come up, we talk through them. I guess the only thing that bothers me now is that we haven't had a fight."

"And that's a bad thing?"

She smiled. "In a way it is. I mean, it's good that we don't, but we need to know that we can fight healthy." She shrugged. "Some people fight mean."

He nodded. He understood. "I don't fight mean. I withdraw."

"I thought as much, my concern is whether you come back."

"I do. It takes me a while. Or at least it used to. I seem to have done a lot of changing lately."

"All for the better from what I gather, too."

"Oh, yeah? Have you heard that I was an asshole before you met me?"

She laughed. "Not exactly."

He frowned. He wasn't exactly surprised. He knew his own reputation, but he was curious as to what she'd heard.

She smiled. "Not an asshole, just that you had your head up your ass."

He nodded with a rueful smile.

"You don't have anything to say to that?"

He shook his head. "I guess all I can say is thank you for helping me get it out of there!"

She laughed. "You're welcome."

Chapter Twenty-Two

Ruby came to him the next morning and hugged his legs when he was trying to get out the door. He was running late.

"I've got to go, Ruby."

"I don't want you to."

"I have to. And you have to go to school."

"I don't want to. I want to stay here with you."

"I wish we could, pumpkin, but we both have to go."

Her eyebrows knit together. "But I don't want to."

He scooped her up and hugged her to his chest. "I know, but it won't be long until tonight and then we can all snuggle on the sofa. How about that?"

She nodded sadly.

"What have you got going on today?" asked Corinne.

He laughed. "I have to engage in a battle of conscience."

She raised an eyebrow.

"With myself. Guy Preston wants to make an offer on a house. It's a stupid offer and I think it's an attempt to screw me over. I'm tempted to let him, because I know he'd only be screwing himself." He shook his head. "But I'm not sure I can bring myself to do it."

Corinne frowned at him.

Shit! He shouldn't be talking about screwing people over in front of Ruby. "Sorry."

She shook her head. "No, I'm sorry. You do what you think best, but I should have warned you. I have very high ethical standards."

Damn! So it wasn't his language in front of Ruby that had bothered her.

"Okay. Good to know. I guess I'll see you tonight, then."

She nodded, but didn't come to him for a kiss.

"I was only joking, you know. I couldn't bring myself to do it, much as he has it coming."

"I hope you were joking, but either way, I don't find it funny."

"Point taken." He didn't get why she needed to be like that about it. He put Ruby down and kissed the top of her head. "You have a good day. I'll see you later."

"For snuggles?"

He smiled. "Yep, for snuggles." He looked at Corinne. "For snuggles?" He wanted to see her smile before he left.

He was relieved when she did. "Yeah. I'm sorry. I guess I'm just a bit crabby this morning."

He went to hug her. "No problem. I look at it as a good thing. I just learned something else about you."

She nodded. "Yep, I'm afraid I can be uptight about some things."

He laughed. "We're definitely two of a kind then."

She finally relaxed. "I guess so."

When he got to the office, Wanda was sitting at her desk sipping her coffee. "G'morning, boss."

"Morning, Wanda. What have you got for me?"

She made a face. "Nothing much, other than a message from Guy Preston. He wants you to call him back. Wants to know if you've written up his offer yet. I can't stand that man."

Beau nodded. "I know how you feel. In fact, do you know what? You can call him back and tell him that I can't do it."

She raised an eyebrow. "And the commission?"

He laughed. "I know you think I'm a tightwad, but some things are more important than money."

She grinned. "That girl is so good for you. When are you going to pop the question?"

"Where did that come from?"

"Well, the Beau of old, wouldn't have hesitated to take Guy's money. Only one thing can make a man open up his eyes the way you have these last few weeks, and that's love. You may as well just admit it and get on with it."

"I have admitted it. It's her who's been taking her time, but I think we're almost there."

"Good. I hope I'm invited to the wedding?"

"Of course you are."

"Okay. Well, in that case I'll get right on the phone and tell Mr. Preston where he can stick it!"

Beau laughed and made his way into his office. "Thanks, Wanda."

It was lunchtime before he lifted his head. He'd had a lot of paperwork to catch up on. He wandered out into the reception. "What do you say, do you want to come for lunch?"

She stared at him as if he'd grown two heads. "Are you buying?"

"I sure am."

"Sorry, I can't. I'm meeting Terry today."

"So why ask if I was buying?"

She grinned. "So that you owe me one!"

He laughed. "You are a piece of work."

She nodded happily. "That'd be me. Oh, and by the way, Guy Preston was well and truly pissed. I don't know what his game is on that place, but he asked me to let you know that you'd be sorry."

Beau nodded. It was hardly surprising. "I just don't want to play his games. It's not worth it."

"I agree, but watch your back. He's a vindictive bastard."

"I will." Beau knew he was, but he didn't see any way Guy could get at him. The only way would be to cause trouble with Corinne, but they'd already talked about it and he was confident that she wouldn't let Guy get to her. He smiled. They were too solid. As he walked down the street toward the coffee shop, he had no clue just how vindictive Guy could be, or any idea how soon he was about to find out.

Once he'd bought his sandwich he decided to go back to the office for his car. He wanted to run home and get some more clothes. He was slowly transferring his stuff to Corinne's cabin. Everything he took there, he left. He still didn't have everything he wanted yet though.

He noticed a man sitting in a beat-up old pickup truck as he turned into his driveway. He smiled to himself. There were plenty of those around here, he wasn't worried. He realized that he wasn't so anal anymore about locking doors and drawers and everything else. Corinne really had opened him up.

He let himself in and ran up to the bedroom to grab a couple more pairs of jeans and shirts. It'd be nice to maybe take them out riding this weekend. Have that picnic in the foothills. He knew Ruby would love that, though he hadn't managed to get Corinne on a horse yet.

He thought about eating his sandwich while he was here, but decided against it. This house didn't feel like home anymore. Home was with Corinne and Ruby. He smiled as he remembered this morning's conversation about snuggles. He had that to look forward to at the end of the day, and hopefully more with Corinne come bedtime.

He locked the door and ran back down the steps. On a whim, he got into the Mercedes instead of his truck. Ruby loved it, she called it his posh car. Maybe a ride in it would cheer her up later if she was still cranky.

He started it up and pulled out into the street. It happened so fast and yet it felt like slow motion. The pickup that had been sitting there was gone, but as Beau looked to his left he saw it heading his way. He had time to think the guy driving it must be an idiot as he hit the gas. He started to think the driver might be crazy as the truck veered toward him. The grill of the truck filled his view. Then came the sound, the sickening noise of crumpling metal. The truck rammed into the driver's door sending the car crashing into the wall. Beau was vaguely aware of pain in his leg; he looked down to see bent metal. He couldn't process it and looked up again, only to see the grill of the truck backing away from him. Hopefully the driver would be able to disentangle the vehicles and he might be able to free his legs. Instead, the truck kept going, reversing away from him. Was the guy just going to leave?

No. Beau started to panic when he heard the engine rev. It was coming again. He scrabbled at the door, but it was no use. The thing was crumpled, buckled inward, as his leg could vouch. The impact came and Beau saw stars. Then everything went dark.

~ ~ ~

"Hello?" Mason didn't recognize the number on his cell phone display.

"Mason? It's Luke Wallis."

"Oh, hey Luke. What's up?" Luke was with the sheriff's department up in town. They'd been friends in high school, but didn't get to catch up much these days.

"This isn't a social call. It's about Beau."

"Beau? What's up?"

"He was involved in an RTA. He's in the hospital."

"What?" Mason shook his head in disbelief. "What happened? Is he okay?"

"He's going to be okay, but he was unconscious when we got to him. Maybe some broken bones."

"What happened?"

"We don't know. We had a report of a hit and run. Two kids walking down that end of Main said they saw a beat-up old pickup ram him as he came out of his driveway."

"Ram him? What the fuck?"

"Yeah. That's what I thought. But it gets worse."

"How?"

"They said after it hit him, the truck backed up and then rammed him a second time."

"Jesus!" Mason didn't know what to make of that.

"We're talking to the kids to see what they can remember. We're going to get to the bottom of this."

"Damned straight we are. I'm on way up there."

"Okay. If I'm not around, have the nurses call me."

"Will do." Mason hung up and strode out of the barn. He started to make his way up to the big house then thought better of it. His first thought had been to go get his folks and take them up to town. But the person he should be taking was Corinne. He changed tack and headed down to the guest lodge. He dialed his folks as he walked.

His dad answered. "Hey, son. What's up?"

"I'm heading up to town. Apparently Beau had an accident in his car. He's going to be okay, but he's in the hospital."

"We're on our way."

"See you there."

Next he called Carter.

"Hi, Mase. Is everything okay?"

"For once, I can't laugh at you for asking that. It's not. Beau's had an accident. He's in the hospital."

"Shit! What happened? I'm in town. I can be over there in five."

"Apparently a truck hit him, that's all I know. You'll be the first there, so call me when you find anything out?"

"Will do."

Mason was almost to the lodge now. He didn't know if Shane would be there, but he called him anyway.

"Yo, bro!"

"Hey. Where are you?"

"I'm in town, why?"

"Can you get your ass to the hospital? Beau's in there."

"Oh, fuck! Why?"

"A truck ran into him. Luke Wallis said he was unconscious and maybe some broken bones."

"Shit. Are you still at the ranch?"

"Yep."

"Do you want to tell Corinne? Bring her up here?"

"Why do you think I'm not on my way already?"

"Yeah, I should've known. I'll see you at the hospital."

"Yup."

Mason hung up and ran up the steps to the lodge. Corinne was standing at the reception desk. She smiled as she saw him approach, but her smile faded as he got closer. "What's wrong?"

He tried to smile. He didn't want to scare her. "Beau had a little car accident." He took hold of her arm and started to lead her out. "We're going up to the hospital to see him."

"He's in hospital? How bad is he?" She'd turned as white as a ghost.

"The deputy I talked to said it wasn't serious. Maybe some broken bones."

She visibly pulled herself together. Mason liked her. She was strong, not easily panicked. "What happened?"

"We don't know yet. I'll tell you the little I do know on the way."

~ ~ ~

The ride up to town seemed to take forever. Corinne called Susie and asked her if she could keep Ruby for a while longer when she picked her up. She had no idea what time she'd get back. Of course Susie was as accommodating as ever, just told her to let her know how Beau was when she knew anything.

Mason called Gina. She would meet them at the hospital.

When the phone calls were done she turned to Mason. "What happened?"

"Apparently he was coming out of his driveway and some kids saw a truck drive into him and then drive away."

"A hit and run? I didn't think things like that happened here."

"Neither did I. I can't believe a local would do something like that."

Corinne couldn't imagine anyone ever doing something like that. She knew it happened, but she never would have thought it could happen here. And not to Beau.

Her cell phone rang and she fished it out of her purse. She recognized the number. It was Beau's office.

"Hello?"

"Hi. Is this Corinne?"

"Yes. Hi, Wanda."

"Hey. I'm sorry to bother you, hon. But Beau isn't with you by any chance, is he? He's got appointments this afternoon and I can't find him. He went out for lunch and didn't come back. He's not answering his phone. I'm worried."

"He had an accident, Wanda. Someone ran into him. They're saying it's not serious. I'm on my way to the hospital with Mason."

"Oh my God! Please let me know how he's doing when you get there? I'll come straight over after work."

"Okay, I'll keep you posted." She hung up.

Mason gave her a rueful smile. "Wanda loves him more than anyone."

"Not more than I do!" The words surprised her, they came out so fast.

Mason looked taken aback.

"Sorry. I think that was me telling myself, not telling you. I've been holding back too much for too long."

Mason smiled. "No worries. It sounds like you've figured it out now."

She smiled back. "I have! Why is it that it takes a shock like this to give us the wake-up call we need?"

Mason shrugged. "I can't speak for you, but I know for me the answer would be a combination of fear, stubbornness, and pride."

She let out a little laugh. "I think you are speaking for me."

He nodded. "I think it's the same for all of us if we're honest with ourselves. I wasn't sure how honest you liked to be with yourself, so I used myself as the example instead."

She smiled. He was a wise one.

When they got to the hospital, there was quite a crowd waiting. It seemed the entire family, minus Chance and Summer had beaten them to it.

"Beau's still in surgery," said Carter. "He has a broken leg and took a nasty knock to the head, but he's fine other than that."

Corinne heaved a sigh of relief. It was bad enough, but she'd been fearing much worse.

"I called Luke," said Shane. "He's on his way over."

Mason nodded.

Corinne watched him closely. There was something he wasn't saying, but she didn't know what.

She took him aside and held his gaze for a moment. "I'm not a damsel in distress; if there's something that needs saying, please say it."

He pursed his lips and nodded. "Sorry. Gina gets pissed at me all the time. I can't help it. It's instinct with me to try to protect the ladies. I have to remember how strong you are."

Corinne nodded, wishing he'd just hurry up and spit it out.

"So, Luke, the deputy told me that the kids who witnessed it said that the truck didn't just hit him and drive away…"

Corinne's heart was hammering in her chest. "What then?" she interrupted.

"They said it backed up and rammed him a second time."

"What the hell?"

Mason nodded. "Exactly! Either he got real unlucky and ran into the path of some crazy bastard, or…"

"Or it was Guy Preston!" Corinne knew it. It had to be him!

Mason shook his head. "No. He wouldn't do something like that."

"He wouldn't? From what I've heard about him he's the only one around here who would."

Mason wasn't buying it, she could tell.

Gina came over to join them. "What's up?"

Mason explained what he'd just told Corinne. "And she thinks it must have been Guy," he finished.

Gina shook her head. "No. He wouldn't do that."

"But who else would?"

"I have no idea. I know Guy must seem a likely candidate, but it's just not his style. He likes to get inside people's heads, but at heart he's a coward. And he's too smart, the chances of getting caught are too high."

Corinne knew they were making sense, but she had a feeling she just couldn't shake. It had to be Guy.

A doctor came out, and went straight to Dave and Monique. Monique turned and beckoned for Corinne to join them. The others followed her and crowded around.

"He's out of surgery now. His leg was broken in two places, but we've set it, put a few pins in and he's in plaster. He'll be in recovery for a while. The nurses will let you know when you can see him."

"Thank you," said Dave.

Corinne eyed a guy in uniform as he approached. He must be Luke. He nodded at her and looked around the group.

"What's going on, Luke?" asked Mason.

"I do have a bit more information." He looked hesitant to speak in front of all of them.

"You may as well just tell us all," said Dave. "We all want to know."

"Okay. Well, according to the witnesses, Beau was pulling out of his driveway when a pickup apparently veered off the road and ran into him." He hesitated. "And then, the truck backed up and came at him a second time. That second impact did the most damage before the truck drove away."

"Oh, my God!" said Monique. "Someone hit him on purpose?"

Luke nodded grimly. "That's how it sounds."

"It was Guy Preston!" Corinne blurted out.

Luke turned to look at her. "What makes you say that?"

"He's had it in for Beau for a while now."

"But you don't have any evidence that he intended to injure him in some way?"

Mason shook his head and put an arm around Corinne. "No. She's just upset. You know there's been bad blood between us for years. There's no reason to believe he'd step things up to this level."

Luke raised his eyebrows.

"What?" asked Corinne. "You think I'm right don't you?"

Luke looked over his shoulder before he replied. "I shouldn't tell you this, but the description the kids gave of the truck, sounds a lot like the one belonging to a ranch hand out at the Preston place. We had him in a couple of times for drunk and disorderly. Found him sleeping in that truck on Main a couple of Sunday mornings, too. I'm going to take a ride out there."

Corinne nodded. She was convinced that he would find the truck had damage consistent with having run into Beau's car.

Mason followed Luke as he walked away and they spoke for a few moments before he left. As he went out through the doors Chance came in with Summer by his side.

"How is he?" he asked.

"He's going to be fine," said Dave. "His leg's broken in a couple of places, but nothing worse than that."

Corinne saw the relief on Chance's face. He cared. He really cared. She smiled at him and he came to hug her.

"Damn, I was scared for a while there."

"Me, too," she said. "He's going to be okay though."

"Thank God."

Chapter Twenty-Three

Beau opened his eyes and stared at the ceiling. It wasn't the right ceiling. It wasn't his bedroom. It wasn't Corinne's bedroom. Where the hell was he? He tried to sit up but his head swam and his left leg hurt like crazy. He lay still, trying to figure it out. Then it came back to him. The crazy bastard in the truck!

"Are you awake?" Corinne leaned over him.

He smiled. Even his face hurt.

"I'm okay."

She leaned in and kissed his lips gently. "The doctors say you will be, though you'll be on crutches for a while."

"It's broken?"

She nodded. "Do you remember what happened?"

He tried to nod, but thought better of it. "I do. The crazy…drove straight at me! Twice! He backed up and did it again."

"Did you get a look at him?"

Beau closed his eyes. "No." All he'd seen was the grill of that truck headed straight at him. "No wait. I did see him. He was there when I pulled in." Could he have been waiting for him? He screwed his eyes shut, not wanting to consider that possibility.

"The police are looking for him."

"Good. I can tell them what the truck looked like, and what I remember of the guy when I arrived home."

"They got a description from some kids who were nearby."

Chance stuck his head around the door. "Is he awake?"

Beau smiled. "Come on in."

Chance stood just inside the door. "How you feeling, buddy?"

"Like I got hit by a truck!"

Chance laughed. "Funny how that works, huh? Listen. I'm going to run back down the valley to get Ruby and bring her up here."

Beau smiled. How about that? "Thanks."

"I just wanted to ask you something before I go. Have you seen any more of Preston, since we ran into him at the Mint?"

"Yeah." Beau thought it odd that Chance wanted to know about him right now. "I showed him a house and then told him he'd have to find another realtor. Why?"

Chance and Corinne exchanged a look he didn't understand.

"What did he have to say about that?"

Beau frowned. "He told Wanda to tell me I'd be sorry. Shit! You don't think…"

Chance's eyes were narrow. He had that wild look about him.

"Don't, Chance. Whatever you're thinking. Don't, okay?"

Chance gave him a long measured look. "Don't worry."

How could he not? He didn't want Chance jumping to conclusions and riding off to exact vengeance. Beau couldn't believe that Guy had anything to do with it.

Chance turned around and beckoned outside. His mom and dad appeared in the doorway with Mason and Gina just behind them. "I'm going to go get Ruby. I'll be back."

The others crowded in and Beau didn't get to ask Corinne what that look had been about.

The next morning, Corinne woke up in Beau's bed. It was the first time she'd stayed the night at his house and she'd slept here alone. Well, at least she was alone in his bed. Chance was in one spare room and Carter and Summer were in the other. Dave and Monique had taken Ruby home with them last night and would make sure she got to school this morning. The others all had work to get back to.

Chance had insisted that she shouldn't stay by herself, and Carter had wanted to stay up in town to be near Beau. It was sweet to see how much he cared. He looked like a big tough guy, but Corinne had soon figured out he was a big softy at heart.

She lay in bed for a few minutes thinking about everything that had happened yesterday. She was convinced that Guy Preston had something to do with it. She was going to call that deputy, Luke, this morning to see what he'd found out. First of all, though, she wanted to go see Beau. The doctor had said they might release him today. She hoped so. She wanted him home where she could take care of him.

By the time they got to the hospital he was sitting up. His leg was elevated, encased in a cast from hip to toe.

He smiled when he saw her. "Hey, sweetheart."

"Hey. How are you feeling?"

"Like I want to go home. Hopefully they'll let me out soon. I can't sit around here. I've got work to do."

"Not for a while you don't. I talked to Wanda, she's taking care of your schedule. You're coming home with me where I can keep an eye on you."

Chance laughed. "So consider yourself told."

Beau smiled. "Oh, I will. She's a tough one."

Corinne made a face at him. "I just love you, that's all."

He nodded and held his arm out to her. "Come here and give me a hug then."

She went to him and perched on the bed beside him.

They all looked up as Luke appeared in the doorway.

"Beau. Good to see you up."

"Well, I'm not exactly up, but give me a pair of crutches and I will be."

Luke nodded.

"What did you find out?" asked Corinne.

"I went out to the Preston place to see if I could take a look at the truck."

"The truck that hit me?" asked Beau.

"We can't confirm that. It matched the description of one of the ranch hand's truck. We got to know him quite well over the last few months. However, when I got out there and asked to speak with him, he'd left. Packed up and gone. Yesterday morning apparently."

"Shit! I knew it!" exclaimed Chance.

"Slow down," said Beau. "That doesn't prove anything."

"It makes it look a lot more suspicious though." Corinne was even more convinced than she had been.

Beau shook his head.

"I'm not saying anything, yet," said Luke. "Other than to tell you that I don't consider this investigation to be over."

Corinne was glad to hear it.

~ ~ ~

"My Beau's home!" cried Ruby and came running to him. He was sitting on the sofa in the cabin with his leg propped up on a pile of pillows.

"There's my pumpkin!" He wrapped her in a hug.

"Please don't go away again. I missed you." She planted a kiss on his cheek.

"I won't."

"I mean it. I don't like it when you're not here anymore."

He caught Corinne's eye and she smiled. "Neither do I. You gave me a scare. I don't ever want to think about our life without you in it."

He smiled. Then it was time. Except now of course he was house bound, dependent on her for anywhere he wanted to go. How could he work a surprise like that?

As if to answer his question, there was a knock at the cabin door. Corinne went to get it and came back with Chance.

He twisted his hat in his hands. "How are you feeling? I'm just coming by to see if there's anything you need? Anything I can do?"

Beau grinned. Not only was he glad to see him, but there was something he wanted his help with. "How would you feel about springing me from here tomorrow?"

Corinne turned a stern look on him. Now he knew how Ruby felt! But he wasn't backing down, this was too important.

Chance looked from him to Corinne and back again. "I'm up for it, if the missus gives us the okay."

Corinne laughed. "How can I put my foot down now without looking like an old battle-axe?"

Beau laughed with her. "You could never look like one of those, sweetheart. But humor me on this one, okay?"

She nodded reluctantly. "But you," she shook a finger at Chance. "I'm going to be holding you responsible."

Chance made an exaggerated gulping sound and looked at Ruby who laughed. “Okay, boss lady.”

Chapter Twenty-Four

Corinne worried all the next day about him. The doctor had said he should try to stay off his feet as much as possible. He needed rest and to keep his leg elevated as much as possible. He'd insisted he had things he needed to do, though, and Chance had promised he wouldn't let him overdo it.

Shane came into her office mid-afternoon. "Why don't you take the rest of the day? It's quiet and I bet you could use some down time."

"No. Thanks, but I'm better off here, staying busy."

"Go on," he insisted. "Why don't you go home? You've got to be exhausted taking care of that brother of mine."

She smiled. "I don't mind at all. I'm glad he's with me."

"So am I and I know he is. Go home have a rest, then you might be able to enjoy the evening with him when he gets back."

"Okay, then. I will. I think I'll make him a lasagna for dinner, it's his favorite."

Shane grinned. "You spoil him."

She shrugged. "I love him." She kept surprising herself by declaring to anyone who would listen that she loved him. She certainly wasn't afraid of letting her feelings be known.

It felt odd to be home alone. She wasn't sure she liked it anymore. She'd grown used to having Beau around. She thought about calling him to see how he was doing, but she didn't want to nag. He was a grown man; he didn't need her reminding him to take it easy. And Chance would look out for him, she knew that. She loved the way the two of them had gotten so close lately.

Her cell phone rang and she ran to get it.

"Hey, sweetheart."

"Hey. I hope you're calling to tell me you're on the way home?"

He laughed. "Almost, but we're going to stop in to see my folks on the way back. I wondered if you and Ruby would meet us up there?"

"Okay." She'd rather he came home to get some rest, but she could hardly tell him not to go see his parents. "What time do you think you'll be there?"

"We shouldn't be long now. How about I call you when we get there."

"Okay, I'll see you in a little while."

"I love you."

"And I love you."

~ ~ ~

Beau hung up and grinned at Chance. "She's going to come up when I call her."

Chance grinned back. "Good, that'll give us time to make sure everyone's there."

When they got to the big house, his dad led him through to the living room and made him sit on the sofa. His mom brought some cushions and piled them under his foot.

His dad squatted down beside him. "I'm so glad you wanted to do this here, son."

He nodded. "Me too. I don't know, but for years I've felt as though I was somehow on the outside. Not quite one of the family in the same way as everyone else…"

"I know. And I'm sorry. I don't know what I did to ever make you feel that way."

"You didn't, Dad. It was me, only me. I did it to myself. What matters now is that I can see it, and I've changed it. Corinne played a big part in helping me come around."

"And Ruby," said his dad with a smile.

"Yep, definitely. And they're my family now. I want to do this here, with all of you, because it will lay the foundation for my new family as part of our big family. I don't want to feel distant anymore. I don't want to be distant anymore."

"You're coming home in more ways than one, aren't you?"

Beau nodded. "In every way. I want to build a house down by the cottage."

His dad grinned as his mom came back to join them. "Did I hear that right?"

"Yeah. What do you think? Can you stand to have us as neighbors?"

She hugged him. "It's what I was hoping for, Beau! We'll have you on our doorstep and…" she smiled. "I'll get to play with Ruby more."

"You really love her, don't you?"

She nodded enthusiastically. "I do! I know she's not blood, but she is my first granddaughter!"

Beau nodded. "Yeah. I know where you're coming from."

His dad held his gaze. "And I hope you understand now where I've been coming from all these years."

Beau hugged him. He knew he was talking about Chance and he really did understand now. It had taken Ruby to help him, but he'd finally gotten there.

"Are you going to call her yet?" called Cassidy. "We've got everything ready in here, and I for one am going to burst if we have to wait any longer."

Beau smiled at her. He knew she hadn't thought much of him in the beginning, but it seemed they were all growing in their understanding of each other—and their love for each other, as the family evolved. "Okay, bossy boots. I wanted to wait for Wanda to get here."

Cassidy's eyes widened and for a moment he thought he'd offended her, maybe it was too soon to start teasing like that? He was relieved when she laughed.

"So it's like that, is it? The gloves are off now?"

He grinned, knowing he'd no doubt take some crap from her in the weeks and months to come. "They sure are."

She grinned back. "Game on!"

"And I'm already here!" Wanda appeared from the kitchen. "So will you get on and call her up here? Or I'm going to burst, too!"

"Hey, Wanda!" He held his arm out to her for a hug, but she waved a hand at him, looking embarrassed. "You can save that for later. Get on with it, would you?"

He laughed and looked around at everyone. "Okay, here goes." He fished his phone out of his pocket.

"Hey," Corinne answered, "are you back yet?"

"Yeah. Do you want to come up?"

"We'll be there in a few minutes."

As he hung up he looked around at his family. This felt so good. So right. He'd spent so many years keeping them out. He'd kept the doors to his heart locked as well as the doors to his house and his office. It had taken Corinne and Ruby to help him unlock them.

Now he felt as though he was throwing the doors wide open and letting not only the two of them, but his whole family back in.

Chance caught his eye and nodded. He'd never have believed that the two of them could become so close. He had something he wanted to spring on him, too. But first and most important was Corinne.

"She's coming," cried Summer who was peeking out of the window.

Beau's heart began to race. He was really going to do this!

His mom went to the door and let them in.

"Come on through, he's lounging around on the sofa."

Corinne laughed and came to him. Ruby let go of her hand and ran over, climbing up beside him to plant a kiss on his cheek. He hugged her tight then pulled Corinne to him with his free arm. This was where he wanted to be—with the two of them and surrounded by his family.

"Are you okay?" Corinne asked.

He looked up into her eyes. "Never been better."

She gave him a puzzled look. "Are you sure?" She looked around at everyone. "Is someone going to tell me what's going on?" She looked at Chance, but he jerked his head toward Beau.

She turned back to him and he smiled. "I've got something to tell you and something to ask you."

Her eyes grew wide as he fished in his pocket for the ring. "What I need to tell you is that you've made me the happiest man alive. I thought I was doing okay until I met you. I didn't know just how lost I was. I'd closed myself off from my family and my feelings. You…" he smiled at Ruby, "…and my little pumpkin here, helped me open up my eyes and my heart. I can never thank you enough." He tried to swallow the lump in his throat, but it wouldn't quite go away. "But I would like to spend the rest of my life trying."

He saw tears well up in her eyes as he flipped the box open and held it up to her. "I can't exactly go down on one knee right now, but I love you Corinne. I love you with all my heart." He couldn't help it, he grinned over at Wanda and Cassidy. "Yes, I do have one!" That had everyone laughing. He turned back to Corinne. "What I'm trying to say is, will you marry me?"

"Yesss!" cried Ruby, making everyone laugh again.

Corinne smiled through her tears as she nodded. "Yes." She wiped at her tears. "Yes, I will."

He felt as though his heart might burst, it was so full of happiness. He slid the ring out of the box and onto her finger. She threw her arms around his neck and Ruby wrapped her arms around both of them as everyone cheered.

~ ~ ~

Corinne wiped her eyes as the others congratulated them. She got lost in a sea of hugs and smiles. She was happy to become a part of this family and even happier for Beau that he was reclaiming his place in it.

Monique came and hugged her. "Will you be my grandma now?" Ruby asked her.

"If that's okay with your mommy?"

Corinne nodded. "I'd love that!"

Ruby beamed. "I have a new grandma. And a new Grandpa Dave, and my Beau." She looked up at Monique. "A Beau is better than a daddy."

Monique smiled at her. "He certainly is."

Wanda came to congratulate her and to admire the ring. She winked at Corinne as she took her hand and held it up to Beau. "Nice ring, boss! Are you still telling me you can't afford to give me a raise?"

Corinne laughed. It was a beautiful ring and the diamond was huge. She laughed even more as Beau scowled at Wanda. "Think about it, would you? After I bought that ring you may have to take a pay cut!"

Wanda laughed and shook her head at him.

"Don't worry," said Corinne. "We can gang up on him now."

Wanda linked arms with her and grinned at Beau. "Did you hear that, Mister?"

He groaned. "What have I done?"

Chance came and sat down beside him on the sofa. "The smartest thing I've ever seen you do."

Beau smiled at him and Corinne loved him even more when she heard what he had to say. "I want to do another smart thing, too. But that will depend on you."

Chance raised an eyebrow at him. "Name it. I'll help if I can."

"I want you to be my best man."

Chance didn't tend to show much emotion, but Corinne could see his eyes were glistening as he nodded. "I'd love to."

She smiled to herself as they gave each other one of those awkward man hugs before Chance stood up and nodded. She realized everyone else was watching them too, and she knew that between Beau choosing to ask her to marry him here with all his family present and the moment he and Chance had just shared, this family was healed. Beau had come home, in every sense.

Gina came and hugged her then pecked Beau on the cheek. "I told you so."

"You told him what?" asked Corinne.

"That there would be four Remington weddings this year."

Beau smiled. "We'll have to see about the timing on ours. We'll do whatever Corinne wants."

"I think you should all go for one big celebration," said Wanda. "One weekend, four big weddings, right here at the ranch!" She stopped herself and looked around. "Sorry, not that it's any of my business."

Beau laughed. "Don't get carried away, Wanda."

"I think it's a great idea!" said Cassidy. "Wouldn't that be awesome?"

Monique smiled. "It'd work for us. We're going to leave town after Mason and Gina's wedding. Of course we'll come back for the rest of you when you set a date."

Carter looked at Beau. Corinne could tell they were having a silent conversation about it. Beau turned to her and she nodded. She loved the idea!

It was Dave who stepped in. "Don't get carried away, just yet. I say you should all think it over, talk about it and no one should feel any pressure if they don't like the idea."

Corinne nodded. The logistics would be a nightmare, but she still loved the idea. Looking around it seemed that the others did too. Maybe it would pan out, but they didn't need to decide right now. What she wanted most right now was to go home. She'd loved this, but she wanted Beau to herself now.

He caught her eye. It seemed he felt the same way.

"This has been awesome guys. Thank you all for sharing this moment with us, but we're going to go home."

Everyone congratulated them again as they left. Chance helped Beau into his truck and drove them back down to the cabin. Once they had Beau settled on the sofa with Ruby sitting beside him, Corinne walked Chance to the door.

"Thanks, Chance. Thanks for everything."

He nodded. "I want to thank you, too. You've made all the difference. You've changed my life for the better and I don't think you even know it."

She smiled. She hadn't known it, but now he said it she could see what he meant. "I think we're all affecting each other's lives for the better and I couldn't be happier."

He nodded. "I predict blue skies ahead, but there is still one dark cloud I want to deal with."

Corinne thought she knew what he meant. "Guy Preston?"

He nodded.

"You think it was him, too, don't you?"

"I think he had something to do with it, and I can't let that go."

She put a hand on his arm. "Please don't do anything stupid?"

He smiled. "I won't. I'm just letting you know that he's not going to get away with it."

She nodded.

"Help!" called Beau from the living room. They could hear Ruby giggling.

Chance smiled. "Get back to them. I just wanted to let you know."

"Thanks, Chance."

She had to laugh when she went back in and saw Ruby sitting on Beau's chest tickling him. "Help me!" he shouted.

"No, help me!" said Ruby.

Corinne laughed and started to tickle him, too.

"Hey! I thought you were supposed to be on my side!"

She laughed. "I am. We're a family, we're all on each other's side. Sometimes you're the tickler and sometimes you get tickled, but we're all in it together no matter what, and you'd do well to remember that."

As he smiled, his eyes told her he understood. It wasn't going to be plain sailing from here on out. Life didn't work that way, but he needed to understand that they were in it together. There were no sides, and he didn't need to go putting himself on the outside. Ever again;

;

A Note from SJ

I hope you enjoyed your visit to Montana and spending time with the Remingtons. Please let your friends know about the books if you feel they would enjoy them as well. It would be wonderful if you would leave me a review, I'd very much appreciate it.

You can check out the rest of the series on my website www.SJMcCoy.com to keep up with the brothers as they each find their happiness.

Chance has finally talked me into giving him his own three book spin-off – Look out for it in Spring 2017.

In the meantime, you'll see glimpses of him in my Summer Lake series, too. If you haven't read them, you can get started with Emma and Jack in Book One, Love Like You've Never Been Hurt which is currently FREE to download in ebook form from all the big online book retailers AND early in 2017 the whole series will be available in paperback as well!

There are a few options to keep up with me and my imaginary friends:

The best way is to Sign up for my Newsletter at my website www.SJMcCoy.com. Don't worry I won't bombard you! I'll let you know about upcoming releases, share a sneak peek or two and keep you in the loop for a couple of fun giveaways I have coming up :0)

You can join my readers group to chat about the books or like my Facebook Page

I occasionally attempt to say something in 140 characters or less(!) on Twitter

And I'm in the process of building a shiny new website at www.SJMcCoy.com

I love to hear from readers, so feel free to email me at SJ@SJMcCoy.com if you'd like. I'm better at that! :0)

I hope our paths will cross again soon. Until then, take care, and thanks for your support—you are the reason I write!

Love

SJ

PS Project Semicolon

You may have noticed that the final sentence of the story closed with a semi-colon. It isn't a typo. Project Semi Colon is a non-profit movement dedicated to presenting hope and love to those who are struggling with depression, suicide, addiction and self-injury. Project Semicolon exists to encourage, love and inspire. It's a movement I support with all my heart.

"A semicolon represents a sentence the author could have ended, but chose not to. The sentence is your life and the author is you." - Project Semicolon

This author started writing after her son was killed in a car crash. At the time I wanted my own story to be over, instead I chose to honour a promise to my son to write my 'silly stories' someday. I chose to escape into my fictional world. I know for many who struggle with depression, suicide can appear to be the only escape. The semicolon has become a symbol of support, and hopefully a reminder – Your story isn't over yet

Also by SJ McCoy

Remington Ranch Series

Mason (FREE in ebook form) and also available as Audio

Shane

Carter

Beau

Four Weddings and a Vendetta

A Chance and a Hope

Chance is a guy with a whole lot of story to tell. He's part of the fabric of both Summer Lake and Remington Ranch. He needed three whole books to tell his own story.

Chance Encounter

Finding Hope

Give Hope a Chance

The Davenports

Oscar

TJ

Reid

The Hamiltons

Cameron and Piper in Red wine and Roses

Chelsea and Grant in Champagne and Daisies

Mary Ellen and Antonio in Marsala and Magnolias

Marcos and Molly in Prosecco and Peonies

Coming Next

Grady

Summer Lake Series

Love Like You've Never Been Hurt (FREE in ebook form)

Work Like You Don't Need the Money
Dance Like Nobody's Watching
Fly Like You've Never Been Grounded
Laugh Like You've Never Cried
Sing Like Nobody's Listening
Smile Like You Mean It
The Wedding Dance
Chasing Tomorrow
Dream Like Nothing's Impossible
Ride Like You've Never Fallen
Live Like There's No Tomorrow
The Wedding Flight

Summer Lake Seasons

A return to the wonderful small town so many readers have grown to love. We'll see our old friends around town and they'll feature to a greater or lesser extent in the new stories. I want you to be able to catch up on their lives if you know them - and to not feel like you're missing anything if you didn't read the original series.

Angel and Luke in Take These Broken Wings
Zack and Maria in Too Much Love to Hide

Love In Nashville

Matt and Autumn in Bring on the Night

About the Author

I'm SJ, a coffee addict, lover of chocolate and drinker of good red wines. I'm a lost soul and a hopeless romantic. Reading and writing are necessary parts of who I am. Though perhaps not as necessary as coffee! I can drink coffee without writing, but I can't write without coffee.

I grew up loving romance novels, my first boyfriends were book boyfriends, but life intervened, as it tends to do, and I wandered down the paths of non-fiction for many years. My life changed completely a few years ago and I returned to Romance to find my escape.

I write 'Sweet n Steamy' stories because to me there is enough angst and darkness in real life. My favorite romances are happy escapes with a focus on fun, friendships and happily-ever-afters, just like the ones I write.

These days I live in beautiful Montana, the last best place. If I'm not reading or writing, you'll find me just down the road in the park - Yellowstone. I have deer, eagles and the occasional bear for company, and I like it that way :0)

Printed in Great Britain
by Amazon

30251780R00148